Island Heat

by

Debby Grahl

Carolina Series

Island Heat

Cover Art by *Kim Mendoza*

The Wild Rose Press, Inc.
PO Box 708
Adams Basin, NY 14410-0708
Visit us at www.thewildrosepress.com

Publishing History
First Edition, 2023
Trade Paperback ISBN 978-1-5092-4871-1
Digital ISBN 978-1-5092-4872-8

Carolina Series
Published in the United States of America

Suzanna breathed in the salty air. *Right now, my life in Charlotte might as well be a million miles away, and I haven't a care in the world.*

"There's Orion." Austen pointed. "Studying the constellations is a hobby of mine."

"I find astronomy fascinating. And I love having my fortune told, though I know that's astrology."

"I can tell you what your future will bring," Austen replied.

"What's that?"

He took her into his arms. "This." His lips covered hers.

The warmth of his mouth made Suzanna's skin tingle. This moment came right off the pages of the romance novels she so loved—a moonlit night, a handsome man, and the faint sound of a piano in the distance. She wrapped her arms around his neck and kissed him back.

He held her close. His kiss, gentle at first, his lips moving slowly across hers, skillfully coaxed her lips apart. Their tongues met, and Suzanna let out a low moan as the kiss deepened. Her body molded to his. She slid her fingers through the hair on the nape of his neck. His hand glided up and down her back, while he held her close. His hard erection rubbed against her, and Suzanna's passion soared.

Austen broke their kiss and gazed into her eyes. In a husky voice, he said, "I want you."

Dedication

To my girlfriends on Hilton Head and to Captain Phil
Smith. You're all the best!

Part One

Chapter One

"Mama, you'll never believe what's happened," Suzanna Shay exclaimed as she burst through the front door.

"For Heaven's sake, Suzanna, what are you shouting about?" Augusta Shay replied.

Suzanna, following her mother's voice, found her in the family room, her feet up, a rerun of *I Love Lucy* on the television. "Mama, I won. I'm going on a cruise."

"A cruise. What cruise?" her mother asked.

"The contest Preston Books had for their employees." Suzanna twirled and danced across the room. "I'm going to Costa Maya."

Augusta muted the television. "When is this cruise, and how long will you be gone?"

Suzanna didn't miss the sharp edge in her mother's voice. "It's a five-day cruise in September sponsored by H&H Publishing and the I Love A Mystery Association."

Her mother's mouth formed a thin line. "Are you going with other people?"

Here it comes, Suzanna thought, trying to hold on to her excitement. "Not anyone I know. There will be others who have signed up for the mystery part of the cruise."

"A single girl alone on a cruise ship. Suzanna, that doesn't sound safe to me. There are men who will take advantage of a situation like that."

"Mama, I'm twenty-four years old. I'll be perfectly fine."

"Isn't September hurricane season?"

"I suppose, but that doesn't mean there will be one."

"And what am I to do while you're gone?"

Suzanna prayed for patience. "Why don't you go to the ranch and visit with Gramma and Gramps?"

Augusta snorted. "They're off again going who knows where in that RV of theirs. Honestly, at their age, gallivanting all over the country."

"I'll only be gone for a few days. Perhaps you can get together with the book club ladies. Or get your hair done. You always enjoy hearing all the gossip at the salon."

"None of that makes up for me being alone. You know how lonely I've been since your father died. First you go off to college, then your sister takes off to that school in Savannah."

Suzanna counted to ten before replying. "Mama, Dad has been gone for seven years. We've had this conversation many times. Savannah and I have our own lives. You need to get out more. Volunteer somewhere, or get a part-time job."

Augusta's eyes narrowed. "Suzanna, I'm fifty years old. No one is going to hire me."

Not if you don't try. Suzanna rose. "I don't know what to say, but I'm going on this cruise." *And I might not come back*, she thought as she left the room.

Suzanna's cell rang, and she smiled when her

friend Amy's name showed on the display. "Hey, Amy. Did you get my voice mail?"

"I did," Amy replied. "I can't believe you won the trip. I'm so envious. We'll have to go shopping for cruise clothes."

"Exactly my thoughts."

"How did your mother take the news?"

"How do you think? September can't get here fast enough."

"Who knows? You might meet the man of your dreams, and he'll whisk you away."

Suzanna laughed. "Yeah, right. The only way I'll get out of Charlotte is on my own."

Amy sighed. "Tell me about it. We both need a fresh start. Sorry, I have to run. Violet's hungry. Let's plan on going shopping this weekend."

"Sounds good." Suzanna disconnected as her mother called, "Suzanna, have you started dinner?"

Visions of turquoise water filled Suzanna's mind as she opened the refrigerator.

Chapter Two

Suzanna paused at the entrance to the Neptune Room. *Oh my.* She smiled in pure delight at the panoramic view of the Gulf of Mexico through the wall of glass. As she made her way to the registration table, she took in the room's underwater motif of colorful tropical fish, deep-blue cloth-draped tables, and blue-and-white-striped chairs.

"Hello, I'm Suzanna Shay," she said to the friendly looking woman checking people in.

"Hi, welcome aboard. I'm Maggie O'Toole. Here's your I Love A Mystery participant information bag. It includes your name tag and the number of the person you'll be paired with. Also, there's a program booklet, swag provided by H&H Publishing, and a notebook to write down clues."

Suzanna took the offered bag. "I'm paired with someone?"

"There are forty participants, and the Mystery organizers thought it would be easier, and more fun, to pair up the singles. If you find you'd rather try and solve the mystery on your own, that's fine."

"Okay, thanks." Suzanna stepped to the side and glanced at her name tag before attaching it to the top of her peach-and-white sundress. Her number was twelve, and she was paired with thirty-two. *Male or female?* she thought as she scanned the crowded room. *No matter. I hope my partner is as excited about solving the mystery as I am.*

As she approached the oval bar, a man turned, and their eyes met. *Wow. Can I be lucky enough to have Mr. Mega Hunk as my partner?* He stood around six-foot with thick light-brown hair and smoky gray eyes. His nose was thin and straight, above a sensuous mouth set beneath a thick mustache. *Oh, my, he's good-looking enough to be on the cover of a romance novel.* She managed to tear her gaze from his and focus on his name tag—Austen Kincaid—and he was number thirty-two.

Suzanna hesitated. "Come on, take a deep breath, and repeat your mantra. I'm on my own, I can do as I please, and I have no one to answer to," she murmured. She wiped her damp palms on her dress and casually headed toward him.

"Hi, it seems you're to be my partner," she said, holding out her hand. "I'm Suzanna Shay."

He took her hand. "Austen Kincaid." His smile showed even, white teeth, and he spoke with a slight Southern drawl. He indicated the bar. "I just ordered a drink. Would you like something?"

"Yes, cabernet, please."

Austen placed her order, and when he gave his cabin number to pay for her wine, Suzanna protested.

"Oh, you don't have to do that."

He handed her the wineglass. "My pleasure. Now, let's find somewhere to sit. I see a couple of seats over by the windows."

"Oh, how pretty," Suzanna said, indicating the shell and coral centerpiece. She gestured at the gently rolling waves beyond the window. "It's wonderful, isn't it?" Not waiting for a response, she continued. "This is my first cruise, and I keep telling myself I'm actually on my way to Costa Maya. Have you been on other cruises?"

"This is my second. I went to the Bahamas researching a book."

Suzanna's brows rose. "You're an author?"

Austen nodded. "Well, kind of. I have a couple of finished manuscripts."

"Good for you. What do you write?"

"Thrillers." He hesitated. "In fact, I'm waiting to hear back from H&H on a manuscript I submitted."

"Is that why you're on the cruise?"

"No, my friend purchased the ticket, but he had a family emergency and asked me if I'd like to go instead. He told me it was a mystery cruise. I had no idea H&H was a sponsor until I got on board. As it happens, the editor I sent my manuscript to is also here."

"Who is that?"

"Clarice Abbot."

"I'll bet you're dying to ask her about your book."

"I sure am, but I'm afraid that might turn her against me."

"I've always wanted to write," Suzanna said. "But I don't have the talent. So, I just work among books."

"What do you do?"

"I'm the manager for Preston Books in their Charlotte store. I won this cruise in a contest the company held."

"That's terrific. I've never won anything."

"Up until now, neither had I."

"Are you a mystery lover?" Austen asked.

"Mystery and romance are my favorites. How about you?"

"Mystery and suspense. I enjoy David Baldacci, Harlan Coben, and Lee Child."

"Good choices. I love the classics: Christie, Sayers, and Ngaio Marsh."

"Considering our taste in authors, we should solve this mystery without any problem."

Suzanna raised her glass. "Here's to my Miss Marple and your Jack Reacher. May they both bring us luck."

Austen tapped his glass with hers. "Absolutely."

As their eyes met and held, Suzanna's thoughts fled from books and solving mysteries to a vision of his sensuously sculpted lips kissing her. Good grief, what was she thinking? Horrified he might have read her mind, she stared out the window, willing away the blush that stained her cheeks.

Austen cleared his throat. "I believe they're about to begin tonight's program."

Thankful for the distraction, Suzanna adjusted her chair for a better view.

"Please, may I have everyone's attention?" Maggie O'Toole asked through a microphone from a raised platform at the far end of the room. "I know we're all anxious to begin tonight's program. In your booklet, we've provided you with a list of the characters in our mystery and information on what you'll need to solve the murder. Tonight, we'll present the opening two acts. Tomorrow, the murder will occur."

In unison, the crowd made an "ooh" sound.

"I'll also go over the rules with you. Then while we're cruising to Costa Maya, you'll have time to put your little gray cells to work. After tomorrow, in designated shops on board, you can pick up clue cards with more information on the suspects. On our last night, we'll present the conclusion and see if we have an ace detective on board. Our winner will get a gift certificate for one hundred dollars at Preston Books. If we have more than one winner, each will receive a fifty-dollar certificate. We have our sponsor, H&H Publishing, to thank for the appetizers on the far table. Please help yourselves. After tonight's presentation, we'll have supper in the Mermaid dining room. In your packet, there's a card listing your table seating. So, if you'll get your notebooks out, in a few minutes we'll get started."

Austen got to his feet. "I'd like another drink. How about you?"

Suzanna nodded and rose. "This one is on me."

"To tell you the truth, I'm kind of hungry. Would you mind getting us some appetizers while I go to the bar?"

"Sure, but the next round is my treat."

****

While he waited in line, Austen marveled at his luck. He'd hesitated about coming on the cruise but thanked the stars, or whatever, for bringing him here. Suzanna Shay was sexy as hell with long dark-red hair, big blue eyes, and a very shapely body. The mystery part of the cruise might be entertaining, but spending time with Suzanna may prove more pleasurable. And if he read her correctly, the feeling was mutual. He hadn't dated since his last girlfriend got tired of the hours he dedicated to his writing, and broke off their relationship.

If H&H offered him a contract for *Upheaval*, the first in his series, his lifetime dream would finally come true. Not to mention getting his father off his ass. He loved the horses and enjoyed watching them win races, but if he had his way, the Kincaid horse farm would not be part of his future. In the meantime, here he was on a Caribbean cruise with an attractive woman.

"What can I get you?" the bartender whose name tag read *Steve* asked.

"A cabernet and a stout," Austen replied.

"Add a martini as well, please."

A woman with strawberry-blonde hair wearing a tight dress stood next to him, giving him a pleasant view of her impressive cleavage.

"Hello," she said with a smile. "I need a drink before I go on. I'm Haley Henderson and"—she glanced at his name tag—"you're Austen."

Surprised, Austen cleared his throat. Haley, married to Brad Henderson, the owner of H&H Publishing, was one of the *New York Times* list's top mystery writers. "It's nice to meet you. I enjoy your books."

"Thanks." She sipped her martini and studied him with her big green eyes. "So, you're a mystery fan. I hope you enjoy our little skit."

"Are you part of the production?"

"Star performer, and I have to confess I also wrote it."

"Then I'm sure it will be great."

She cocked her head, and a slow smile spread across her face. "Are you here alone?"

Austen hesitated. If he wasn't mistaken, the woman was flirting with him. Great, just what he needed. Her husband's publishing house might hold his future in their hands. "I'm here with a friend."

"A female friend?"

Austen tamped down his annoyance. He didn't want to insult her, but what business was it of hers? He gave her what he hoped was a friendly smile. "I need to take my seat. I'll let you finish your drink, and good luck with the skit."

"Thanks," Suzanna said as he handed her the wine.

"You're not going to believe who I ran into at the bar. Haley Henderson." He nodded at Suzanna's wide-eyed reaction. "I didn't recognize her at first. She said she wrote the mystery skit and is starring in it."

"No kidding," Suzanna replied. "When her new releases come into the bookstore, they fly off the shelves. She did a book signing for us once. I have to admit she wasn't the friendliest author we'd had."

"She stays at the top of the *Times* best seller list. Fame can inflate people's ego to the point of being obnoxious. If I make it big, I hope I never get that way." He glanced at the plate piled with food in the middle of their table. "Looks good."

"I wasn't sure what to get, so I got a little of everything. Is it okay if we share?"

"Sure." He popped a crab puff into his mouth. "Yum."

"They're about to begin, and we haven't gone over our introduction sheet explaining who all the characters are," Suzanna said.

Austen draped his arm along the back of Suzanna's chair. "We'll figure it out as it goes along."

Chapter Three

Murder skit cast of characters —
Haley Henderson as Vanessa Grimes.
Brad Henderson as Thomas Grimes, Vanessa's husband.
Clarice Abbot, editor for H&H, as Belinda Pool, Vanessa's sister.
JJ Jackson, literary agent, as Gordon Pool, Vanessa's brother.
Melinda Pearce, marketing director for H&H, as Amelia Stone, Vanessa's aunt.

The curtain parted to reveal a posh hotel room. Vanessa sat at a dressing table. Behind her stood her husband, Thomas.

From a jewelry case, Vanessa removed a stunning diamond necklace. Smiling at her reflection in the mirror, she draped it around her neck. "Thomas, darling, would you please help me with this?"

"For Heaven's sake, Vanessa, why did you bring that with you?"

"Because it's mine, and I plan on wearing it every chance I get."

"We're on an island in the Caribbean, not Park Avenue. Isn't it a bit out of place?"

Vanessa narrowed her eyes. "There are those in my family who are determined to take it from me, so I plan on keeping it close at all times."

"Good God, Vanessa, it's worth half a million dollars."

She stroked the glittering diamonds. "Each time I look at it, I think about how upset those sniveling relations of mine are knowing I have it, and they don't."

"They're contesting the will. Perhaps you shouldn't get too attached to it."

Vanessa slammed her hand on the dressing table. "I'm the one who made something of myself. I'm a famous supermodel. Who are they but a bunch of nobodies living their boring little lives? Where would they ever wear a necklace like this, Thrift Mart?"

"I imagine they'd sell it."

"Over my dead body. This necklace belonged to my grandmother, the woman I'm named after and once the darling of Hollywood society. She would want me to have it, not any of them."

"What if they overturn the will?"

"They can try all they want. Mother signed the will, and you and I witnessed it. It's perfectly legal. Besides, that cheap lawyer they hired is a nobody like them. He'll never be able to prove anything."

"I'm concerned about Amelia."

"I don't care if Amelia is my mother's sister and believes the necklace should be hers. It's not my fault she's nothing but a dowdy frump and can't get a man to marry her. Besides, Mother did leave her a few nice pieces of jewelry."

"Financially we're doing extremely well. Give your family the necklace and let them sell it. It's not worth all this turmoil."

"We're doing well, my dear husband, because of

my popularity. I'm the most sought-after model in a decade. I'm the one who makes it possible for us to live in a fabulous Manhattan apartment, take wonderful trips, and live the life we love. If we had to depend on the pittance you bring in with your little stories, we'd be living in squalor."

Thomas's face hardened. "My little stories, as you call them, supported me just fine before I married you."

Vanessa rose, her eyes narrowed in anger. "This necklace belongs to me, and no one is going to take it away. I've always outshone the others, and I always will. If that bothers you, just leave."

"You'd like that, wouldn't you?" Thomas snarled. "Then I wouldn't be in the way of all your little affairs." He leaned forward until his face was inches from hers. "But don't forget, I know the truth about the will, so think about that the next time you crawl into bed with one of your boyfriends."

Vanessa laughed. "Is that right? Well, my dear husband, your little secret could bring your career tumbling down. So, I suppose that's checkmate."

"You're nothing but a bitch," Thomas said through clenched teeth. He stormed from the room, slamming the door behind him.

Haley and Brad took their bows to a round of applause.

"Thanks, everyone," Maggie said. "Give us just a minute to prepare for the next scene."

"My goodness," Suzanna said. "I want to kill her, and I don't even care about the necklace."

Austen chuckled. "I agree."

"The acting was excellent. The tension between them seemed real."

"Perhaps it was. Rumors are their marriage isn't doing well."

"Really? That's a shame." Suzanna checked her program. "The next scene introduces Vanessa's relations. Clarice Abbot is Vanessa's sister. JJ Jackson plays her brother. I don't recognize Melinda Pearce who plays Vanessa's aunt." Suzanna grinned at Austen. "Perhaps you should applaud loudly when Clarice takes her bow."

Austen grinned back. "If it would help, I would."

The lights dimmed, and the curtain opened.

A woman stood with an airline ticket in her hand. A man sat with a suitcase at his feet, and a gray-haired woman clutched a large black purse.

"Belinda, are you sure we should be doing this?" the older woman asked.

"For the thousandth time, Aunt Amelia, yes," Belinda replied. "If we can't break Mother's will, that bitch Vanessa gets away with cheating us out of what should be ours."

"That's right," Gordon interjected. "She's always been embarrassed by the rest of us. She thinks she's entitled because Grandmother was a Hollywood star, and she's—" He made an exaggerated face. "—famous like her."

"She comes from the same small town we do. Screwing her way to the top doesn't make her anything better than a whore."

"Belinda," Amelia gasped.

"Well, I'm tired of her haughty ways. The necklace should be sold and the money split between the three of us. Vanessa is always bragging on how rich she is. She sure as hell doesn't need the money like we do."

Amelia cleared her throat. "If you want to be fair, as your mother's only living sister, I'm next in line, but don't think I wouldn't divide the money with you two. I'm sure if the situation were reversed, you'd share it with me."

Belinda and Gordon glowered at Amelia, then a slow smile spread across Belinda's face. "Of course, we would, Aunt Amelia, but first we have to get the necklace."

"And just how do you intend doing that?" Gordon asked. "When it's not in her safe, the damn thing is around Vanessa's neck."

"We're going to have to be very cunning," Belinda replied. "That's why I should be the one to approach her."

Gordon narrowed his eyes. "And what are we supposed to do in the meantime?"

"Wait for me at the hotel. When I have the necklace, we'll all leave."

"Do you actually think Vanessa is going to just hand it over to you?"

"I can be very persuasive."

"What, holding a gun to her head? No, I'm the one who should talk to Vanessa. She always liked me better anyway."

Belinda scowled. "That's because you were always a suck-up."

"The two of you, stop," Amelia said. "Bickering among ourselves isn't going to accomplish anything. I'll speak with Vanessa. When I explain our circumstances, I'm sure she'll do the right thing."

The lights came up, and the audience clapped. Once again Maggie took the stage.

"Thanks, everyone. Tomorrow is our murder. Now, please head up to the Mermaid dining room for supper."

Chapter Four

"Okay, super sleuth, which one of them is our murderer?" Austen asked.

"Aunt Amelia," Suzanna replied, placing her program in her bag.

"Really, why her?"

"She's the most innocent-acting. But I might change my mind after we're shown how Vanessa is killed."

"You're sure Vanessa will be the one?"

"She's the most obvious."

"That's right. So, she'd be the least likely."

Suzanna stood. "If not her, who?"

"Perhaps Aunt Amelia."

"Why?"

"The necklace has been handed down to each sister, and she's the only one left. If the challenge goes to court, she might have greatest clout."

"One can tell you're a thriller writer. I'm afraid you're putting more into the skit than can be explained."

Austen laughed. "You're probably right."

"Do you know our table number?" Suzanna asked as they entered the dining room.

"It's 261. There it is." Austen headed for a table where five other people were seated.

"Hello, welcome," an older man said with a smile.

"I'm Dwain, and we're the Paige family, and this pretty lady is my friend Kay. Please join us."

Austen and Suzanna sat and introduced themselves.

"Are you here for the mystery?" Suzanna asked.

Dwain nodded. "I am. My son Darrin, his wife Joy, and the kids are along for the cruise."

"We're here for both," Suzanna said.

At that moment, the waiter arrived and said his name was Mathew. While he took their orders, Suzanna's attention was caught by the adjacent table. Haley Henderson glowered at her husband while a disapproving scowl creased his face. The others from the skit fidgeted, appearing extremely uncomfortable. Brad leaned close to Haley and whispered in her ear.

Her body went rigid, and her eyes blazed with anger. She threw down her napkin, said something to Brad, rose, and stormed from the room. For a moment, those remaining at the table were still, then Clarice Abbot took Haley's seat and spoke quietly to Brad. JJ Jackson poured himself more wine, and Melinda Pearce's eyes shot daggers at Haley's retreating back.

Suzanna's interest was piqued. *That, I'm sure, was a little tableau that wasn't scripted.*

"Are you still with us?" Austen asked, bringing Suzanna's attention back to their table.

"Sorry, just people-watching."

Austen glanced from her to the adjacent table and lifted a questioning brow.

"Later," Suzanna mouthed.

"So, who do you two think the murderer will be?" Dwain asked.

A lively discussion lasted through dinner.

"We're off to sing karaoke," Dwain said after

they'd finished dessert. "Would you like to join us?"

"I can't sing, but I enjoy listening," Suzanna said. "What about you, Austen?"

"Sure, why not?"

"Great," Dwain said. "We'll see you there."

"I don't know where the karaoke bar is," Suzanna said as she and Austen waited for the elevator.

"Here's a map of the ship." Austen stepped to where it hung on the wall. "It's on eight."

When the doors of the elevator closed, and they were alone, Suzanna described what she'd seen at Haley's table.

"No kidding. You may be right. We might have a plot beneath a plot."

"I'm telling you the anger in Brad's face was thunderous."

"As I said, there are rumors she fools around on him and that the marriage is in trouble."

"Where did you hear that?"

Austen shrugged. "I belong to a few writers' social media groups. People love gossip."

When they arrived at the karaoke bar, the room was packed. Suzanna pointed. "There's Dwain."

"We got the last table," he said when Austen and Suzanna took their seats. "I put my name in and chose the song I'll sing."

"What song?" Suzanna asked.

" 'Mack the Knife.' "

"That's great. I can't wait to hear you."

"He does it very well," his granddaughter Amanda said.

"I'm curious to see what song Austen will sing," Dwain said.

"Me too," Suzanna replied.

"You two make such a cute couple," Dwain said. "You'd never know you've just met."

"Austen is certainly a hunk," Joy said with a grin.

"And what about me?" her husband Darrin asked good-humoredly.

Joy patted his cheek. "You're still *my* hunk."

Suzanna studied Austen as he made his way back to their table. Her instant attraction to him surprised her. They'd hit it off as if they'd known one another forever. In the last few years, her relationships with men were practically nonexistent. She'd dedicated her life to finishing college and working to pay off her student loans. Not to mention, being at her mother's beck and call. A serious relationship wasn't something she'd had the energy or time for. Now, here she was in the middle of the Caribbean with this handsome guy, and no work and no responsibilities. Romantic encounters didn't happen to her. Suzanna smiled to herself. Her cousin Jenn would tell her, "Go for it."

Why not be daring for once? Suzanna inwardly sighed. *What am I thinking? Austen may not be attracted to me. He's nice, but that doesn't mean he's interested in anything but having fun and solving the mystery.*

As Austen sat down, Phil, the karaoke DJ, called Dwain to come up.

Suzanna leaned toward Austen. "Not only are you a writer, but you can also sing."

"I sit in with a band now and then back home."

"Where is home?"

"Louisville, Kentucky."

"I have family in Lexington."

He nodded. "Nice city."

Dwain began his song, and they all clapped and cheered.

Suzanna touched Joy's arm. "He's really good."

"He loves to show off," Brendan, Dwain's grandson, replied.

"He definitely enjoys himself," Joy added.

When Dwain returned beaming, he ordered a round of drinks for them all.

Suzanna opened her mouth to decline, but she was having a good time. What would one more hurt?

Phil called Austen's name. When he sang the first words, Suzanna's breath caught. The country song was one of her favorites. Austen's voice was slightly husky as he sang about having nothing on but the radio. Her eyes met his, and desire spread through her body as she imagined the two of them bringing the song to life. The more he sang, the hotter she became. When Austen finished and made his way toward her, the heat showed in his own eyes.

Everyone around the table clapped and cheered as he took his seat next to Suzanna.

"You sounded great," Suzanna said. "That's one of my favorite songs."

"Mine too. For some reason, the words kept playing in my mind." He leaned closer. "There's a full moon. How about a stroll out on the deck?"

Suzanna, you don't know him. Think about what you're doing. Her mother's voice rang through her head. But as she gazed into Austen's face, careful was the last thing she wanted to be. She stood. "Let's go."

They said goodbye to the Paiges and headed for the doors leading onto the deck. The night was warm with a gentle breeze. Stars filled the velvet sky as moonlight sparkled upon the water.

Suzanna breathed in the salty air. *Right now, my life in Charlotte might as well be a million miles away, and I haven't a care in the world.*

"There's Orion." Austen pointed. "Studying the constellations is a hobby of mine."

"I find astronomy fascinating. And I love having my fortune told, though I know that's astrology."

"I can tell you what your future will bring," Austen replied.

"What's that?"

He took her into his arms. "This." His lips covered hers.

The warmth of his mouth made Suzanna's skin tingle. This moment came right off the pages of the romance novels she so loved—a moonlit night, a handsome man, and the faint sound of a piano in the distance. She wrapped her arms around his neck and kissed him back.

He held her close. His kiss, gentle at first, his lips moving slowly across hers, skillfully coaxed her lips apart. Their tongues met, and Suzanna let out a low moan as the kiss deepened. Her body molded to his. She slid her fingers through the hair on the nape of his neck. His hand glided up and down her back while he held her close. His hard erection rubbed against her, and Suzanna's passion soared.

Austen broke their kiss and gazed into her eyes. In a husky voice he said, "I want you."

Suzanna, never one to jump into bed with a man she'd just met, hesitated. Again, for a second, her mother's disapproving scowl flashed through her mind.

She defiantly brushed it aside. *There's no one here to question your actions. Don't let this perfect night pass you by. Besides, who would ever know?* the adventurous part of her brain screamed, drowning out any misgivings. Who was she kidding? Nothing would keep her from having sex with Austen. "Yes," she whispered.

"I suggest we get off this deck before we go any further. Your cabin or mine?"

Struggling to gather her wits, Suzanna nodded. "Mine."

Without another word, hand in hand, they headed inside, maneuvering around happy, intoxicated people leaving a dance bar.

"What floor?" Austen's voice rose over the din as they reached the elevators.

"Seven."

"Let's take the stairs," Austen said. "We'll be here forever waiting on an elevator." Suzanna held on to his hand as they headed for the carpeted steps. "What's your cabin number?"

"714."

Austen rounded a corner and cursed.

"What's the matter?"

"We're on the wrong end of the ship."

"What?"

"Because of the pool deck, we can't get through. We either have to go outside or down and around."

"Okay, where's your cabin?"

"On six, but it's on the other side as well."

Suzanna burst out laughing. Here was her perfect romantic night, and they couldn't get to a bed.

Austen scowled. "What's so amusing?"

"Oh, I'm sorry, but you have to see the humor in this."

For a minute Austen didn't speak, then he grinned. "In a way, this could be funny, but considering I about made love to you standing on the deck of a ship, and now we're half a ship away from either of our beds, I'm not totally certain that it is."

Suzanna's laughter faded, and she sighed. The romantic mood was broken. "You're right." She kissed him lightly. "This is our first night. We have four more."

Disappointment showed in his eyes, but he took her hand, and they headed for the stairs.

By the time they'd reached the hall that led to her cabin, Suzanna feared their romance was dead in the water. Austen hadn't said a word the entire way back.

"Well, here's where I turn," Suzanna said. "I can make it from here."

"I'll take you to your door."

They were halfway down the hall when they encountered Christopher, Suzanna's cabin steward.

"Good evening, Miss Suzanna," Christopher said with a big grin. "I hope you've been enjoying yourself."

"Yes, Christopher, thank you."

"I didn't see a breakfast order on your door. Will you be wanting morning coffee?"

"Yes, please. I'm sorry I forgot to put it out."

"No problem, no problem." Christopher glanced from Suzanna to Austen. "Will you also be wanting breakfast in your cabin?"

Embarrassment colored Suzanna's cheeks. She hesitated. "I'm not sure."

"That's okay. There's plenty of time for you to

decide. If you do, place your form on your door."

"Thank you, I will."

As they continued to Suzanna's cabin, Austen chuckled. "What's so funny?" she asked.

"The way you blushed when he indicated you might have a breakfast companion."

At her door, Suzanna rummaged in her bag for her key card. Austen stood close, and she inhaled his musky cologne. Images of what they'd be doing if they'd made it here on their first try made Suzanna's fingers tremble. As she fumbled with the card, Austen took it from her and opened the door.

She stepped in, and Austen followed. When she faced him, he reached for her.

"Are you going to kiss me good night?"

Hope leaped in Suzanna's heart. Perhaps their romance wasn't over. "I'd love to." She stepped eagerly into his arms.

His kiss was full of promise, and happiness flowed through Suzanna.

He broke the kiss and took a step back. "Tomorrow we're at sea. How about meeting me for breakfast?"

Suzanna's mind still on his toe-curling kiss, it took her a minute to comprehend what he'd said. "Um, sure, what time?"

"If you want to miss the crowd, we should eat early. How about we meet around eight?"

"Okay, sounds good. I'm an early riser anyway."

He brushed her lips with his. "See you then."

Minutes passed as she stood staring at the closed door. What was wrong with her? She'd let a handsome sexy man who wanted to make love to her leave. She gnawed on her lower lip. Had he also felt the mood slip away? If his goodnight kiss was anything to go by, the flame had dampened, not gone out.

She glanced at the clock. If the roaming charges weren't so high, she'd call her friend Amy and tell her about Austen. Although perhaps she should wait. What if her romantic shipboard fling fizzled out? Then it would be nothing but one more disappointment. She let out a long sigh. A minute ago, she was floating on a cloud. Now, here she was, full of gloomy thoughts. *Get a grip, Suzanna. Stop imagining the worst.* She slipped on her oversized T-shirt and climbed into bed with visions of Austen filling her mind.

****

Austen stabbed the elevator button. Too wired to sleep, he'd find a quiet place to have a nightcap, then he'd try and get visions of making love to Suzanna out of his mind. He snorted. *Yeah, good luck. If you'd been paying attention, you idiot, you would have realized you were on the wrong end of the ship. You'd be in her bed, not out here alone.* The way she'd melted in his arms promised incredible sex. He ran his hand over his face. If he didn't stop thinking about her, he'd be awake all night.

He entered the Compass, a dark lounge where people were sitting in comfortable chairs, having low conversations. Austen made his way to a semicircular booth and sank down in the soft leather. Within minutes, the waitress appeared. "Hi, I'm Wendy. What can I get you?"

"Maker's straight up."

She nodded, placed a small bowl of bar nuts on the table, and left to get his drink.

She'd no sooner gone than his thoughts were back

on Suzanna. He didn't just want her in his bed. He enjoyed being with her. She had a great sense of humor, she loved books, and they clicked as if they'd known each other for years. Even though they lived far apart, it's possible their relationship could lead to more than a brief encounter. Although, with his uncertain future, who knew where he might end up.

"Well, hello there."

Austen's musings were interrupted by a woman's voice. He glanced up and cursed under his breath. There, sliding into the booth across from him, was Haley Henderson. He forced a smile. "We meet again."

A sensuous grin spread across her face as she leaned forward. Her cocktail dress barely contained her breasts. "I thought my eyes were playing tricks on me when I spotted you sitting here all by yourself. A handsome man like you shouldn't be alone." She pursed her cherry-red lips. "I stopped in for a nightcap on my way to bed."

Her words were slightly slurred, and she screamed trouble waiting to happen. How in the hell was he to get away from her? Wendy arrived with his drink, and Haley ordered one for herself.

She sat back in the seat. "Tell me, what did you think of our skit?"

Relieved she'd changed the subject, he nodded. "It was quite good. I'm looking forward to tomorrow night's murder."

"I did some acting in college. I've always loved dressing up and pretending to be someone else."

"Your part as Vanessa was very convincing."

She glanced away, then back at him. "Sometimes fiction is closer to the truth than people realize." She held up her glass. "Here's to lonely strangers who hopefully won't be lonely for long."

Austen sipped his bourbon. *I have to get out of here. She has no idea what trouble she can cause me.* From under the table, Haley ran her bare foot up the inside of his leg. He silently cursed. "Where's your husband?" His tone came out sharper than he intended, but, damn it, he didn't mess around with married women, and he wasn't about to start now.

Not seeming to notice his irritation, Haley frowned. "I left him losing at blackjack in the casino. Brad tends to lose at a number of things." Her foot moved higher. "Why don't you order us another drink, and you can tell me why you're sitting alone."

"I'm not alone. I told you I was here with a friend."

Her smile reminded Austen of a cobra about to strike. "But she's not here, and I am."

Austen downed the rest of his drink and rose. He needed to leave before he said something he'd regret. "It's been a long day. I'm going to call it a night. It was nice seeing you again." Then, before she had a chance to reply, he left. He'd been rude, but even though she screamed sex appeal, he wasn't interested in fooling around with her, and fooling around was exactly what Haley Henderson had in mind. Besides, her dismissal of Suzanna pissed him off. She might be a hell of a mystery writer, but as a person, Haley was pretty heartless.

Chapter Five

When Christopher brought her coffee at seven the next morning, Suzanna had showered, dressed, put her makeup on, and fixed her hair.

She'd spent most of the night fantasizing about Austen making love to her and awakened with her body aching for his touch. At five-fifteen she'd given up and gotten out of bed.

She stood on her balcony as the first orange streaks of dawn broke over the shimmering blue water. Never had a man consumed her mind the way Austen did. Even though she had cousins, friends at work, and her best friend Amy, they couldn't take the place of warm arms around her and kisses that left her breathless.

You need to get out from under your mother's thumb and date, Amy kept telling her. She was right, but date whom? She'd contemplated trying one of those online dating sites but was wary of going out with a stranger. She laughed aloud. *Yeah, and now you're ready to hop into bed with a man you just met.*

Was her attraction to Austen nothing more than getting caught up in the excitement of being on her own for the first time, this far from home? No one knew her, and there wasn't anyone to judge her actions. She'd do what she wanted when she wanted to. Again, her mother's disapproving scowl flickered in her mind, and she pushed it away.

"It's my life, and I'll live it the way I wish," she defiantly said aloud. Whatever this was between her and Austen, she'd enjoy every minute and damn the consequences.

At seven-forty-five, Suzanna put on her gold necklace, with its tiny paperback book charm, smoothed down her navy-and-white-striped halter sundress, placed her room key in her pocket, and headed for the Windjammer and Austen. When she rounded the corner at the dining room, Austen stood waiting for her. She paused a minute to admire him in his light-blue golf shirt and navy shorts. *Control yourself, or you'll be jumping him right here in the middle of the hallway.*

"Good morning," Suzanna said.

He smiled. "You look great. Are you hungry?"

Hungry for you. Aloud she said, "Not awfully. I'm just going to have fruit and toast."

He led the way to the breakfast buffet that offered everything from eggs to bacon, sausages, hash browns, and pancakes, an array of fruits and juices, and baskets of breads and bakery goods. They filled their plates and found a table by the window. A waiter soon brought them coffee and juice.

"So, did you sleep well?" Austen asked.

"No," Suzanna replied.

"I didn't either."

"Why not?"

Austen lowered his voice and leaned forward. "Because all I thought about was making love to you."

Suzanna laid down her fork. It wasn't food she wanted. She tried her best not to let her desire for him show, but as she stared into his eyes, she had no doubt he knew what she was thinking. She swallowed hard before she spoke. "I happened to have the same sorts of thoughts."

"This is the way I see things," Austen began. "We could spend the day wandering around the ship gathering clues, pretending we're having fun, or we can go to one of our cabins and do what we'd rather be doing, which is having mind-blowing sex. So, which will it be?"

Suzanna licked her lips. Here it was. Her chance to throw all her inhibitions out the window and walk on the wild side. "Let's go."

Austen rose. "Come on."

Bubbling with anticipation, Suzanna followed him toward the elevators.

"Whose room?" Austen asked as the doors closed, and they were alone.

"Mine."

As the elevator rose, Austen pulled her into his arms and kissed her. By the time the doors opened on her floor, Suzanna's mind had dulled, and she was a little breathless. They hurried toward her cabin, dodging maid carts, food trays, and laundry bags, finally making it to her door.

"Give me your key," Austen said.

Suzanna took the card from her pocket and handed it to him. They entered her cabin to find Christopher had already straightened the room.

Austen went to the sliding glass doors and pulled the drapes closed, leaving the room in semi-darkness. He kicked off his deck shoes, and Suzanna flew into his open arms. Their mouths met, and the sensuous strokes of his tongue increased Suzanna's desire until she about came right there in his arms.

Their bodies were pressed close together, and she moaned in disappointment when he stepped away. He spoke in shallow breaths as he said, "Before we go any further, I have something to tell you."

Suzanna's lust-filled brain fought to comprehend what he was saying. "What?"

"Suzanna, listen to me."

When his words finally penetrated, her heart sank. Was he going to tell her he was married? Or engaged? Or wanted by the police? Or worse? She stammered, "What?"

"I didn't think I'd be in this situation on the ship, so I didn't come prepared. I stopped by last night, but the store was already closed, and they're not open yet. I checked a few restrooms, but they didn't have a machine."

Suzanna blinked in confusion. Again, she asked, "What?"

"Protection, Suzanna. I don't have any."

Understanding dawned, and relief washed over her. "I haven't been with a man in quite a long time, and I'm on the pill. So, if you haven't been with anyone lately, we're okay."

The slow smile he gave her made her knees weak. Austen walked her backward until her legs hit the side of the bed.

"Turn around and lift your hair."

Suzanna did as he asked. He slid down the zipper of her dress and undid the button at her neck. The fabric fell away to reveal her breasts.

"Now let it fall." Austen pressed his body against hers and reached around to cup her firm mounds. He gently squeezed and stroked while kissing the side of her neck.

Suzanna's breath came in shallow gasps, and moisture pooled between her legs. His hard erection pressed against her bottom while he ran his thumb across her taut nipples.

"Do you like this, sweet?" he murmured in her ear.

Her orgasm was building, and she found it hard to speak. She nodded.

"How about this?" One hand left her breast and moved slowly over her stomach to push her dress down, so it piled at her feet. His fingers slipped beneath her panties and found the moist bud nestled within her damp curls. As he continued to press kisses along her neck, caress one breast, and stroke her swollen bud, Suzanna came apart.

"Austen," she cried as the orgasm slammed through her.

"That's it, sweet. Come for me."

Wave after wave of incredible sensation filled Suzanna, and her body went limp.

"Baby, we're just getting started." Austen's low, husky voice whispered in her ear.

Before Suzanna's head stopped spinning, she found herself on her back in the middle the bed with a naked Austen above her. His body was as perfect as she'd imagined, and she ran her hand along his hard shaft. "Very nice."

He gave her a wicked grin. "I'm glad you like it. Now let's see if I can make you come again." He positioned himself between her thighs and eased into her wet warmth.

Suzanna's body throbbed as she lifted to take him

all the way in. As he moved inside her, Suzanna ran her fingers through the thick hair on his chest, her own movement becoming more demanding. "Now, Austen, now."

"Sweet Suzanna," he rasped as he thrust deep inside her. When she screamed his name, he covered her mouth with his and filled her with his release. When he lifted his head, his eyes, dark gray, still blazed with desire. She'd read about passion igniting searing heat between two people, but had never expected it to happen to her, and she wanted more.

****

Austen had had his share of good sex, but damn, Suzanna made him feel like a randy twenty-year-old. "As the saying goes, I hope that was as good for you as it was for me."

Suzanna chuckled. "Considering you're the first man to make me come twice and scream while doing so, I have to say yes."

He rose up on his arms and gazed into her glowing face. The thought of any other man touching her caused a sick sensation in the pit of his stomach. From this moment on, he'd make sure to pleasure her over and over again. "As soon as I have the strength, we'll see if I can't make that three."

Suzanna's fingers slid over his back. "Is that a promise?"

"Sweetheart, count on it." He moved inside her. "In fact, I'm already getting my second wind."

She closed her eyes and sighed. "I have a feeling three times isn't going to be difficult at all."

"You got that one right, darlin'." He lowered his head and kissed her. Easy at first, but as his rhythm increased, his kiss deepened. He made love to her with his mouth as he moved faster.

Suzanna's nails raked his back as she met him thrust for thrust.

When her body contracted around him and she started to climax, Austen breathlessly demanded, "Open your eyes. I want you to look at me while you come."

Suzanna did as he asked, and he smiled with satisfaction. When she cried out, Austen placed his lips over hers and once again muffled her screams.

His body poised for his own release, Austen lifted his mouth and growled, "Raise your sweet ass and take me deep." He arched his back and let out his own cry of pleasure.

When his brain was functioning again, Austen rolled over, taking Suzanna with him. He brushed the damp hair from her face and lightly kissed her lips. "You're beautiful," he whispered.

Suzanna gave him a shy smile. "You're not so bad yourself."

Austen chuckled. "You've also worn me out." He pulled the duvet over them. "After I get some rest, I've decided I'm going to make you come so many times, you'll lose count."

Suzanna snuggled next to him, her head on his chest, and yawned in contentment. "Mmm. I'll take that challenge."

Chapter Six

The rolling motion of the ship woke Suzanna. Still half asleep, she rose to see over Austen to the clock on the night table. She blinked when she read 2:35.

Austen stirred next to her and opened his eyes. "What time is it?"

"Two thirty-five. It seems we've slept half the day."

He ran his hand along her side. "I have to say, how we've spent our time was a lot more fun than searching for clues."

Suzanna pursed her lips. "Perhaps."

He leaned toward her and nibbled on her earlobe. "You aren't sure?" His hand that had been on her hip was now stroking her breast. "I suppose I'll have to try and do better."

Suzanna sighed as his fingers played with her nipples, then gasped as the pitch of the ship changed and she rolled halfway on top of Austen. "Oh."

"We've hit some rough seas," he said, holding her tight. "As long as you're lying on me, let's see what we can do." He caressed her backside.

"Stop that. I need a shower."

He placed kisses from her ear to her neck. "Hmm. A shower. Now that sounds interesting."

Suzanna laughed. "Austen, don't even think about it. You and I can't both fit in that shower."

"You'd be amazed." He placed her hand on his hard erection. "I like making love when I wake up." He nudged her onto her back. His fingers moved between her damp curls. "Have you ever had an orgasm in the shower?"

"What? No." Suzanna was lost in the sensations his fingers created throughout her body. As her climax built, she spread her legs to give him better access. When he paused, her eyes opened wide. "Austen, don't stop."

"Come on, sweet." He stood, bringing her up with him.

"What? Where are we going? Austen, you're crazy." He led her into the tiny bathroom. "This is not going to work."

He opened the doors and turned on the water. "Trust me." They stepped under the spray. Not an inch of room remained. Her breasts pressed against his chest, while his erection pressed against her stomach. "Now what?"

He grinned. "This." In one swift move, he lifted her off her feet and brought her slick heat down on his shaft.

Her back pressed against the shower wall, Suzanna wrapped her arms around his neck as he moved inside her. She rode the wave of passion until, as one, they spun over the edge.

****

He eased her off him. Her legs a little wobbly and her head slightly dizzy, Suzanna knew if there'd been more room, she would have staggered.

"Are you okay?" he asked on a ragged breath.

She nodded. "That was quite something."

He laughed. "No kidding, sugar." He bent down and kissed her. "While we're here, we might as well do this." He placed his hand beneath the shampoo dispenser mounted on the shower wall and squirted a dollop in his palm. As the spray poured over them, he lathered her hair. Smiling, Suzanna did the same to him. Soon shampoo and soap flowed over their bodies as they kissed beneath the spray.

Austen grabbed a white towel and stepped from the shower, while Suzanna rinsed off. "I don't know about you, but I'm starving."

"So am I," she replied. "What time are we supposed to be at tonight's mystery?"

"I almost forgot about it. Five-thirty, I think. There's plenty of time to have a quick bite beforehand. I'll go to my cabin and change clothes, then return with food."

"Don't forget tonight is Meet-the-Captain dress-up night," Suzanna said as she slipped on a terrycloth robe.

"Damn," Austen swore. "I hoped I wouldn't have to wear the tux."

Suzanna's mouth watered picturing how handsome he'd look. "Your cabin is closer to the dining room, so put on casual clothes now, and you can change before the cocktail party."

Austen nodded. "Good idea. I'll be back soon." He kissed her, playfully slapped her bottom, and went out the door.

****

Suzanna applied lotion to her body. With her hair in a towel, she studied her reflection in the mirror. Spending the majority of the day having sex definitely put a satisfied glow on her face. Her lips were slightly swollen and her eyes clear and bright. She grinned. *Wait until I tell Jenn I finally had multiple orgasms and screamed with each one.*

Mascara brush in hand, she stopped and frowned. Was she in danger of falling for Austen? Other than being extremely good-looking and fantastic in bed, she didn't know much about him. He was from Louisville and a writer, but what else did he do for a living? How old was he? Had he ever been married? Did he have a girlfriend? That thought gave her a sick sensation in her stomach. She shook her head. Austen didn't seem to be the type of person to lie or cheat. Standing here speculating wasn't going to get her anywhere. The only way to find out was to ask him. If she discovered something she was uncomfortable with, she could bring their relationship to a halt. That thought made her stomach lurch even worse. She glowered at her reflection in the mirror. *I've had a fantastic afternoon, and I'm not going to allow my insecurities over men bring me down. I'll find an opportunity to talk to Austen and put my fears to rest. In the meantime, I'm going to enjoy being with him.*

She finished applying her makeup and dried her hair, clipping it up so long tendrils hung down her back. She slipped on black lace panties and opened the closet door. She removed the black dress her friend Amy had insisted she purchase for the formal party. The silky fabric slid over her body, and Suzanna took in her appearance with unease. How was she talked into buying a dress this skimpy? Thin straps held up a V-shaped bodice which exposed quite a bit of cleavage, and the handkerchief hem hung inches above her knees. Suzanna bit her lower lip. She didn't normally dress like this, but since she'd boarded the ship, she'd been doing all kinds of things she'd never expected to be doing. She slipped her feet into black strappy sandals with a two-inch heel. She draped a silver chain around her neck, the black pearl at its end nestled above her breasts. She was placing matching earrings into her ears when someone knocked.

Suzanna opened the door to find Austen wearing a dark-red polo shirt and black jeans, holding a pizza and a bottle of wine, a garment bag across his arm. His gaze moved over her from head to toe. He opened his mouth, but nothing came out.

She cocked her head. "I'm sorry. I don't recall ordering a pizza. Perhaps you have the wrong room."

Austen cleared his throat and glanced up and down the hall. "I was told to bring food and wine to the sexiest lady on the ship, and I've found her." He lowered his voice. "I understand if I feed her, I might get one hell of a tip. By the way, you look amazing."

"Thank you, now get in here. I'm starving, and that pizza smells great."

He gave her a quick kiss as he passed. "Let's eat out on the balcony. If we stay in here, I'll have you out of that dress in about two minutes." He opened her closet and hung the garment bag inside. "I brought the tux so I could change here. Grab a couple of water glasses for the wine."

Smiling to herself, Suzanna did as he asked and soon joined him. In the distance, the sky was darkening, the waves cresting higher. "The storm is getting worse. Do you think we'll be all right?"

Austen nodded. "I'm sure the captain will do his best to steer us out of its path."

She ignored her disquiet and sat down. As she did, the hem of the dress brushed the top of her thighs, giving Austen a view of long, shapely legs.

"If your intention was to turn my brain to mush, you've succeeded."

Innocently, Suzanna's eyes opened wide. She reached for a slice of pizza, thick with cheese and piled high with pepperoni. "Whatever do you mean?"

"Sweetheart, you're playing a game you won't win. Before this night is over, I will take that dress off you, and you'll be coming as I do."

At his husky words, a flush spread across Suzanna's face. She'd better divert this conversation, or they wouldn't leave the cabin. She cleared her throat. "Pizza was a great idea."

"I hope cheese and pepperoni is okay?"

"Perfect. Mmm," she murmured as she took a bite. "I didn't realize how hungry I was."

"Wine?" He held up the bottle.

She nodded. As she sipped, her earlier misgivings resurfaced. What would be the best way to ask him without sounding too intrusive? She decided the easiest was to just ask. "Austen, I was thinking, we don't know much about each other."

"I know you're one sexy lady."

Suzanna smiled. "Thanks, but other than sex."

He slid a slice of pizza onto his plate. "Okay, ask away."

"Um, well, are you in a relationship back in Louisville?"

His brows creased in puzzlement before he answered. "Ah, no. If I were, I wouldn't have spent the day in bed with you."

Suzanna let out the breath she didn't realize she was holding. "I honestly didn't think you would, but I needed to hear it. You see, my experiences with men haven't been great."

"Then all I can say is that those guys were idiots and not worth your time," he said, pouring them more wine. "I did have a girlfriend, but a few months ago, she finally got tired of the time I spent writing and working, so she moved on."

"I considered one of those online dating sites, but I didn't have the nerve to sign up."

His brows lifted in surprise. "Sugar, I can't believe you don't have men lined up to ask you out."

"Not hardly, but thanks for the compliment." She reached for another slice of pizza. "What do you do besides write?"

"I drive a cab."

Suzanna almost choked. "Do you really?"

"I have a degree in journalism, but when I decided I wanted to write novels, I needed a job that would allow me to do both. So, while I wait for passengers, I can work on my next manuscript."

"A cab driver. I would have never guessed that one. Okay, one more. How old are you?"

"On July twenty-fifth, I turned thirty." He leaned back in his chair and sipped his wine. "Now it's my turn. How old are you?"

"I just turned twenty-four. And to save you the trouble of asking, I have a degree in marketing, and my dream is to one day own my own bookstore somewhere interesting."

"Such as?"

"I haven't really decided. I like Charlotte, but I

grew up there and want to be somewhere different. My family originally comes from Pine Bluff, a small town outside of Asheville, and I considered going there, or Hilton Head Island. I do love the beach." She sighed. "But that will take money, and right now that's not happening. How about you? Do you want to stay in Louisville?"

He hesitated. "For the time being. If H&H offers me a contract, I might move to New York City."

"I've never been there. Have you?"

"No. I'd be a country boy in the big city."

"Is your family in Louisville?"

"Yep. My sister and brother and their spouses all help out with the horses."

"Your parents own a horse farm?"

He nodded.

Suzanna, her slice of pizza halfway to her mouth, paused. Recognition dawning, she gaped. "Kincaid? As in the Kincaids who breed racehorses?"

Again, he nodded.

"Holy crap, Austen," Suzanna screeched. "Why didn't you tell me you come from one of the premier families in Kentucky?"

"Because it's not important to me. The farm is my parents' business, not mine."

"Don't you live there?"

"Nope. I have an apartment in Louisville." He sipped his wine and sighed. "I'm the youngest child. In fact, I'm pretty sure I was a boo-boo. I loved growing up on the farm, and I love the horses, but that's not the life for me. When I got my journalism degree, my parents were extremely disappointed. When I told them my dream was to become an author, my dad had a fit.

He said that was fine as a hobby, but the chances of making a living at it were near zero. How was I supposed to provide for my family without an income? When I pointed out I was single and didn't have anyone to support but myself, the conversation went south. That's one reason getting the contract is so important to me. I want to show him I can make a living writing. Don't think I'm naive about making it as an author. It's going to be a horrific challenge; I just want the opportunity to prove myself."

"I can totally relate. Since my dad passed away, my mother has tried to run my sister Savannah's and my lives. She has the personality of a steamroller, and that's one of the reasons I want to leave Charlotte. She and I have never gotten along. She's incredibly bossy and opinionated. No matter what I do, or how I do it, it's wrong. This trip is the first time I've been somewhere she can't call and check up on me. She about drove me crazy during college, constantly wondering what I was doing and who was I doing it with." Suzanna shook her head. "She's nothing like my aunts and uncles. If she didn't resemble my grandmother, I'd wonder if she was adopted."

Austen squeezed her hand. "I have to say that when I'm told I can't do something, I'll do it or die trying."

Suzanna nodded. "I'm a little like that myself." She grinned. "Here we are. You want to write books, and I want to sell them. Hopefully, someday both our dreams come true."

Austen poured the last of the wine into their glasses. "So, have I satisfied your curiosity?"

Again, a blush crept across her cheeks. "I honestly wasn't trying to pry."

He reached over and squeezed her hand again. "You weren't prying. Most people get to know each other a little before jumping into bed. We just bypassed the first step."

"I, um, need to say something about that. This is going to sound like such a cliché, but I honestly don't hop into bed with a man I've only known for hours. I don't know what came over me."

"Are you sorry we spent the afternoon making love?"

"No. Not at all."

"Neither am I. And, if you're worried I'll think any less of you, you're wrong. I'm not going to say I didn't enjoy the sex, but I also enjoy being with you."

Suzanna's heart soared. *Perhaps he is the man of my dreams.* She smiled. "I'll agree with both of those."

Austen glanced through the open door to the clock on the side table. "I'd better change if we don't want to miss the murder."

Suzanna gathered up their glasses and the empty pizza box. "I can't wait to see if I'm right, and it's Vanessa who gets killed." While Austen changed, Suzanna applied her lipstick and placed items in her evening clutch. When she caught sight of Austen in his tux, her mouth went dry. He was handsome enough for the cover of *Gentleman's Monthly*.

His eyes full of heat, he stepped toward her. "Why don't we stay right here? We'll sit on the balcony, watch the storm, and create some turbulence of our own."

Suzanna took a step back. "Stop right there. We don't want to miss the murder, and besides, I'm looking forward to meeting the captain and drinking champagne."

Austen bowed and held open the cabin door. "If the lady wants champagne, champagne it will be. But I have to warn you, champagne makes me horny as hell."

Suzanna glanced back over her shoulder and whispered, "Me too."

They entered the Neptune room, already crowded. As they searched for an empty table, they waved at Dwain and his family. "There's one near the bar," Suzanna said, heading in that direction.

"Would you like something to drink?" Austen asked.

"Some iced tea, please. I've had enough wine for the time being."

****

As Austen headed toward the bar, Haley Henderson stepped in front of him.

"Well, if it isn't Austen," she said, giving him a slow smile while moving closer. "We meet again."

"Hi, Haley," he replied. "How you doin'?"

"Good, thanks. I enjoyed meeting up with you last night." She lowered her voice. "Perhaps we'll run into each other again tonight."

Damn it, what the hell was she up to? Austen glanced at Suzanna and silently swore at the hurt and confusion on her face. He had to defuse this situation. He shrugged. "Considering our encounter was simply chance, I doubt it. I told you I stopped in for a nightcap because I couldn't sleep." He placed his arm around Suzanna. "I had a pretty active afternoon, so I'm sure I won't have any problem sleeping tonight."

Haley glanced at Suzanna and smiled, but her eyes were full of venom. "I hope you two enjoy the show."

When Haley was out of hearing range, Austen leaned toward Suzanna. "After I left you last night, I stopped off at the Compass bar on my way to my cabin. Haley came in and sat down across from me."

Suzanna held up her hand. "Austen, stop. You don't owe me any explanation. It's okay."

"I don't want you to get the wrong idea."

"She's a flirt, and she likes you."

"Well, I'm not interested." Haley got her drink and headed toward the stage. "She's gone. I'll be right back."

"It seems everyone decided to get a drink at the same time," a tall guy whose name tag read *Rob* said as he made room for Austen at the bar.

Austen smiled. "No kidding."

"I tended bar in college. I could offer to help out," Rob's wife, Kelli, said good-heartedly.

Austen placed his order and returned to the table as Maggie took the stage.

"Good evening, everyone," Maggie said. "I hope you all enjoyed your day at sea."

Austen leaned toward Suzanna and whispered, "I certainly enjoyed mine."

"Stop it," she whispered back.

"As I said yesterday, tonight will lead up to our murder," Maggie continued. "So, sit back, put your detective hats on, and good luck."

The curtain parted to show Vanessa once again seated at her vanity, the necklace securely around her neck. She smiled at her reflection in the mirror. A knock came at her door, and she frowned.

She rose to answer, and her eyes opened wide in surprise. "Aunt Amelia, what on earth are you doing on

St. Pats?"

"Hello, Vanessa. May I come in?"

Vanessa shrugged. "You're here. You might as well."

Amelia stood in the middle of the floor and cleared her throat. "Vanessa, I'd like to talk to you about my mother's necklace, which I see you're wearing."

"Yes, Aunt Amelia, I'm wearing it because it belongs to me. And if you came all this way thinking otherwise, then you've wasted a trip. Not to mention the expense of getting here, money I'm sure you could have spent more wisely."

"I had hoped you'd decide to do the honorable thing and give me the necklace."

"Evidently my mother wanted me to have it, or she wouldn't have left it to me."

Amelia shook her head. "Your mother promised me the necklace would be mine. Since I didn't have children of my own, I then would leave it to you. If you had something to do with her changing the will, I implore you to follow her original wishes."

Vanessa's face hardened. "I have no idea what you're talking about. Besides, it's not my fault you never found a man to marry and take care of you. It's not my fault you've always had a boring low-end job that left you penniless. You must have some kind of pension. Isn't there somewhere you can go and live with other poor people?"

Hurt and bewilderment crossed Amelia's face. "Vanessa, I'm family. How can you do this?"

"Because if you owned the necklace, you'd sell it, and what you didn't keep you'd give to those loser siblings of mine."

"And what do you plan on doing with it? Wear the necklace like a trophy?"

Vanessa smiled. "Exactly. I worked hard to get where I am, and I deserve a reward." She cocked her head. "Besides, where would you ever go to wear a necklace this fabulous? I would think that fake pearl choker you have around your neck would be sufficient for your limited social life"

Amelia's cheeks flamed with anger. "You evil witch. You know nothing about my pearls."

Vanessa's eyebrows rose.

Amelia seemed to gather herself. She took a deep breath. "I hope that necklace brings you nothing but misery." Without another word, she left the room.

Vanessa reseated herself at her vanity and held the diamonds against her cheek. "You sparkle and shine just as I do, and we'll always be together." As she lifted her brush to fix her hair, another knock came at the door. Once again frowning, she rose to answer.

Belinda and Gordon didn't wait to be asked in. They pushed past her, and Belinda spoke.

"We've come for the necklace, so hand it over."

Vanessa shut the door and scowled. "I should have guessed Aunt Amelia wasn't here alone. Well, I'll tell you two what I told her, which is 'no.' The necklace is mine, and you'll have to get used to it."

"You're a lying bitch. You made Mother change her will, and we'll prove it," Belinda said.

Vanessa snorted. "Good luck."

"I should just rip it off your neck and see what you do then," Gordon said with a snarl.

Vanessa took a step back. "Try it, and I'll call the police."

"You know damn well Mother expected the necklace to be sold and the money split among Gordon, me, and Aunt Amelia," Belinda said. "Since you're so wealthy, you weren't supposed to have any of it. You're nothing but a selfish, self-centered bitch."

Vanessa's brows rose. "According to Aunt Amelia, Mother said the necklace was to go to her, then me. She didn't say anything about you two."

Dismay creased both their faces. Vanessa smirked with satisfaction. "I take it she didn't inform you of this."

"You're lying," Gordon snarled. "Mother wouldn't do that to us."

Vanessa stroked the diamonds. "Believe what you want. This necklace will bring me nothing but joy because every time I put it on, I'll know that I have it, and you don't. So, why don't you go back to your loser lives in your loser town and leave me alone."

"You're going to pay for this," Belinda stated. "Somehow, someway, you'll get what's coming to you. And I hope that necklace brings you nothing but pain."

Vanessa cocked her head. "Speaking of pain, heard from your husband lately?"

Belinda lunged at Vanessa, and Gordon grabbed her. "Don't. It's what she wants." His eyes blazed as he glowered at Vanessa. "You think you're so clever, but you're nothing but a whoring little gold-digger who will step on anyone to get what you want. Well, sis, paybacks are hell."

Vanessa's breath came in shallow gasps. "Is that right? And what would you know about paybacks? How far in debt are you, Gordon?"

At that moment Thomas entered the room. "What

the hell is going on?"

"These people were leaving," Vanessa said.

"Rot in hell, you evil bitch," Belinda shouted as she and Gordon stormed from the room. Vanessa kissed the necklace and laughed.

The curtain closed, and the room erupted with applause.

Maggie took the stage. "Weren't they great?"

"Yes," the room said as one.

The entire cast appeared and bowed.

Again, applause filled the room.

"Thanks, everyone," Maggie said. "Here's what you need to do to be a winner. We're taking our rules from the board game. As you read in your packet, there are certain shops where you can gather clue cards. They will list our suspects, choice of weapon, and crime scenes. In order to win, you have to guess who is murdered and by whom, with what, and where. We'll see all of you back here on our last night. Don't forget to turn in your sheet with your solutions. Also, since we dock in Costa Maya tomorrow, we won't have any other mystery activities. But while we're at sea, on the way back to Miami, in the Compass bar I'll be hosting mystery trivia games if you'd like to attend. All this information is in your packet."

"That was well done," Suzanna said. "It's going to be hard to figure out which one murders Vanessa."

Austen nodded. "They all have a motive, but I'm not convinced Vanessa is the victim."

"No kidding. Who's your other choice?"

"Aunt Amelia. At first, I took her for the murderer, but now I wonder if she's the one who legally threatens Vanessa."

Suzanna paused in thought. "I see what you mean." She glanced over the program. "It says here that the cards we can pick up from the shops have more background on each suspect."

"That's good. Hopefully, they'll give us more insight into who has the nerve to kill. But Vanessa is my first choice."

"I'm sticking with Vanessa as the murder victim and Thomas as the murderer. He's crazy about her. If she's cheating on him, he might be hurt enough to kill."

Austen sipped his soft drink. "Don't forget Vanessa's holding some kind of secret over him."

"Something to do with his past."

"How about his publishing career?"

"Good idea." Suzanna took her notebook from her bag. "Let's start writing down all our suggestions, so we don't forget."

"We could type them into our phones," Austen said.

"Yes, but using the notebook seems more detectivelike."

Austen grinned. "You're right, Miss Marple. What was I thinking?"

Chapter Seven

"This is so exciting," Suzanna said. "I always loved that board game."

"So did I." Austen rose, and they headed out of the room. "If you'd like to go to one of the shops, we have time before Cocktails with the Captain begins."

"Yes, let's." They made their way to the Coral Boutique, a trendy store carrying casual clothes.

"Hi, I'm Jamie," the salesperson said. "Can I help you with anything?"

"We'd like one of the clue cards," Suzanna said.

"Sure."

As Suzanna followed Jamie, the ship listed sharply to the right, and the two of them lost their balance and fell against a clothes rack, landing in a tangle of clothes and hats.

"Austen," Suzanna called.

"Are you hurt?"

"I don't think so. How about you?"

"I'm fine." Austen helped Suzanna to her feet.

Jamie sat on the floor, rubbing her foot, grimacing with pain. "It's my ankle."

Austen knelt next to her. "It's already beginning to swell. We need to get you to the infirmary."

Tears flowed down Jamie's cheeks. "I just got hired for this trip, and now I'll probably lose my job."

"Don't worry about that now," Suzanna said. "The

accident wasn't your fault. I can't imagine they'll fire you."

Jamie sniffed. "I hope you're right. Behind the counter, there's a number to call for help."

Austen located the card and dialed the extension. After explaining what had happened, he hung up. "Someone will be right here."

"We'll stay with you until they come," Suzanna said.

Jamie shook her head. "I'll be fine. Please go. You don't want to miss meeting the captain."

At that moment, the captain's voice came over the intercom.

"May I have everyone's attention. This is Captain Dave Murry from the bridge. We're going to encounter rough weather, but please don't be concerned. This ship is designed for these conditions. Unfortunately, we're going to have to close the pools and the outdoor lounges. For the time being, all indoor facilities will remain open. I apologize for any inconvenience, and hopefully the storm will pass quickly. I have to ask that everyone obey any instructions given to you by crew members. I'll see you soon on the promenade deck for our champagne gathering."

Austen and Suzanna said goodbye to Jamie and headed for the promenade deck. As the ship rolled, people grabbed onto anything that seemed stable.

"This is getting dangerous," Suzanna said as she peered out the window at the gray, heaving ocean and threatening sky. "I don't see how they'll serve champagne with the ship pitching like this."

Austen nodded. "I also don't see how they'll serve dinner in the dining room."

As the ship rocked and lurched, Suzanna clung onto Austen for balance.

As he held her close, he nuzzled her neck. "Although, this makes a great excuse for me to put my hands all over you in public."

"Stop that," Suzanna said, laughing.

They stood next to the piano bar as the piano player broke into a sexy blues song. "Oh, yeah," Austen whispered as he swayed to the music.

Suzanna wrapped her arms around his neck, laid her head on his shoulder, and let the music and the scent and feel of Austen carry her away.

"I suggest we skip meeting the captain, find our own dinner, then get a bottle of champagne and go back to your cabin," Austen whispered in her ear. "Then I can see how many times I can make you come while we sit on the balcony and watch the storm."

"Mmm, how could a girl turn down a proposition like that?"

"I was hoping you'd say that." He took her hand, and they headed for the elevators. "You know what, I've changed my mind. Let's go up to Rocket Burgers."

"You can't be hungry. We just finished pizza."

"All of a sudden, I'm in the mood for a big, cheesy burger."

Suzanna hesitated. "Won't the motion of the ship be worse up there?"

"Sure, that's half the fun. Come on. It will be fine."

The fifties-style diner was almost empty. The jukebox played Elvis as they sat near the window.

"Austen, I'm not sure about this," Suzanna said as the motion of the ship increased.

Before Austen replied, the waitress appeared. "Hi,

folks. Because of the storm, we may have to close the restaurant soon, so I need to take your order."

"No problem." Austen indicated the menu. "How about two burgers with the works, onion rings, and iced teas?"

Suzanna nodded and, with apprehension, stared out the window at the distant lightning. "I'm getting a little nervous about this storm. It's September and hurricane season. My mother went on and on about how dangerous it would be to go on a cruise now. I'll never hear the end of it if her prediction comes true. What will happen if we can't avoid it?"

"I suppose we ride it out and hope for the best, but I doubt it's even as bad as a tropical storm." He reached across the table and took her hand. "It might get a bit rocky, but I'm sure the captain won't allow us to be in any danger."

Their food arrived, and they both dug in. "This is the first time I've eaten a burger while wearing a tux."

Suzanna chuckled. "I was in a wedding once up in Michigan. After the reception, we were all starving, so we went to White Castle, which happened to be the only place open." She laughed. "We were quite the sight all dressed up in our bridesmaid dresses and the men in their tuxes. What made it funnier is the wedding couple came as well." She licked sauce from her finger. "This is really good. I can't believe I ate the whole thing."

"It's all those orgasms. You burned off lots of energy."

"Austen, stop it. Someone might hear you."

Austen chuckled and motioned for the check.

The jukebox was playing a twist as they finished

their meals. "Are you ready?"

She sipped the last of her tea. "Yes."

He signed for the food, and they made their way onto the outer deck. Wind buffeted against them, and Suzanna held on to him for balance.

"My hair," Suzanna yelped as the long tresses blew in her face. "Austen," she shouted above the wind. "Get me inside."

"We're okay," he shouted as he took her into his arms. He tried to guide them out of the wind, stumbled against a lounge, and fell onto it, Austen on the bottom with Suzanna sprawled on top. Both laughed uncontrollably as Suzanna wiggled to lie more comfortably.

Austen cupped her face and kissed her. His hand slid down her back to clasp her bottom.

"Have you ever made love outside?" he whispered.

Intoxicated with the taste of him, she replied, "No."

"There's no one around, and it's awful dark. I'll bet we wouldn't be seen."

His hand had left her bottom and moved between their bodies to slip his fingers beneath her bikini panties.

With what sanity remained in her lust-filled brain, she stopped him. "Austen, we are not making love on a lounge on the deck of a ship in a storm."

He placed soft kisses along her neck. "Are you sure?"

Being daring was one thing, but the thought of them being caught was more than Suzanna could handle. "Yes, I'm sure." She scrambled off Austen and straightened her dress. As she brushed her hair from her face, at the edge of her vision, a shadow moved. She lowered her voice. "Austen, someone's here."

Now on his feet, Austen peered into the darkness. "I don't see anything."

Suzanna shivered and rubbed her arms. "I have the strangest feeling we were being watched."

"It was probably a trick of the light."

"Perhaps, but let's get out of here." She led the way, and as they passed a DJ playing '80s music, Austen grabbed her hand.

"I love this song." He tugged her into the crowd of dancers and twirled her around the floor.

"You're crazy," she shouted with laughter while keeping up with him step for step. When the song changed, she gave him a mischievous grin and dirty-danced toward him.

He grinned back. "Oh, yeah, baby, bring it on."

She wiggled and shimmied against him as he circled her. By the time a slow song began, they were both out of breath and clinging to each other.

Suzanna waved her hand in front of her face. "I have to have something to drink."

"Me too. The champagne bar is right outside, and I promised you champagne."

When they stopped at the bar, Suzanna expected him to ask for two glasses. When he ordered a bottle, she protested. "Austen, that will cost a fortune."

He lightly kissed her. "It's a night for champagne." He handed her the empty flutes. "You carry these. I'll try and keep us upright." The motion of the swaying ship sent people careening against walls, tables, chairs, and other passengers. They made it to her cabin and stumbled through the door.

Chapter Eight

"Open the champagne," Suzanna said. "If we're going down, I want to be high when I do."

The cork popped, and Austen poured the bubbly liquid. "Stop worrying." He tapped his glass with hers. "Here's to us."

Suzanna took a pleasurable sip and smiled. "I love champagne."

Austen topped off their glasses and placed the bottle in the ice bucket. "Let's sit out on the balcony."

With uncertainty, Suzanna glanced toward the sliding doors. "Is it safe?"

"I'll hold you on my lap." He shrugged out of his jacket and undid his bow tie. "But first, take your panties off, but leave the dress and heels on."

She did as he asked. "Now what?"

Austen smiled. "You ride me." He slid the door open onto the balcony. The wind wasn't as strong as on the upper deck. He sat in one of the outdoor chairs and placed both their glasses on the side table. He opened his fly, released his already-hard shaft, and motioned for Suzanna to straddle his lap.

"Hop aboard, darlin'."

Suzanna, so turned on, feared she might come before she even had him inside her. She positioned herself above him and eased him into her wet heat. She sighed in pure pleasure as he filled her completely.

He slipped the thin straps of her dress off her shoulders and exposed her breasts. He ran his tongue across her nipples as Suzanna's orgasm rocketed through her. Crazed with lust, mindless of anything but the glorious sensations still throbbing through her, Suzanna moved over him as another climax built. She gripped his shoulders and ground against him. Thunder boomed as she cried his name.

Austen cupped her bare bottom and thrust his hard shaft deep and growled. "That's it, darlin', bring me with you."

Lightning flashed as the motion of the ship increased. So did Suzanna's rhythm.

"Baby, you're going to kill me." He slid his thumb between her legs and stroked her swollen clit.

Suzanna arched back and, for the third time, screamed his name.

"Christ," Austen cried as he erupted inside her.

Suzanna collapsed against his chest, her body molten silk. "Austen, I can't get up."

"That's fine with me, because I can't move either." He nuzzled her neck and whispered, "If it were possible, I'd keep you right where you are forever."

"If it were possible, I'd stay," Suzanna whispered back.

Another crack of lightning and a burst of wind, and rain soaked them both.

Suzanna squealed as the icy drops drenched her bare back. She extricated herself from Austen's lap and hurried inside.

"Talk about putting a damper on a romantic mood," Austen said, joining her in the cabin.

Laughter bubbled up in Suzanna as she slipped off

her soaked dress. "Tell me about it."

She stood wearing nothing but her two-inch heels. "You're so beautiful."

A stillness came over them as they stood, their eyes locked on one another. Without saying a word, Austen removed the rest of his clothes and reached for her. "I believe the mood is back."

Pale sunlight streaked across the rumpled bed as Suzanna opened her eyes. Austen lay beside her, his arm draped across her waist. *If there was a way to stop time, I'd do it now. This trip is a magical dream I never want to wake from.*

She snuggled closer to Austen's warm body. Unfortunately, the logical portion of her brain that wasn't full of sexual delights took that moment to rear its ugly head. *Suzanna, be careful. Don't let yourself become too emotionally involved with him. After the cruise is over, you may never see him again.* That unwelcome thought brought a stab to her heart. Was it already too late? Was she too attached to him?

Suzanna, reality check. He lives in Louisville and you in Charlotte. What kind of relationship could you have? Besides, he said if he gets the contract with H&H he might move to New York. And you plan to leave Charlotte. Suzanna let out a long sigh, willing her common sense to shut up. *I have three more days with him. I'm not going to worry about the future until I step onto the plane.*

Austen's hand slid up her leg. "Morning, sweet," he whispered, sending tiny goose bumps over her skin.

When his fingers found the heat between her legs, Suzanna moaned, knowing that when it came to Austen Kincaid, her common sense was nonexistent.

Chapter Nine

"We're docking in Costa Maya." Suzanna pointed out the window as they sat in the Windjammer, having breakfast.

Sunlight sparkled upon the water beneath fluffy white clouds in a clear azure sky.

"Thank goodness the storm is behind us. I read where the area with the hotels and shops was developed specifically for cruise ships and tourists."

Austen's mouth turned down at the corners. "Tourist trinket shops are last on my list of things to do. What about the Mayan water park?"

"Sure, that sounds like fun. I have the brochure." She reached in her straw bag and removed a handful of shiny pamphlets.

Austen shook his head. "That bag of yours is like Hermione's purse."

She grinned. "It's good to be prepared. They have various levels of waterslides running through a fake Mayan temple. There's also a zip line where you end up in a pool, and my favorite, the Lazy River."

"Perfect. After we eat, we'll sign up."

"According to this," Suzanna continued reading, "you can rent lockers. I'm going to change into my bathing suit and wear it under my clothes. We can place our extra items in the locker."

An hour later, they climbed aboard the bus to the

water park. Once there, it didn't take long to store their things in the locker. Suzanna removed her shorts and top and slipped a sheer sleeveless cover-up over her tangerine-striped bikini and slid her feet into matching water shoes.

Austen, in swim trunks and a T-shirt, frowned. "That suit doesn't leave much to the imagination. You're going to have every man here ogling you."

Suzanna inwardly smiled. *So, he's a little jealous. Good.* "I doubt it. Plenty of pretty girls are wearing less than me."

"Not by much," he murmured.

Suzanna swallowed back her mirth. "Let's go through a few shops before we get wet."

The thatch-roofed stores were full of the usual tourist souvenirs. Suzanna headed toward a display of hats and clothing. She was admiring a peasant-style blouse when Austen startled her with an extremely lifelike rubber iguana.

She scrunched up her face. "Yuck."

"Cool, isn't it?"

"No, it is not. Take it away."

"You'd better get used to it. There are real ones running around outside."

"I'll ignore them."

"I'm ready to go. How about you?"

Suzanna hung the blouse back on the rack. "I'm going to get this on our way out."

"Whatever."

"You're not much of a shopper, are you?"

"Nope."

Suzanna rolled her eyes. "You remind me of my cousin Dillon. What do you want to do first?" she asked once they were outside.

"How about if we begin with the slide, then the zip line. Then we can dry off a bit and go find lunch."

"The slide has different levels. I'm not going down the seventy-eight-foot one, but I'll do the Lord of the Dead, Yum Kimil. It's a forty-foot drop."

"Chicken."

"That's right. You'll also not get me on the rope bridge."

"Ah, I'll pass on that as well."

"If you want to go on the tall slide, I'll wait for you at the bottom."

"Isn't there one we can go down together?"

Suzanna nodded.

He placed his arm around her shoulder. "Let's do it."

They made their way through the park and came upon an outdoor table where Haley, Brad, Clarice, JJ, and Melinda sat drinking tropical concoctions. They tried to hurry past. Haley, in a wide-brimmed hat and sunglasses, waved. "Hey there, Austen," she called.

"Damn," Austen said under his breath.

Suzanna wasn't pleased either, but it would be rude not to stop.

"Hi, how y'all doing?" Austen asked.

Haley crossed her legs, and her short skirt rode high on her thigh. With her hand, she indicated the table. "I don't believe you've met Austen Kincaid." Ignoring Suzanna, she continued. "He's one of our mystery guests." She smiled. "I'll bet Austen is clever enough to follow all the clues and win the prize."

Shocked at Haley's flirtatiousness in front of her husband, Suzanna surreptitiously studied Austen's reaction. Judging by his scowl, he wasn't pleased.

Austen clenched his jaw so tightly, he thought it might crack. Not only did the rude woman act as if Suzanna wasn't there, she purposely came onto him in front of her husband. It took everything he had not to tell her off, but it wouldn't accomplish anything, just embarrass Suzanna and Brad. He held Suzanna close to him. "Suzanna is the clever one. My money is on her."

"Well, good luck to you both," Brad said.

Austen nodded. "Thanks. If you'll excuse us, we're on our way to the waterslide." Without another word, they walked away.

"What an awful person Haley is," Suzanna said. "I swear that if someday I have my own bookstore, I won't carry her books."

Austen kissed her cheek. "Forget her. She's Brad's problem, not ours."

"While you were talking with Haley, I was studying the others. When your name was mentioned, Clarice Abbot's attention sharpened."

"Really?"

"She may have recognized your name from your manuscript. It might be a good sign."

"I hope you're right. I didn't want to say anything for fear of jinxing myself, but I have the sequel to the book ready to go."

"Oh, Austen, she might offer you a multi-book contract."

"Let's not get ahead of ourselves. At this point, any offer would be great. Here's the elevator to the slide. Ready?"

"As ready as I'll ever be."

****

Haley's eyes glittered in anger as Austen disappeared into the crowd. She sure as hell didn't appreciate being dismissed, nor would she accept it. She made a vow to herself: she would have Austen in her bed.

Brad chuckled. "He doesn't seem interested, my dear. Better luck next time."

Haley tossed her head. "Don't be silly. I have no idea what you're talking about."

"You're walking on thin ice," Brad said. "Watch your step."

"That can go both ways." Haley finished her drink. "Who's ready for another round?"

****

Side by side on a mat, Austen and Suzanna flew down the slide, Austen laughing, while Suzanna, holding his hand in a death grip, screamed.

"Awesome," Austen exclaimed when they reached the ground. "Want to do it again?"

"No. I need a drink."

"Ah, come on, it wasn't that bad."

"Okay, it was fun, but once is enough. If you want to go again, I'll find somewhere to sit."

"No problem, I'll wait for the zip line." He guided her to an umbrella table. "What will you have?"

"I'd love an ice-cold beer."

"Me too." The waitress appeared, and they ordered a couple of the local beers.

"Are you hungry?" Austen asked. "The loaded nachos sound good."

"Sure, and some chips and salsa."

"So, what do you think of Costa Maya?" Austen asked after the waitress left.

"It's touristy, but I like it. I still want to do some shopping, but you don't have to go with me."

Austen nodded. "I'll head back to the ship and lie by the pool. With most people on shore, it shouldn't be crowded."

After they ate, the zip line proved to be another experience Suzanna wasn't eager to repeat. Now she and Austen lay floating on the Lazy River. His arm was around her as she gazed into the brilliant blue sky. There had been happy moments in her life, but none compared with her utter contentment with this man. A future spent with the sun on her face and Austen by her side as they glided through life sounded perfect. She sighed. *Suzanna, you've been reading too many romance novels.* But these days with Austen could be from the pages of a book.

"What are you smiling about?" Austen asked.

"How perfect life is at this moment."

"Yep, this would be easy to get used to."

She stared into his handsome face. *But could you get used to spending it with me?* she wanted to ask.

"I won't be long," Suzanna said as they parted in front of the souvenir huts. "I'll meet you by the pool."

Suzanna stood debating between a peasant blouse and a skort with tropical flowers when a female voice said, "They'd look great together."

Suzanna glanced up to see Melinda Pearce standing next to her. "I agree, but I've already bought quite a lot on the ship."

"Oh, go for it. What are vacations for?"

Suzanna grinned. "You're the kind of lady I enjoy shopping with."

Melinda grinned back, then paused. "This is none

of my business, but I'd like to give you some advice."

"What's that?"

"Watch out for Haley."

Suzanna cocked her head. "What do you mean?"

"Let me ask you this. Have you and Austen been together long?"

"No, why? We just met on the ship."

"I wouldn't want Haley spoiling any relationship you might develop."

"Why would she do that?"

"Because she's a conniving witch who doesn't care who she hurts." Melinda touched Suzanna's arm. "I wouldn't put it past her to have her sights on Austen."

Suzanna, totally taken aback, wasn't sure how to respond. "Okay, um, thanks for warning me."

Melinda gave her a slight smile. "Good luck."

After Melinda left, Suzanna stood stock-still. Was she right that Haley's interest in Austen went beyond flirtation? Unease twisted Suzanna's stomach. How could she ever compete with someone as famous and outgoing as Haley? Although Austen didn't show any interest in her. Perhaps Melinda read the situation wrong. Suzanna, clothing in hand, headed for the checkout. As she stood in line, a display of necklaces and bracelets made of coral and shell caught her eye. When she stepped closer, she noticed Clarice Abbot on the other side of the glass counter.

"Oh, hello," Suzanna said.

Clarice glanced up and smiled. "Isn't it gorgeous?" She pointed at a gold-and-coral hair clip shaped like a shell.

"It's very pretty."

"It's awfully expensive, but I have to have it."

Suzanna grinned. "Go for it."

"I believe I will." Clarice motioned for the clerk to remove the clip from the case.

Suzanna's eye was caught by a pair of delicate coral earrings. Thinking they'd be perfect with her new sundress, she looked for the price. "Oh," she gasped at the three-digit figure. Regretfully, she left the earrings and got in line to pay for her clothing. When she arrived at the area to catch the bus back to the ship, she found she'd just missed it. Packages in hand, she sat on a bench to wait.

Chapter Ten

"Excuse me, Austen."

Half drowsing in a lounge chair on the deck, Austen jumped when the female voice spoke. He opened his eyes. Standing in front of him was Clarice Abbot. Speechless, he stared, willing his brain to form a coherent response.

"I'm sorry if I woke you. I'm Clarice Abbot, but I'm sure you know that by now. Would you mind if we talked?"

Damn, was this it? Was she about to tell him she read his book and wasn't interested? Or was this the break he'd hoped for? He opened his mouth, but when nothing came out, he nodded. He swallowed hard and motioned to the chair next to him. "Please have a seat."

"I don't normally talk to authors who have sent me a manuscript until a contract has been finalized, but when I realized who you were, I wanted to speak to you in person. I've read *Upheaval*, and I loved it. With good marketing, I believe you could hit the NYT best seller list. I'd like to set a date to discuss a contract with H&H."

Austen's pulse raced. Barely able to contain his excitement, Austen smiled. "I'm glad you enjoyed the book. I'd be happy to talk with you." He hesitated. Should he tell her about the sequel? No guts, no glory. "Actually, if you're interested, I've written a sequel."

"I'm definitely interested. Do you have it with you?"

"No. I didn't bring my laptop."

"No problem. Send it to me when you can. Here's my card. When you get home, contact my scheduler, and she'll set up a time for us to go over everything."

Austen, hoping his hand was steady, took the cream-colored card she handed him.

"By the way, where are you from?"

"Louisville, Kentucky."

"Would you be willing to come to New York for some promo?"

"Sure, like what?"

"Local television and bookstore appearances. It's a way to get your name out there." She rose. "I'll go into more detail later." She held out her hand. "It was nice meeting you." She cocked her head. "You and your friend seem like a nice couple, so I'm going to give you some advice. Stay as far away from Haley as you can. If she has her sights on you, she'll do anything to get what she wants. Trust me, I know."

Austen gaped in surprise. How was he supposed to respond? "I can tell you, besides the fact Haley's married, I have no interest in her."

Clarice laughed without humor. "That won't stop her." She turned to leave. "Enjoy the rest of your cruise."

Austen, unable to filter everything that had happened in the last few minutes, sat until Clarice was out of sight. My God, he'd done it. After all the disappointments and all the rejection letters, now a contract with H&H. Wait until he told Suzanna. He hoped she wasn't too tired from their day, because tonight they were celebrating. He glanced around. Would people think he was crazy if he started jumping up and down and let out a loud yee-haw? Grinning like a fool, Austen rose and went to make reservations for dinner in the Steak House restaurant.

Suzanna, loaded down with packages, opened her cabin door, and Austen swept her off her feet. "What are you doing?" she exclaimed as her packages went flying.

"I did it, Suzanna. I did it."

"Austen, you're making me dizzy. Put me down."

"I've been offered a contract with H&H."

Suzanna gaped. "Seriously?"

"That's right." He relayed his conversation with Clarice. "So, I might be going to New York after all."

She hugged him tight. "I'm so happy for you. You'll be in the big leagues now."

"Well, that might be a long way off, but it's a start. I hope you're not too tired, because we're celebrating. I've already made dinner reservations. Then we're going dancing."

"Okay, sounds like fun. Give me time to change." She gathered her shopping bags.

"What is all that?"

"Some souvenirs for my friend Amy and her little girl." She smiled. "And a few things for me."

"A few things, yeah right." He glanced at the digital clock. "I'll go clean up and meet you at the Steak House in an hour."

Suzanna took a quick shower, then slipped on a yellow sundress with colorful, tiny beach chairs and umbrellas stitched around the hem. She put on yellow-and-white strappy sandals and grabbed her straw bag.

In the central hall, she impatiently waited for the elevator. The doors opened, and Suzanna hesitated. "You're pretty full. I'll take the next one."

"Come on, pretty lady, we can make room for one more." A man in a cowboy hat motioned her in.

Suzanna smiled. "Thank you."

"She's making a fool out of him," a woman behind Suzanna whispered.

"Yes, but what's he supposed to do about it?" a man replied.

"Divorce her, that's what," the woman said in a harsh tone.

"He won't."

"I wouldn't be so sure. There comes a time when you have to say 'enough.' "

"Yeah, well, look what she did to me," the man said. "Her ruthlessness is well-known."

"You don't have to remind me," the woman added. "There has to be a reason he won't leave her."

"I'd give anything to know what that might be."

The elevator doors opened, and Suzanna exited with the others. Curious who the people behind her were, she glanced over her shoulder. Her mouth formed a silent "oh." JJ Jackson and Melinda Pearce exited in the opposite direction. Suzanna continued on her way to meet Austen, her brows knitted together in thought. Were they referring to Haley? If so, what had she done to make them dislike her so much? She certainly flirted with Austen. A pang of jealousy shot through Suzanna.

Austen would soon be in New York working with H&H. Her steps slowed. If Haley were known to cheat on her husband, what would stop her from setting her sights on Austen? Melinda had warned her. What if

Austen and Haley did have an affair? *Suzanna, you have no claim over him. He's a shipboard romance, nothing more.* Suzanna snorted. *Keep telling yourself that, but deep inside, you know the truth. You're falling in love with Austen Kincaid, and there isn't anything you can do about it.*

****

Austen smiled with pure pleasure as Suzanna walked toward him. *It's amazing how close to her I've become in such a brief time. When I get home, I'm going to miss her.* The thought of never seeing her again was something he didn't want to contemplate. Besides, even if he ended up in New York, Charlotte wasn't that far away.

"You look great," he said when she stopped in front of him. "As if you've just come from the beach."

"Thanks. My sister in Savannah designed this dress for my birthday. It's her own line called Beachi."

He took her arm and guided her into the restaurant. Deep-red cloths covered the tables. In the center, hammered metal holders contained white rosebuds. After the waiter took their order, red wine for her and a bourbon and water for him, Austen studied the menu.

"They have a porterhouse for two, with garlic mashed potatoes and a vegetable. How does that sound?"

"Great." She lowered her voice. "Did you see the price?"

"Don't worry about it. We're celebrating. Besides, if my book does as well as Clarice expects, I'll be rolling in money."

She toasted him with her glass. "You and Grisham."

He grinned. "In my dreams."

"You never know. You might become so famous you forget I exist."

He reached across and took her hand. "Not on your life, darlin'. There's no way I'd forget you or this trip."

The joy in her eyes touched his heart. After his last breakup, he'd decided until his writing career was doing well, another relationship would have to wait. But Suzanna understood the dedication it took to succeed in the writing world. Even though they lived in different states, they shared the world of books, and hopefully they could make this work.

Suzanna's smile turned into a frown, and Austen glanced over his shoulder to see what had caught her eye. There, waiting to be seated, were Haley and Brad. What kind of weird fate was it that no matter where they were, Haley showed up?

Suzanna slipped her hand from his and sipped her wine. "It seems we weren't the only ones wanting a steak."

"Hopefully, they won't see us."

Suzanna snorted. "Not a chance. Here they come."

"Well, hello again," Haley said, her words slightly slurred.

Austen and Suzanna both nodded.

Haley ignored Suzanna and directed her question to Austen. "Did you enjoy your day on Costa Maya?"

"Yes, we both did," Austen replied.

Brad tugged at Haley's arm. "Come on. Let them enjoy their evening."

Haley pulled away from Brad and flung out her hand, not noticing she'd knocked over Suzanna's wineglass. "We had a wonderful time."

"Oh," Suzanna shrieked as the red liquid landed in her lap.

Brad's brows drew together, and he let out an exasperated sigh. "For God's sake, Haley, look what you've done."

Haley barely glanced toward Suzanna and shrugged. "Oh, well, accidents happen. I'm sure that dress can easily be replaced."

Suzanna jumped from her seat. Austen's mouth formed a thin line. "Suzanna, what can I do?"

Suzanna gritted her teeth. Her self-control was about to snap. She wanted nothing more than to toss her full glass of water in Haley's face. Instead, without a word, she headed for the ladies' room. When she examined her dress, she discovered the heavy cloth napkin had absorbed most of the wine. If she got cold water on the remaining spots, they should come out. Tears filled her eyes as she dabbed at the stains. The bitch did it on purpose. It was too bad her murder in the skit was pretend because Suzanna wouldn't think twice about strangling her for real.

"Oh, my, what a shame," a woman said. "That's such a cute dress."

Suzanna glanced up to see an older woman standing next to her. "I think it's coming out."

"Wait a minute." The woman rummaged around in her purse. "I'm a klutz and carry stain remover with me. Yes, here you go." She handed Suzanna a small spray bottle. "This should help."

Grateful, Suzanna applied it to the spots. "This is the first time I wore this dress. It was a gift from my sister." Suzanna sighed in relief as the red started to fade. "Thank you so much." She handed the bottle

76

back.

Austen, furious, glowered at Haley, who ignored him. She continued drunkenly prattling about her day in Costa Maya, until Brad interrupted.

"Please tell your friend how sorry we are. If the stain won't come out, let me know, and I'll reimburse her for the cost of the dress." His grip tightened on Haley's arm, and he practically dragged her to their table.

Suzanna returned and sighed in relief to see Haley was gone.

"I didn't order yet. I wasn't sure you'd still want to eat here," Austen said.

"I thought about leaving, but I won't give Haley the satisfaction of knowing she ran us off. It's your night to celebrate, and that's what we'll do."

He took her hand in his. "If you're sure."

The waiter took their order, then Austen continued. "I have to say, this entire situation with my contract offer has me both excited and apprehensive."

"Why?"

"If I go to New York, I'll have to deal with Haley, which is something I'd rather avoid."

"You'll have to make her understand you're not interested."

Austen snorted. "I'm not sure that matters to her. Damn it. This is the beginning of my career, and I don't want her messing it up."

"All you can do is be firm and stay away from her as much as possible." She debated whether to tell him what Melinda had told her, and decided he was better off warned. "Austen, after you left the island earlier, I ran into Melinda." She proceeded to explain. "So, you see, you might have more of a problem than you thought."

Austen nodded. "Clarice told me the same thing. Now, enough of Haley. Let's not let her ruin our night."

"I agree. I'm starving. And I'll have another glass of wine."

They tucked into a perfectly grilled steak, creamy mashed potatoes, and steamed asparagus.

"Oh my," Suzanna said when she'd finished. "That was the best steak I've ever eaten."

"Don't forget we have chocolate mousse for dessert."

"Are you kidding? I can't eat another bite."

"That's okay. We'll take it with us, and I'll feed it to you in bed." He lowered his voice. "Or I'll dab some on your body and lick it off."

The image that created made Suzanna's mouth water more than the thought of chocolate mousse. She smiled. "Or I might lick it off you."

"I'd say we'd better leave before we do something in public we're not supposed to."

They left the restaurant and were passing the casino when Austen paused. "I know I promised you sexual delights, but let's postpone our carnal dessert and go in."

Suzanna nodded. "Sure. Besides, anticipation is half the fun."

Austen and Suzanna entered the glittering casino to the sound of bells and whistles from slot machines, the ticking of a small ball as it fell into a spinning roulette wheel, and a young man calling craps.

"What would you like to play?" Austen asked.

"I've only been to the casino on the Cherokee

reservation once," Suzanna replied. "And all I played was the slot machines."

"I enjoy roulette. Let's start there." Austen found them two seats at the table.

"What do I do?" Suzanna asked.

Austen explained, and Suzanna placed one dollar chip on Red and another on sixteen.

Austen nodded and placed his chips on the four corners around eight with one in the center.

Suzanna held her breath as the wheel spun, and the ball clattered to a stop.

"Sixteen," the croupier called.

Suzanna squealed in delight. "Austen, I won."

"Good for you," Austen said with a grin. "Do you want to try again?"

"Can I place my chips like you're doing yours?"

"Sure." He did as she asked, and the wheel spun.

When she hit again, Suzanna leaped from her chair, clapping. "Austen, this is such fun."

Austen laughed. "At least one of us is winning."

Suzanna noticed his dwindling stack of chips. "Oh, I'm sorry." She pushed chips toward him. "Here, you can have some of mine."

"No, those are yours. I still have some, and I haven't given up yet."

"Would you mind if I cash out and go play the slots? I love pulling the arm and hearing the coins fall."

He kissed her. "Go have fun. We'll buy another bottle of champagne with your winnings."

Suzanna made her way along the rows of machines until she found one she liked. Her thrifty nature would normally kick in, and she'd play the quarter slots, but tonight she was feeling reckless and chose the dollar ones.

Suzanna's tray was brimming with coins, when a voice behind her said, "Well, well, look who's sitting all alone. Did your luck run out with Austen?"

Suzanna swung around to find Haley, drink in hand, leaning against the chair next to her. Still pissed over the wine being spilt on her dress, Suzanna, her words dripping ice, replied, "Excuse me? I have no idea what you're talking about."

"What happened? Did he buy you a nice dinner, then send you on your way? I knew it was only a matter of time before he became bored with you." Haley's glance traveled over Suzanna. "Some backwoods farmer might find you appealing, but, seriously, someone as handsome as Austen, no way. I'm sure he saw you as nothing more than an easy shipboard fling."

Suzanna was well aware that people took her for a quiet mouse, but there were those who had discovered she could hold her own if provoked.

Suzanna smiled sweetly and thickened her North Carolina accent. "There's only one little bitty problem with your theory. I may not be so sophisticated, but I can assure you, Austen would rather be with me than a pathetic tramp who can't keep her own husband and who has to throw herself at men in order to get their attention." Suzanna scooped up her coins and left Haley gaping.

****

Austen, happy he had managed to win back his losses plus a little, was stacking his chips when Suzanna approached. "Hey, that's an impressive bucket of coins. I don't have to ask how you did." Austen, noticing the tears brimming in her eyes, hesitated.

"What's wrong?"

Suzanna shook her head. "Not here. Let's go."

"Okay, I'll cash us out."

Austen knew from experience with emotional sisters to keep silent as he followed Suzanna through the ship to her cabin. Once inside, he placed their dessert in the small refrigerator. "Okay, what happened?"

Suzanna's tears flowed down her cheeks, and she sniffed. "Haley approached me while I was playing the slots." She repeated all Haley had said.

"That bitch."

"Austen."

"Well, she is. I hope you told her where she could go."

"I said a few things and called her a tramp."

Austen smiled. "Good for you."

Suzanna stared at her hands clenched in her lap. "Is she right?"

"Right about what?"

"That I'm not glamorous enough for you."

"What?" Austen sat next to her on the love seat. "Suzanna, she's jealous and lashing out. I didn't grow up in an uptown fancy-ass neighborhood. I'm from the country, like you." He gathered her in his arms. "You're exactly right for me." He kissed her. "We still have our chocolate mousse. How about I get it and we feed each other in bed?"

Suzanna laughed. "That sounds wonderful."

Austen rose and headed for the refrigerator, vowing that the next time he saw Haley, he'd make sure she understood, without a doubt, that he had no interest in her and never would.

Chapter Eleven

"What's on the schedule for today?" Austen asked, pouring coffee from the carafe. Exhausted after the previous day—and night—they decided to have breakfast delivered to Suzanna's room, then carried it out to the balcony.

"Since this is our last day, and the murder is tonight, we'd better gather our clue cards and see what kind of detectives we are."

"Sounds good. Anything else?"

"Sure, I understand they're playing bingo at one o'clock." The incredulity on his face made Suzanna laugh. "Just kidding. Actually, I plan on kicking your ass at miniature golf."

Austen's brows rose. "Is that right?"

Suzanna nodded.

"Well, if you're so sure you'll kick my ass, let's make a bet."

Suzanna hesitated. "What kind of bet?"

"If I win, you have to strip for me, then feed me in bed."

She rolled her eyes. "And if I win?"

He leaned close and whispered.

At his words, a warm tingling sensation flowed through Suzanna.

"So, is it a bet?"

A mischievous light danced in his eyes. She

nodded. "You're on."

Austen grinned. "Okay, well, I need a shower and clean clothes. I'll go to my cabin and meet you where?"

Suzanna stepped into the room and removed the instruction booklet from her purse. "It says the cards can be picked up at the coffee shop, general store, ice cream parlor, the wine bar, and the coral boutique, which we need to go back to. The shops are all up on the promenade. Give me an hour to get ready, and I'll meet you at the general store. We'll work our way to the wine bar. I'm sure we'll need a break by then."

"Okay." Austen folded his napkin and placed it on the tray. He stood and bent to kiss her. "Did I tell you how sexy you are in the morning?"

Suzanna snorted. "Yeah, right."

"I'm serious. Your hair is kind of mussed, and your cheeks are rosy pink. You glow as if you've been thoroughly made love to." He kissed her again. "And I'm glad I'm the one who made you look like that."

After he left, Suzanna sat staring at his empty chair.

I'm falling in love with him, and I'm probably in big trouble. It's my luck to find someone I'm comfortable with, who makes me laugh, is fun to be with, and is every woman's fantasy in bed, only to have him live in another state, and who may soon forget about me. She let out a long sigh. *Suzanna, you don't know how he feels. He might be as crazy about you as you are about him. He sure acts like he cares. Give it a chance. Don't make the glass half-empty until you have to. Tomorrow, you dock in Miami and will go your separate ways. Enjoy him while you can and hope you have a future with him.*

But as she rose and headed for the shower, Haley's words from the night before wouldn't leave her mind.

An hour later, Austen peered at Suzanna's notebook and smiled. Across the top of the page for writing clues, she'd written, "Think Like Miss Marple."

"Miss Marple, huh?"

She nodded. "This skit reminded me of one of her stories."

"Okay, then who should I be?"

"If you want to stay in the time period, I'm crazy about Roderick Alleyn."

"I haven't read any of those books, but if you're crazy about him—" He stepped close and kissed her lips. "—I'll do my best to act the part."

The promise in his eyes sent waves of pleasure through her. She cleared her throat. "I would imagine that would be the biggest thrill Miss Marple ever received."

Austen laughed and took her hand. "Let's go collect clues so we can set our minds on other activities."

As they went from shop to shop, they met other mystery sleuths. Suzanna, unable to resist, also took the opportunity to shop. By the time they'd collected all the clues, along with several shopping bags, Austen was ready for a break.

"It amazes me that after everything you bought yesterday you can still shop." Austen sighed when Suzanna handed him another bag.

"I never get tired of shopping."

"Tell me about it. Let's drop these off at your cabin, then instead of going to the wine bar, let's try the Galley pub for a sandwich and a beer."

"Fine with me. I'll bring the cards, and we can go through them. I'm curious as to what they say."

Soon they were eating roast beef on rye and drinking cold mugs of beer. Suzanna laid out the five cards. "Remember the skit takes place on St. Pats. The rules say we have to decide who the murderer is—who done it, where the murder took place, and what weapon was used. Our choices for the place are Vanessa and Brad's hotel room, the outdoor bar near the pool, and the beach. The weapons are a knife, poison, or a gun."

Austen nodded, and Suzanna continued.

"Here are the character profiles." She read them off:

"Vanessa Grimes, supermodel. Was she supposed to inherit the necklace? Or was Aunt Amelia telling the truth, and she was the next in line? Did Vanessa coerce her mother into changing the will?

"Thomas Grimes. What secret does Vanessa hold over him? Does he genuinely love his wife, or is there another woman? Does the secret have something to do with his writing?

"Belinda Pool, Vanessa's sister. Does she resent Vanessa's fame? Is she still jealous over the affection Vanessa received as a child from their grandmother? Does she blame Vanessa for her divorce?

"Gordon Pool, Vanessa's brother. Does he truly have a gambling problem, or is his wife overly fond of expensive jewelry?

"Amelia Stone, Vanessa's aunt. How upset is she over not inheriting the necklace? Does she resent the cruel way Vanessa has always treated her?"

"That's it," Suzanna said. "Who's your first choice for our murderer?"

"Aunt Amelia," he replied. "She suspects Vanessa is lying. And she needs the money more than the others."

Suzanna gnawed on her lower lip. "I agree, but I also don't trust Belinda."

Austen hesitated. "She's an excellent choice, but if I were writing this, Amelia would be the one."

"Belinda acts as if she's super jealous of Vanessa and comes across as a real bitch."

Austen laughed. "Well, I'll give you that. What's your choice of weapon?"

"The knife. It can't be a gun because they flew, and they couldn't have carried it through security. And how could someone put poison in a drink or food? They would have to bring it with them."

"I agree."

"We also have to choose where the murder takes place. I'd say this would be somewhere there isn't a lot of people, such as their hotel room."

"One thing we weren't told is what time of day the murder happens."

Suzanna tapped her pen against her chin. "So, if it were late at night, the murder could happen at the bar or on the beach."

"I think the hotel room is too obvious," Austen said.

"Me too. How about the outside bar? Her murderer could have lured her there."

"Sure, why not? "Okay, Miss Marple. Vanessa is our victim, Aunt Amelia our murderer, with a knife at the outside bar."

Suzanna smiled. "But Chief Inspector Alleyn, I choose Belinda as the killer."

Austen threw up his hands. "I give."

Suzanna laughed and finished filling out their form. "All done. We can drop this off on our way to miniature golf." She stood and spotted Clarice and Brad sitting at a table behind a potted plant.

"What are you staring at?" Austen asked.

Suzanna motioned for him to keep walking. When they were in the hall, she told him what she'd seen. "I'm telling you, Brad's face looked thunderous. Clarice's back was to me, but their conversation seemed pretty intense."

Austen shrugged. "Probably something to do with work."

"Perhaps, but I'll bet it's about Haley. Darn. I left my notebook on the table. I'll be right back." She hurried to where they'd been seated. As she passed Clarice and Brad, Clarice, her voice slightly raised, said, "Seriously, Brad, she's making a fool out of you in front of everyone. I'm afraid that nice young man Austen is her next victim. She's like a black widow about to strike. Austen has talent and doesn't need the harlot interfering in his life. It's time you tossed her out on her ass."

Suzanna, not wanting them to see her, grabbed the notebook and fled. She spotted Austen by the elevator and hurried to him.

"What's wrong?" he asked.

"Quick, get in."

"Why?" he asked as the elevator doors closed.

Suzanna related what she'd overheard. "Austen, you can't let your guard down around Haley."

Anger and disgust filled his eyes. "Why the hell did she have to choose me? If Brad knows she's got her sights on me, he could destroy my career."

"Clarice was defending you," Suzanna said. "I'm sure you have an ally in her."

Austen sighed. "Let's forget about this bullshit." He took her hand. "Get ready to get your ass kicked at golf."

They'd arrived at the stern of the ship where the miniature golf was located. Two couples were finishing, so Austen and Suzanna stepped to the rail where the Gulf of Mexico was spread out before them.

"I was raised in the mountains," Suzanna said, "but I always loved the water. Growing up, we'd take vacations to the Outer Banks or Hilton Head."

"Didn't you say your family owned a ranch?"

"My grandparents did, but now my cousin Dillon does. It's called the Lazy M."

"What kind of ranch?"

"Horses and cabin rentals. When I was young, I spent summers there, but it's too rural for me."

"It sounds perfect."

"You and Dillon would get along great. No one loves horses more than he does. He used to ride the rodeo circuit, but he recently got married and now has the ranch."

Austen cocked his head. "That wouldn't be Dillon McCoy, would it?"

Suzanna nodded.

"No kidding. I love rodeo and used to follow him when he competed. You'll have to introduce me to him."

"Perhaps once you get everything settled with your book, we can go to the Lazy M."

"It's a date."

"Hey, look, sharks," a woman near the railing called.

Suzanna glanced down at the dark fins and shuddered. "I love the ocean, but I'm absolutely terrified of sharks."

"I take it that means no snorkeling."

Again, she shuddered. "I'll walk along the edge, but that's as far as I'll go." Suzanna noticed a woman seated nearby doing a charcoal drawing of a young girl holding her doll. "Austen, let's have her do one of us."

"Sure, why not?"

"Hello," the woman said as Suzanna and Austen stopped next to her. "I'm Charlene. Would you like a sketch of the two of you?"

"Yes, please," Suzanna replied.

"How about standing next to the rail," Charlene suggested. "I can get the water behind you."

"Perfect," Suzanna said. She and Austen stood where Charlene indicated. Austen placed his arm around Suzanna, and she laid her head on his shoulder.

"Oh, how nice," Charlene said. "Don't move."

Minutes later, Suzanna smiled in delight as Charlene handed her the finished drawing. "I love it. Thank you."

Austen also thanked Charlene, signed his cabin number on the check, and motioned. "The miniature golf course is clear. Are you ready to get your butt kicked?"

Suzanna rolled her eyes and picked up a club. "In your dreams."

An hour later, Suzanna whooped with joy as her last ball slid into the cup. "I win."

Austen shook his head in disbelief. "You must

have cheated."

"I did not. I'm a better player, that's all." She grinned. "According to our bet, you owe me."

"My cabin is closer." His eyes turned smoky gray, and the smile he gave her sent butterflies swirling in her stomach.

The digital clock on the bedside table read three-thirty. Once again, they'd spent the afternoon making love. Suzanna sighed in total bliss. Who would have ever guessed winning a writing contest would lead to Austen and the most romantic time of her life? Now they were sailing closer and closer to land and reality. How would she ever tell him goodbye and keep her self-control? *Suzanna, you have to be prepared for the worst. No matter what it takes, you can't let Austen see how leaving him is tearing you apart. You'll stay calm and kiss him goodbye. It will be up to him to make the next move. And if he doesn't tell you he wants the relationship to continue, you'll be strong and wait until you're out of sight before you fall apart.*

Austen's hand slid up her leg, distracting her from these gloomy thoughts. "Your skin is like silk," he whispered. His fingers found the damp curls between her legs. "And this…"

"Austen, it's getting late, and I have to clean up. We're supposed to be in the murder room at five."

He nuzzled her neck. "You can shower here."

"It's easier if I go to my cabin. All my toiletries are there."

His hands found her breasts. "If you're sure."

She gently removed his hands and rose. "I'm sure. I'm going to have to hurry as it is." She reached for her clothes. "You'll be ready before me, so I'll meet you in the Mermaid room." She bent and kissed him.

Chapter Twelve

Suzanna headed for her cabin knowing her disheveled appearance left no doubt what she'd been doing for the last few hours. Talk about the walk of shame. Eyes on the ground, she hurried along the hall to her room. Once inside, she jumped into the shower, washed and dried her hair, applied makeup, and slipped on white capri pants and a blue-and-white-striped top. She was out the door in less than an hour.

When she entered the Mermaid room, she waved at the Paiges and wove her way to where Austen waited by the window.

"Have you been here long?" she asked as she took her seat.

"No, but I almost body-slammed another guy out of the way to get this table."

Recognition dawned. "We sat here the night we met."

He grinned. "How could I forget?"

A sudden lump formed in Suzanna's throat. The clock was ticking on their time together, and depression threatened to overtake her. She forced a smile. She had to stay upbeat and carefree. The last thing she wanted was for Austen to see she was falling in love with him. "So, where's our drinks?"

He rose. "I didn't want to lose the table, so I waited for you."

Suzanna took her seat. "Thanks. You'd better hurry. Maggie is about to take the stage."

Austen made his way to the bar, glancing back at Suzanna. Something was wrong, and he thought he knew what it was. They'd become too close too fast, and now their future together was unknown. Leaving Louisville and moving to New York was increasingly appealing to him. He was ready for a change, and H&H might be giving him that opportunity. He wanted Suzanna in his life, but until he knew what was ahead for him, he couldn't give her any answers.

Drinks in hand, he arrived at their table as Maggie took the stage.

"Hello, everybody," Maggie called. "I hope you've all enjoyed the cruise."

"Yes," came their unanimous reply.

"Great. I'll bet you're anxious to see who our super sleuth is. So, instead of telling you the solution, we're going to show you."

Whistles and applause erupted from the crowd.

Maggie smiled and motioned for silence. "We love an enthusiastic group. So, here's our murder."

The lights dimmed to show a backdrop of a full moon and ocean waves. Vanessa was seated at the outdoor bar, gazing into her glass, the diamond necklace sparkling around her neck.

Behind her, Amelia crept, a shiny knife gripped in her hand.

Vanessa swung around. "Aunt Amelia, what are you doing here? I thought you left with Belinda and Gordon."

"I'm not leaving without what belongs to me. Your days of selfishness and cruelty are over. I want my necklace, and I want it now."

Vanessa laughed. "Well, dream on. You should have gone with the others, because in order to get this necklace, you'll have to kill me, and we both know you're a coward. If you had any self-respect or backbone, you wouldn't have allowed people to walk all over you your entire life."

"How's this for backbone?" Amelia plunged the knife into Vanessa's heart.

Vanessa's eyes opened wide, and her mouth gaped. She slumped forward, blood covering the front of her blouse.

Silence filled the room.

Suzanna grabbed Austen's arm. "Is she dead?"

Austen's face mirrored Suzanna's confused one. "It's only a skit. I'm sure she's fine."

Anxious murmurs spread throughout the room. Someone screamed. A man dressed in a suit appeared on the stage.

"Good evening. I'm Justin Conway, president of the I Love a Mystery Association. It's my great honor to announce the name of the detective who solved our murder."

Vanessa stood, and the rest of the cast joined her on the stage.

"Oh, my God, for a minute, I honestly thought she'd been killed," Suzanna said.

"It was well-done," Austen replied.

"We have two detectives who got all four elements correct. Amelia kills Vanessa with a knife, at the outdoor bar."

Suzanna leaned toward Austen. "We almost had it right."

Justin Conway held up two completed clue forms. "Our super detectives are Dwain Paige from Michigan, and Sarah Nielson of Florida."

The crowd clapped and cheered.

"On behalf of the I Love a Mystery Association, we'd like to thank everyone who participated and joined us on the cruise. We hope you've enjoyed our game of clues and will come again next year. Now, Maggie will fill you in on what we have planned for our last night on the ship."

Amidst more applause, Maggie retook the stage. "After dinner tonight, we're planning on meeting at the piano bar for dancing and a sing-along. We hope to see all of you there. Now, please mingle and enjoy the hors d'oeuvres. We'll head for the dining room in an hour."

"That's great Dwain won," Suzanna said. "Let's go congratulate him."

They found a beaming Dwain and his family surrounded by well-wishers.

"I have to say I never trusted Amelia, but my grandson Brendan helped me put it all together," Dwain was saying when Suzanna and Austen were able to get close. "So, how did you two do?" he asked.

"We got three elements right," Austen replied.

Dwain nodded. "It was hard to choose. I put a number of scenarios together before deciding on the final outcome. Will you two be at the piano bar later?"

"I suppose so," Suzanna replied. Her time with Austen was slipping away, and she didn't want to think past this moment.

Dwain patted Austen on the back. "Perhaps we can sing a duet."

"Sure thing," Austen said with a grin.

More people arrived to congratulate Dwain, so Austen and Suzanna stepped aside.

"Are you hungry?" Austen asked.

Suzanna's emotions were in such turmoil, she wasn't sure if she'd eat another bite while on the ship. "I'm okay until dinner." Hopefully, she'd have more of an appetite by then. "But if you want something, go ahead."

He shook his head. "I'm fine. Let's go for a walk on deck."

Chapter Thirteen

The sun was setting, and the sky was streaked with shades of blue and orange. They passed two empty lounges, and Austen indicated they should stop. "Let's sit and watch the sun disappear into the water."

"Sounds nice." Suzanna stretched out and made herself comfortable.

"I'll be right back," Austen said.

"Where are you going?"

"It's a surprise."

Suzanna smiled. "I love surprises."

He returned carrying two flutes of champagne.

"Oh, what a wonderful way to enjoy this beautiful night." Suzanna took the glass he offered. A gentle breeze lifted her hair. Lights from another cruise ship twinkled in the gathering darkness while the waves slapped against the ship. Austen took her hand in his. "I have an idea. Instead of spending our last night with other people, what do you say we get some food and eat on your balcony?"

"I'd say you read my mind."

"Pizza and more champagne?"

"Perfect."

"We're both scheduled to debark the ship at the same time," Austen said. "But first I have to go to my room and pack so I can place my suitcases in the hall. I'll do that, pick up the pizza, and meet you at your cabin."

"I'll get the champagne." Suzanna held up her hand to stop his protest. "And no arguing. You've bought all the drinks. It's my turn."

Suzanna hurried to the champagne bar, bought a bottle, then stopped at the Deck Side café for a cheese tray. Impatiently she glanced at the clock. She hoped to have everything ready before Austen arrived. Finally, champagne and cheese tray in hand, she arrived at her door.

Once inside, she placed the bottle in the ice bucket and arranged the tray, glasses, and plates on the balcony table. She found a smooth jazz station on the ship's radio and slipped into a short, silky, black nightgown and robe. She was dabbing perfume behind her ears when Austen knocked.

"Wow," Austen mouthed when she opened the door. "Staying here was the right idea." He placed the pizza box on the dresser, took her into his arms, and kissed her. His growing erection pressed against her. He broke their kiss. "How hungry are you?"

Pleased with his reaction, Suzanna stepped from his embrace. "Starving. Come on, I have us all set up." She led the way onto the balcony.

A thousand stars sparkled in the velvet sky as a warm breeze surrounded them.

"I got us a little appetizer to start," Suzanna said as she spread cheese on two crackers.

"Great." Austen poured the champagne and tapped his glass against hers. "Here's to us."

Suzanna smiled. "To us."

They sat enjoying the soft music, listening to the sound of the waves as the ship glided through the water.

"Oh." Suzanna pointed. "There's a falling star. Quick, make a wish." She closed her eyes. *Please don't make this be the last night I have with him.*

"What did you wish?"

Suzanna shook her head. "I can't tell."

Austen gazed into her eyes. "Whatever it was, my wish is that it comes true."

Her feelings for him were most likely clear on her face, but at this moment she didn't care.

He took her empty glass and placed it on the table. He stood and reached for her. "Come here."

She stepped into his arms, and they swayed to the sultry sounds of a saxophone coming from the radio.

When he quietly sang along, Suzanna wrapped her arms around his neck and let the sexy words flow over her.

A shaft of moonlight illuminated them as they held each other. Austen found her lips and tenderly kissed her.

Suzanna abandoned herself to the feel of Austen's mouth over hers, his strong body pressed against her, and this magical night.

He ran soft kisses along her cheek, whispering, "I'm going to spend the night making slow love to you." He kept one arm around her and grabbed the champagne bottle. "We'll finish this in bed."

Anticipation had every cell in her body tingling. "That sounds perfect." Her eyes fell on the forgotten pizza box. "Aren't you hungry?"

He laid her upon the bed. "Only for you, darlin'."

Hours later, as moonlight spilled across the rumpled sheets, Suzanna, her head on Austen's chest, sighed in complete and total bliss. He'd done as he promised. With both his hands and mouth, he had made love to her, sending her soaring over and over again. When he finally entered her, their bodies moving as one, he brought them to the peak of passion before hurling them over the edge.

Austen brushed her hair from her face. "I want to say something now before we go our separate ways tomorrow."

Please, not now. Don't ruin this perfect night. Suzanna's stomach did the elevator fall. *This is when he tells me it was nice, but it's over.* She willed herself not to cry. She opened her mouth to speak, but he placed his finger over her lips.

"First, I have a present for you." He rose and removed a cloth pouch from his pocket and handed it to her.

"Austen, what is it?"

"Open it and see."

With slightly trembling fingers, Suzanna undid the tied string and reached into the bag. "Oh, Austen, it's beautiful." In her hand lay a gold charm of the ship.

"I thought it would make a nice memento of our time together."

A lump formed in Suzanna's throat. "I'll always cherish it."

He sat next to her on the bed and took her into his arms. "I want you to know these few days with you have been some of the best in my life, and I care deeply for you. I only wish the timing were different, but it's not. I've been wanting to leave Louisville, and the book contract is my opportunity to make the move."

With each word he spoke, Suzanna feared her fantasy world with Austen was slipping away. She wasn't sure how much longer she'd be able to sit there without bursting into tears.

"Our relationship would be easier if we lived closer, but it can be managed. It will take time for me to get settled in New York, but as soon as my life isn't so upside-down, I'll come to Charlotte."

Suzanna blinked. Had she heard him correctly? "What?"

"I'm saying, I want to have a relationship with you, but you need to understand I have to straighten out my life." He frowned. "Did you think I was going to tell you that this has been fun, but it's over?"

"I honestly wasn't sure," she managed to say.

"It's true we don't know each other that well, but I hoped you could tell I'm not the type of guy who could become as close as we have, then walk away."

He cares about me. The hurt and disappointment was clear in his eyes. She blinked back tears of relief and joy. "I've never been as happy as I've been since I met you. I was afraid to let myself believe we might have a future together."

He gently kissed her. "I don't want to lose you. One way or another, we'll make it work. Okay?"

She smiled. "Okay."

Part Two

Chapter Fourteen

Hilton Head Island, ten months later

"I'm supposed to pick up who?" Suzanna asked with consternation. "Amy, this is a joke, right?"

"Suzanna, I'm so sorry, but no, it's not a joke," Amy Karr replied. "You have to pick up Austen Kincaid at the Hilton Head airport."

"You can't be serious?"

"Ah, yes, I am."

"There has to be a mistake. He isn't one of the conference's scheduled authors."

"He is now. He's the keynote speaker."

"What?"

"I'm as surprised as you are. I just got a call from Tina Blair, the conference chair, informing me Sharon Ball sprained her ankle, and Austen is taking her place."

"Amy, this is getting worse by the minute. You're telling me I have to spend the next four days with a man who broke my heart?"

"Suzanna, I understand how hard this is going to be for you. If Violet weren't sick, I'd go get him. But she still has a high temperature, and I'm afraid to take her out."

"How about if I come sit with Violet, and you go to the airport?"

"She's awfully fussy. If I were to leave, she'd probably just scream."

Suzanna let out a long breath. "And there's no one from the conference committee that can go?"

"Not here on the island. The other editors and agents are flying into Savannah tomorrow and are being driven here. Austen is the only one flying onto Hilton Head. All you have to do is pick him up and take him to the hotel. Later we'll figure out how to keep you away from him as much as possible."

"There must be other authors besides Austen to take Sharon Ball's place. Why did the committee choose him?"

"I have no idea. I read H&H canceled his contract, so I imagine he had time on his hands. The scuttlebutt is Miller and James picked him up."

"He always lands on his feet, doesn't he?" Suzanna sighed. "Why can't he just take a cab?"

"Suzanna, you can't tell an NYT best-selling author, who's willing to come to Hilton Head, to take a cab. Try and focus on what excellent PR the bookstore will receive for being one of the conference sponsors."

"You mean instead of how I'd like to drop him into Port Royal Sound with all the sharks?"

"Yes, well, please wait until after the conference."

"What's ironic, counting Austen, there are now three people coming who were on the mystery cruise."

"Really? Who?"

"Agent JJ Jackson and Melinda Pearce, marketing director for H&H."

"That's quite something. Hopefully, that's the only similarity, and no one is murdered."

"Unless I kill Austen."

"Suzanna."

"All right. I won't murder him, and I'll go pick him up, but that's all. I will not socialize with that man."

"Okay, call me later, and let me know how it went."

Suzanna hung up the phone and turned to Peg Daily, a retired librarian who worked part-time in the store. "Peg, I have to go to the airport. Can you manage things until I get back?"

Peg nodded. "Sure. I couldn't help overhearing your phone conversation. Whoever it is you have to pick up, I'd be more than happy to go for you."

"Thanks, but Amy is right. Since we're part of the conference, I should be the one to get him."

"Do you mind if I ask who it is that you dislike so much?"

Suzanna hesitated. Her cousin Jenn and Amy were the only two she'd confided in about her and Austen and what had happened on the cruise. When she thought about how lovestruck she'd been and what a fool he'd made of her, it tore open a place in her heart she'd hoped was sealed and locked. Willing back unsettling emotions, she replied, "It's Austen Kincaid."

"The author who writes those great thrillers? I read both his books and loved them. I can't wait for his next one."

"Yes, well, he might be a good writer, but as a person, he's a…" Suzanna again hesitated. Just because she considered him a low-life scumbag, didn't mean she should burst Peg's bubble. "Let's just say he's not my favorite person."

Peg patted Suzanna's hand. "I'm not going to pry into your personal business. Perhaps when you see him, time will have healed some wounds."

Suzanna, needing to collect her emotions before leaving for the airport, headed for a cup of coffee in the kitchenette next to the stockroom. As she passed the display of new releases, Austen's latest thriller caught her eye. Unable to pass by, she took it from the shelf.

She stared at his picture in the back of the book. *Am I strong enough to get through this?* She traced his lips with her finger, remembering how his kisses alone brought her desire to fever pitch. No matter how hard she fought against them, the memories flooded back. Their instant attraction had led to intimate breakfasts in bed, romantic dinners, dancing to their favorite music, and making love as the ship gently rocked. A smile touched her face, as images of Austen's lean, naked body moving on top of her, bringing her to heights of excitement she hadn't experienced before—or since—filled her mind. For five glorious nights, she'd lost herself in his arms. When the ship docked, they'd hurried to catch their flights. In the Miami airport, they'd kissed goodbye, and he'd promised to call and see her soon.

At first, they'd talked every night, and he'd managed to come to Charlotte twice. New Year's Eve was the last time she'd seen him.

****

"What do you think?" Suzanna asked as she pirouetted on her two-inch stiletto heels.

Austen's gaze traveled down her ruby-red dress as it clung to her body. "Wow, sexy lady, you look incredible. You'll have every man in the restaurant drooling over you."

Laughing, Suzanna tossed her long hair over her

shoulder. "You're the only man I want drooling over me. Besides, I'll be busy keeping all the women's hands off you in that tux. Talk about sexy."

Austen lowered his voice and stepped closer. "We could stay home and enjoy ourselves by removing each other's clothes."

Suzanna put her hand up, stopping his advance. "No way. I spent a fortune on this dress, and I'm going to wear it. You can undress me later."

"Oh, darlin', you can plan on that."

Suzanna slipped on her black fake-fur coat, blew him a kiss, and headed for the door.

"I've never fondued in a restaurant," Austen said as he fed Suzanna a piece of seasoned steak.

Suzanna closed her eyes in total bliss. "Yum. That's so good. I don't know what I like best, the meat or cheese."

Austen nodded. "I know. These mushrooms are great."

Suzanna made a sour face. "You can have those; I'll take the other vegetables."

Austen cut a slice of bread from a small loaf. "This is really fun. Much better than spending New Year's with a bunch of people."

"With your publicity tour beginning next week, I'm still surprised you were able to get away."

"My first stop is a bookstore in the city, so it's not a problem. I wish you could come to New York and be there."

Suzanna sighed. "So do I. But we're shorthanded at the store, and with my grandfather's health failing, I couldn't leave."

"Is this your grandfather who owns the ranch?"

"No, my dad's father. After my dad died, my mother didn't stay in touch, but my sister and I did. He's a great guy, and I love him dearly."

Austen took her hand. "I hope his health improves. Grandparents are a blessing to have."

"Are yours still living?"

"On my mom's side. They live in a town called Prestonsburg in the mountains of eastern Kentucky."

"Really? I've never been in that part of the state."

"It's pretty. I'll have to take you to meet them."

Suzanna's heart swelled. *He wants me to meet his family.* She loved him so much, she thought she'd burst with it. She glanced down at the sparkling gold heart necklace he'd bought her for Christmas and smiled.

"Speaking of meeting family," Austen continued. "When do I get to meet your mother?"

Suzanna coughed, choking on her wine. Introducing him to her mother was the last thing she wanted to do. "That's not a good idea. Every guy I brought home to meet her never asked me out again."

Austen grinned. "She can't be that bad."

Suzanna let out a long breath. "She'll grill you about everything, from your family to your work. Then she'll complain about my sister moving to Savannah, and how she hopes I don't abandon her as well."

"Does she know about us?"

"No. The only ones who do are my friend Amy and my cousin Jenn."

"Why's that?"

Because I don't want too many people to know I've been a fool when you break my heart, she thought. Aloud, she said, "Those are the two I share all my secrets with."

107

He gave her a mischievous grin. "Oh, and how much of our secrets did you share?"

Suzanna licked her lips. "All of them."

Austen laughed. "I hope they were jealous."

Afterward, he held her in his arms as they danced in the New Year in his hotel room.

"Happy?" he whispered.

Suzanna wrapped her arms tight around his neck. "Oh, yes."

"Let's see if I can make you happier." His fingers tugged on her zipper, when his cell rang. "Damn," he cursed. "Who the hell is calling me at this hour?"

"You'd better check. It might be important."

Austen went to where his cell lay on a table and glanced at the caller ID. "What does she want?"

"Who is it?"

"Haley."

Suzanna's euphoria evaporated. What timing the woman had. "You'd better answer, or she'll probably call back."

Austen, his mouth in a thin line, answered. "Haley, do you know what time it is?"

Suzanna studied Austen's surprised expression. When a huge grin spread across his face, a sudden premonition of her world turning upside down came over her. *No, go away*, she demanded. *I don't believe in premonitions*. But no matter how hard she tried, the feeling of dread wouldn't leave.

Austen disconnected the call and reached for Suzanna. "I did it," he exclaimed as he picked her up and twirled her around. "I made the *New York Times* best sellers list."

Suzanna, caught up in his happiness, laughed.

"That's wonderful. Congratulations."

"Haley got a heads-up from a friend of hers. She said H&H is going to have a small party for me when I get back."

When Suzanna's dread came rushing back, she willed it away. *This is good for his career. Nothing bad is going to happen.*

****

Soon, his calls became less frequent. Suzanna blinked away the tears that formed. His career was skyrocketing, and she told herself he was involved with promoting his books. She invented one excuse after another for his silence. Then she'd received the photographs, and her world shattered.

She placed Austen's book back on the shelf. *Suzanna, you're going to have to put on your big-girl pants and deal with it. As Amy said, being part of the conference is a wonderful opportunity for the bookstore. When you see him, be friendly but aloof, then dump his sorry ass at the hotel.*

Visions of Austen, his hands and mouth moving over her body, filled her mind. She gritted her teeth. *Stop it, stop it, stop it. Thoughts like that will lead to nothing but trouble. The only way to protect your heart is to stay as far away from Austen Kincaid as possible.*

She undid the chain from around her neck. As hurt as she was, she still wore the golden ship Austen had given her. Perhaps it was a way of reminding herself what a fool she'd been. No matter, she wasn't about to allow Austen to believe she wore it because she still cared.

Chapter Fifteen

Austen Kincaid placed his laptop in the overhead compartment and slipped into his first-class seat. He adjusted the seat belt and opened the magazine he'd brought. The flight attendant stopped next to him.

"Hello, I'm Robyn, can I get you something to drink?"

"A club soda would be great."

Robyn hesitated. "Mr. Kincaid, I have to tell you I loved your books."

Austen smiled. "Thank you." He still marveled at the success of his books. When Clarice Abbot told him she was confident he was good enough to become a best seller, she was right. The contract with H&H had rocketed his life in a direction he'd dreamed of, but, as he discovered, wasn't prepared for. He'd allowed himself to be seduced by his newly found fame and success. He leaned his head back, and once again, the biggest fuckup in his life played through his mind like a bad movie you want to forget.

****

Austen fumbled as he attempted to place the key card in the door to his room. Damn, he'd drunk more than he should have. Thankfully, the celebration was at his hotel, and he didn't have far to go. He managed to get the door open and, a little unsteady, stepped into the suite. He headed for the bedroom and paused. He blinked a couple of times at the naked woman lying in his bed.

"It's about time you got here," Haley purred. "I've been all alone and lonely."

"Haley, what the hell do you think you're doing?"

"I'm waiting for you to get into this bed and make love to me."

Austen's gaze traveled over her voluptuous body. "Haley, I don't fool around with married women."

"Austen, we both know you want me." She lay against the pillows and lifted her arms above her head and thrust out her breasts while spreading her legs wide. "So come here and stop fighting it."

"How many times do I have to say this? I have no desire for you, so get the hell out." He'd gone into the bathroom, and when he'd returned, Haley was gone. He'd stripped off his clothes, fell into bed, and was instantly asleep.

Haley, still naked, crept back into the bedroom. "No one turns me down," she whispered. She eased in next to him and held up her cell phone. "Let's see what your little girlfriend thinks of these."

When Austen awakened the next morning, his head pounding, visions of Haley in his bed seeped into his muddled brain. Relief swept over him. Haley wasn't here. Thankfully it was just a dream, or a nightmare.

After showering and eating breakfast, he packed his belongings. Tomorrow, he'd move into a small apartment in Greenwich Village. He'd placed the last article of clothing in his suitcase, when there was a knock on his hotel room door.

Anger and guilt shot through him when he opened the door to discover his visitor was Haley.

"What are you doing here?"

"Well, hello to you too," Haley said as she breezed in past him. "You were a lot more friendly last night." She tossed her purse on the small sofa.

"What are you talking about? Nothing happened between us."

"Oh, yes it did." She gave him a cat-with-the-cream smirk. She withdrew her phone from her purse and turned the screen so he could see the photos.

Austen gaped in disbelief. Photo after photo showed a naked Haley in bed with him. He slept without clothes, so the viewer would easily believe the pictures were true. Rage like he'd never known pumped through him. "You're fucking crazy." Austen started to slam the phone against the marble bar, when Haley's words stopped him.

"It won't do any good, I have copies."

"What the hell do you want?"

"You in my bed."

"Well, that's not going to happen. Do you honestly think I could get a hard-on, when the sight of you makes me sick?"

Her face hardened. "If you care about your writing career, you'll change your mind."

"What are you talking about?"

"Austen, H&H launched you into the writing world and landed you on the NYT best sellers list. I can ruin you just as quickly."

"There are other publishers," he replied through gritted teeth.

"Not after I put out a rumor you'd do anything to get published, including plagiarizing someone else's work."

"You'd have to prove it."

Haley shrugged. "Once something like that gets out, it's hard to prove it's not true. But, if that isn't enough to convince you to stay in my bed, I'll send your little girlfriend the pictures, explaining exactly what you and I were doing all night and how much you enjoyed it."

"Suzanna won't believe the pictures are real." But as he said the words, he wasn't sure they were true. "If you think for one minute I'll be blackmailed for sex, you're even crazier than I thought." His jaw clenched. He'd never been so angry in his life. His voice was low and menacing when he spoke. "Haley, get out of my sight before I wring your neck."

His words and expression must have penetrated her brain, for she grabbed her purse and headed for the door. Haley's eyes narrowed. "Don't think this is over," she snapped. "I think your cozy apartment will make the perfect place for us to meet." She slammed the door, and Austen stood trembling with fury and revulsion. He ran his hands over his face. How had he allowed Haley to trap him? Jeopardizing his lifetime dreams and his career because of his utter stupidity.

Austen paced across the sitting room area. Did Haley actually have the power to ruin him? Should he go to Brad before Haley had a chance to tell her lies? And say what? *Oh, by the way, I found your naked wife in my bed, and nothing happened, but now she's blackmailing me for sex, so don't believe anything she tells you.* Right.

And what about Suzanna? Did he tell her the truth? What if Haley didn't follow through on her threat, and he'd upset Suzanna for no reason?

His eye fell upon the congratulatory card and bottle of bourbon his family had sent after hearing of his success. Now, would he have to go home in defeat, spending the rest of his life at a job he didn't want? *Hell, no.*

He needed to get out of this room and away from the place where his dreams were about to crumble at his feet. He grabbed his suitcase, laptop, and phone. He'd find another room for the night and decide his future.

Chapter Sixteen

The next day, he settled into his apartment and thankfully hadn't heard from Haley. For the next week, he stayed away from H&H, attending book signings and immersing himself in his next book, only communicating with his editor, Clarice Abbot.

His cell rang, and the ID said it was Suzanna. He hadn't spoken with her since his ill-fated night with Haley. Guilt at letting himself be placed in this situation ate away at his conscience. He took a deep breath and answered. "Hey, how's it going?"

"Hi, I haven't heard from you and was wondering how you like your new apartment."

"It's small but suits me."

"Great. I happen to have the weekend off and thought I'd come see you."

Panic threatened to overtake him. All he needed was Suzanna here and to have Haley show up with her photographs. "Sorry, darlin', but I've got book signings and interviews lined up." This was true, but under normal circumstances, Suzanna being here wouldn't be a problem. In fact, he'd have her come with him.

"Oh, okay. Well perhaps when your schedule slows down."

Austen didn't miss the disappointment in her voice. "Since the first book did so well, they want to release the next in the series as quickly as possible. They're pushing me to finish the third book, so they're keeping me pretty busy."

"I see." She hesitated. "Austen, is everything okay? You sound funny."

Austen closed his eyes and silently groaned. So much for his ability to bluff his way through this. He swallowed hard. "Sorry, darlin', but I'm really busy and a little overwhelmed." How easily the lies rolled off his tongue.

"I understand. Well, call me when you can."

"Sure." He disconnected the call and dropped his head in his hands. *I'm an awful liar, and Suzanna isn't stupid. It won't be long before her suspicions surface.*

He'd no sooner hung up from Suzanna than his doorbell rang. Dread curled in his gut. What if it was Haley? He stood staring at his door, fury flashing through him. *To hell with this.* He wasn't going to live his life under Haley's thumb. He crossed the room and swung open the door.

"Hello, Austen," Haley said. She swept past him in a cloud of expensive perfume. She glanced around. "This is nice. And the location's perfect. No one would expect me anywhere near here." She slipped off her coat and dropped her purse on his couch.

She wore a tight sweater and skintight jeans. She came toward him, smiling. "Want to show me the bedroom?"

Austen's decision was made. "No. What I want you to do is leave."

Haley's eyes flashed. "Didn't I make myself clear? I've stayed away to give you time to think about what I said. You have two choices. Have sex with me or see your future career as a famous author go up in smoke."

"As I said, in order to have sex with you, I'd have to get a hard-on. Considering that the thought of entering your body sickens me, I doubt that would happen."

Haley's cheeks flamed, and she slapped his face. "You're going to regret this. When I'm through with you, you will be dead to the publishing world." She grabbed her coat and purse and stormed out.

Austen went to where he kept his alcohol, grabbed the bottle of bourbon, and poured a generous amount into a glass. *Here's to my short-lived life as a published author.*

The next day, he'd arrived at H&H for a meeting with Clarice, when a note was delivered for him to go to Brad's office. He'd assumed Brad had found out about his night with Haley, and his contract was about to end. Instead, he'd found Haley sprawled across the desk with her dress hiked up.

"I knew you wouldn't ignore a summons from Brad, so come in and shut the door."

"No way." Austen turned to leave.

"Austen, get back in here, or I'm going to send Suzanna the photos and tell her explicitly about our night together. Do you honestly think I didn't realize you're in love with the dowdy country mouse? The satisfaction of breaking her little heart when she learns you gratified your lust in my bed was one of the reasons I seduced you."

Austen, his jaw rigid in anger, slowly crossed the carpeted office floor. He stopped in front of the desk where she lay. "You did not seduce me. That night only happened in your twisted mind. If you contact Suzanna, I'll go to Brad and tell him what a whore he's married to."

"You wouldn't dare," she spat. "What about your precious career?"

"To protect Suzanna from you, I'd give up everything." He was about to leave, when the door opened, and Brad walked in.

What followed was pure hell.

"Brad, honey, he tried to force himself on me," Haley screamed.

"You bastard," Brad shouted as he took a swing at Austen.

"She's lying. I didn't touch her," Austen yelled as he ducked away from Brad's fist. "She came on to me, not the other way around."

Brad's face was suffused with red, and his breath came in shallow gasps. "Get out of my office," he snarled at Austen. "Consider your contract canceled."

The scandal hit the next day. His career teetered on the edge, and his reputation took a nosedive. People were no longer talking about his books. It was all about him and Haley and how they'd been caught. Disgusted by what an idiot he'd been, and despondent over his career, he'd locked himself away in his apartment for several days. He had no idea how many times he'd picked up his phone to call Suzanna. He wanted to hear her sweet voice. He needed to tell her it was all a lie, but each time, his nerve gave out.

When he'd received the call from Miller and James offering him a contract, he couldn't believe his luck. His guardian angel had stepped in, and he was given a second chance.

Hoping his luck would hold out with Suzanna, he called her. When she answered, her words sliced through him. "Austen, I hope she was worth it. You didn't have to send me pictures. A phone call telling me we were through would have been sufficient. Or did you two get a big laugh out of making a fool out of me?"

"Suzanna, please listen. The pictures aren't real."

"Austen, I've seen your body. Trust me, it was you."

"Yes, but I'd had too much to drink, and I was passed out. Haley took those photos. I had no part in it."

Suzanna snorted. "What about Brad's office? Was that a lie as well?"

"Yes, Haley set me up."

"Seriously, Austen, how stupid do you think I am? Pictures don't lie. Haley was naked in your bed. Do not call me again." With that, she disconnected.

****

Austen stared out the plane's window as they banked to the left, and Charlotte was clear below. The last time he'd been here, he and Suzanna had celebrated New Year's. *Is a second chance with her too far out of reach?* There was an hour before he caught the flight to Hilton Head. Should he try and call her? No, it would be too easy for her to hang up on him. He needed to see her in person. Perhaps on his return trip, he'd reschedule his flight so he'd have a longer layover. He'd spend his time on Hilton Head rehearsing what he'd say. And, if she agreed to see him, he'd get down on his knees and beg her to take him back.

Chapter Seventeen

The distant hum of the plane reached Suzanna seconds before it cleared the top of the tall sea pines and headed for the runway. As she waited outside the small Hilton Head Island Airport, dread mixed with anticipation to form a miniature tornado in her stomach.

Calm down, or you're going to make yourself sick. She self-consciously ran her hand down her powder-blue sundress with its pattern of tiny white daisies. *What will he do when he sees me?* As far as she knew, he didn't know she'd moved to Hilton Head and opened the bookstore.

The terminal doors opened, and Austen strolled out. *God, give me strength.* Her pulse quickened, and her palms grew damp. If anything, he was even more heart-stopping than he'd been the last time she'd seen him. Suzanna took a calming breath, pasted a smile on her face, and lifted her arm. "Austen, over here."

He glanced up and headed toward her.

She stood stock-still as his steps faltered.

"Suzanna?" He let go of the handle of his bag and reached out to remove her sunglasses. "It's really you."

His voice was as rich and smooth as the bourbon his home state was known for. Suzanna willed her voice to stay steady. "Hello, Austen."

When he stood staring, she took her glasses from his outstretched hand, surprised her own hands weren't trembling.

He gave her the smile which always caused her heart to skip a beat.

"What are you doing here?"

"I live here." *If you weren't such a lying jerk, you'd know that.* She wanted to scream.

"Since when?"

"A couple of months now. Is that your only bag?" She indicated the duffel next to him.

"Yes, but wait a minute. When my agent set this up, I had no idea you'd be here."

"And I had no idea I'd be the one to pick you up." She headed for her car. "I'm parked over here."

He touched her arm. "Suzanna, I…"

She swung around, fire in her eyes and steel in her voice. "Austen, don't touch me. I realize this is awkward, but after I drop you off at the hotel, hopefully we won't have to see one another again."

"Please, hear me out."

"Trust me, Austen, I've heard more than I care to."

He ran his hand through his hair. "Suzanna, you have no idea how many times I started to call you but didn't know what to say. Damn it, Suzanna, I'm sorry I was stupid enough to walk into Haley's trap."

"Or are you sorry you got caught? She was after you on the ship, and she finally got what she wanted. The reason you stopped the affair is that her husband walked in on you. Seriously, Austen, on the desk in Brad's office? How tacky."

"Christ." He let out a long sigh. "Suzanna, it was all a huge misunderstanding."

She snorted. "Yeah, right. You are aware that Brad didn't hold anything back when he talked to the press."

Austen's mouth formed a thin line. "A lot of it was pure exaggeration. I received a note to go to Brad's office, and I assumed it was from him. When I arrived, Haley was there. She was lying across the desk when Brad walked in. I was standing in front of her, and, yes, it looked bad, but I was fully clothed. Haley set the entire scenario up."

"And the photos? I suppose she set that up as well?"

"Yes. I'd had too much to drink after a party. When I got to my room, she was in my bed. I told her to leave and thought she had. I passed out, and she took the photos. I honestly had no part in it."

"If you weren't having sex with her, why would she do that?"

Austen hesitated. "It's complicated."

"I doubt it's all that complicated. Austen, you're a great storyteller, but you won't fool me again. You and I had fun, and I made the mistake of believing it was more than a shipboard fling. You have your life, and I have mine. I'll take you to the hotel, and we'll go our separate ways."

"Suzanna, Haley doesn't mean anything to me, but you do. Please hear me out."

A mental battle raged inside of Suzanna, with curiosity as to what he had to say almost winning out. She sighed. "I'll think about it, but don't hold your breath. Let's get you settled in the hotel." She motioned for him to place his bag in the trunk of her bright yellow convertible bug.

"Great car. It suits you. All sunshine and spunk. Are you living on Hilton Head?"

"My grandfather passed away and left me some

money. My friend Amy Karr and I both wanted a change, so we left Charlotte and bought Beachside Books, a store here on the island."

"That's great. It's something you really wanted, but I'm sorry to hear about your grandfather."

She slammed the trunk. "I also wanted you."

"How did your mother take you moving?"

"Not well at all."

"That's too bad." He opened the passenger door. "How are you involved with the conference?"

"The local association of mystery writers asked us if we'd help sponsor." She paused. "I understand they were thrilled to hear you would be their keynote speaker."

He gave her a slight smile. "And what about you?"

She narrowed her eyes. "You certainly wouldn't have been my first choice."

"Ouch."

As she slid into the driver's seat, his next words sent her reeling.

"I should let you know that on the plane I decided that as long as I was here, I could use some R&R and maybe do a little writing. So, after the conference, I'm going to check into renting a villa for about a month. I didn't want to drive all the way from New York, so I'll have to rent a car."

Suzanna, speechless, stared.

A shrill female voice startled them both. "Austen, yoo-hoo, *surprise*."

Suzanna twisted in her seat to see a curvy blonde wearing large, round sunglasses, pulling a Louis Vuitton bag.

"What the hell?" Austen murmured.

"Is that Haley?" Suzanna asked with consternation. He jerked the car door open. "Yes."

The last time Suzanna had seen the mystery writer diva had been on the cruise. Now, with her shoulder-length strawberry-blonde hair cut short and spiked, and large sunglasses covering her striking green eyes, Suzanna hadn't recognized her. She inwardly cursed. This was just what she needed to make her day perfect.

When Austen stepped from the car, Haley flung her arms around him and devoured his mouth with hers.

Haley in Austen's arms was more than Suzanna could stomach. Willing herself not to cry, she opened her mouth to tell them both to go to hell, when Austen took a step back and removed Haley's arms from around his neck.

"Haley, what are you doing here?"

Surprised at the irritation evident in Austen's voice, Suzanna didn't move.

Haley's lips formed into a perfect hot-pink pout. "Austen, honey, I've missed you," she purred. "I was shocked when I learned you were coming to beautiful Hilton Head to do some dinky conference. I wanted to surprise you, so I took an earlier flight. I've been waiting in this so-called airport. I'd just stepped into the ladies', and I almost missed you. Let's blow these people off and have our own good time."

Dinky conference indeed. Suzanna gritted her teeth to keep from telling the snooty woman to go stuff it. Well, she'd had enough. They could both find their own way to wherever they wanted to go. She jammed the key in the ignition. Damn it to hell. Austen's bag was in her trunk. Cursing under her breath, she popped the trunk.

Haley said, "Austen, where's the limousine? You don't expect me to ride to the hotel in that, do you?" She pointed a scarlet-tipped finger at Suzanna's car.

Suzanna's temper was at the boiling point. "Excuse me, but this happens to be my car."

"Oh, good, then be a dear and take our luggage." She gestured to where two large bags sat by the curb. "We'll take a cab."

Convinced steam was pouring out of her ears, Suzanna glowered at Austen and through gritted teeth said, "The cabs are over there." She waved toward the curb. "The hotel is the Huntington. Have a nice day." She pulled Austen's bag from her trunk, dropped it on the ground, got into her car, started the ignition, popped the clutch, and hit the gas. As she drove away, Austen called her name. "Don't stop and don't look back," she repeated until he was no longer visible in her rearview mirror.

Chapter Eighteen

"Damn it to hell," Austen cursed, as the little yellow car disappeared around a curve. When he had spotted Suzanna in the airport, he wasn't sure his eyes weren't playing tricks. Had his guardian angel stepped in once again to give him another chance? If so, he'd do everything he could not to let it slip away.

"Austen, honey, let's get the cab. I'm melting in this heat," Haley said, fanning herself with her hand. "I want air-conditioning and something cold to drink."

Austen willed himself to control his temper. Was the woman insane? "Haley, I don't know why you're here, or why you're acting as if we have a relationship. If you believe your own delusional lies, let me make myself perfectly clear. I want nothing to do with you. I know damn well you knew that was Suzanna picking me up, and you put on quite a performance. But listen closely. For some reason, the gods have shown mercy on me and brought me together with Suzanna again. I'm not going to allow you to fuck that up. Besides, you may not care about your career, but I care about mine. I don't need nor want that kind of publicity again. You have to go back to New York and your husband."

To Austen's utter surprise, a tear trickled down Haley's cheek, just before she turned her head away. In a quiet voice she said, "I can't go back to New York. Brad threw me out."

"I heard you were seeing a marriage counselor."

Haley sniffed. "It worked for a while. I thought he'd forgiven me, and we were moving on. Then three days ago, he told me he wanted a divorce, and to leave. I didn't know where to go." Her tears flowed freely. "I found out you were coming to Hilton Head and, well, here I am."

"But why? You have friends all over the world. Why come to me? If Brad finds out, it will make things worse."

She removed her sunglasses and, with a tissue, wiped her streaming eyes. "Brad Henderson doesn't give a damn where I am or who I'm with." She crammed the tissue into her purse. "But if you don't want me either, I'll leave, but I can't just go back into the airport and get onto a plane. I'll need to go somewhere and make some arrangements."

He studied her closer. *Is she truly unbalanced?* Not knowing what else to do, resigned to having her stay for at least one night, Austen grabbed the handle of his bag and headed toward the parked cabs. "Come on, let's find the hotel. I'm sure they can help you with flight information."

Getting Haley settled in the hotel proved to be a time-consuming task made difficult by her insisting on having a suite. This ended with Austen giving her his suite and taking one of the rooms set aside for conference goers.

He'd then arranged for a rental car to be delivered. Now he gunned the engine, hearing the convertible's familiar roar, and turned onto 278, heading for Coligny Plaza and Beachside Books.

He'd been in college the last time he'd visited

Hilton Head, and he and his buddies were more interested in bikini-clad girls and partying than taking in the actual beauty of the island.

Tall sea pines and live oaks dripping Spanish moss lined the street. Restaurants, shops, and businesses were tucked discreetly behind. He reached the Coligny traffic circle and turned into the plaza. Palm trees dotted the parking lot, and seagulls sailed overhead as he parked the car. Mouthwatering aromas filling the air reminded him that he hadn't eaten since the bagel he'd grabbed at the airport in New York. If he were lucky, he'd convince Suzanna to have dinner with him. The concierge at the hotel had told him the bookstore was located in Coligny Plaza, but not exactly where. Austen stared in dismay at all the clothing stores, gift shops, and restaurants. It would take too long to search for the bookstore, so he asked in Fresh Produce and was told Beachside Books was next to Jamaican Me Crazy. Back out on the sidewalk, he maneuvered his way around children licking dripping ice cream cones, giggling girls loaded down with packages, and sunburned tourists. He paused in front of the bookstore before entering to admire the window display. In the middle, surrounded by books, sat a beach chair, flip-flops, and pink sunglasses. Above it all, a sign exclaimed "Summer Reads." He smiled to himself when he didn't see *Backlash*. Was she so pissed she refused to even stock his books?

Suzanna was waiting on a customer when he entered, so he wandered among the shelves. The store wasn't large but was arranged so the different sections were easily found. He smiled to himself, for there, among the mysteries, was a display of his books. So, he wasn't at the top of her shit list after all.

"Oh, my, Mr. Kincaid, I can't believe it's really you."

Austen turned to find an older woman with short gray hair staring at him. "Hello, yes, it's me," he said with a smile.

"Mr. Kincaid, I'm a huge fan. Welcome to Beachside Books. I'm Peg Daily. I was so excited when Suzanna told me she was going to pick you up, and you'd be part of the conference."

Even though his book had hit the NYT best seller list and he'd instantly become well-known, Austen still wasn't used to the public's reaction to his stories. The idea that something he had written gave people such enjoyment both pleased and surprised him.

Austen held out his hand. "Thank you, Peg. It's nice to meet you."

Peg shook his hand, then reached over and took *Backlash* from the shelf and held it out. "Would you autograph this for me? I have it in paperback, but I'd love to have a signed hard copy."

Austen smiled. "I'd be happy to."

Suzanna finished with her customer as Austen handed his book to Peg. The entire way back to the store, she'd rehearsed what she'd say the next time they met. Now, here he stood, and the words wouldn't come. Her traitorous heart spoke instead. Did she honestly believe that in a few months she'd be over him? No matter how much she still cared, she wasn't going down that road again.

She took a deep breath and went to where Austen and Peg stood. "What can I do for you, Austen?"

"Mr. Kincaid was kind enough to sign this for me."

Peg held up her book. "I'll just take it to the checkout counter."

"I like your store," Austen said after Peg left. "It's in a terrific location." He indicated the beach in the distance.

"Thanks. I hope your accommodations at the hotel are satisfactory."

Austen hesitated. "They're very nice."

"I have a folder that I forgot to give to you, with the conference information you'll need. It also contains your schedule of events. There's also a list of restaurants and excursions the island offers. In fact, for Sunday, the conference put together a fishing trip for the men and shopping for the ladies. I have the information in my office. Feel free to look around. I'll only be a minute."

When Suzanna headed for the back of the store, Austen followed. She stepped into the small space, and to her dismay, he closed the door behind them. Her desk took up most of the room, so they were inches apart.

"Austen, what are you doing?"

"If I wanted to kiss you, would you let me?"

Suzanna gazed into his eyes, and her resolve slipped. She willed herself to remain strong. The smell of his cologne brought memories rushing back.

He stepped closer, and they almost touched. "Please, let me kiss you."

The sexual energy between them threatened to ignite both their bodies.

Suzanna's pulse quickened, and her knees were weak. His lips were a breath away from hers.

"Let me, Suzanna."

Her lips parted to say yes, when the ringing of the phone on her desk broke the spell. Suzanna blinked and twisted her face away.

Austen cursed and stepped back.

Suzanna shoved the folder at him. "You need to leave."

"You said you'd have dinner with me and hear me out."

Suzanna was so angry with herself for almost giving into him, she blurted, "That was before your girlfriend showed up."

Austen ran his hand through his hair. "Suzanna, she's not my girlfriend. She followed me. I had nothing to do with it. I told her to go home to New York."

"Why did she follow you?"

"She said Brad threw her out."

"Good for him. I'm surprised he hadn't already done that."

"They tried a marriage counselor. Evidently, it didn't work."

"If you weren't still having an affair, why would she run to you?"

"First, I never had an affair with Haley. And she doesn't hear or react to the word 'no.' She thinks she can maneuver people to get what she wants, and it usually works. That's how she trapped me."

Suzanna stepped behind her desk. Distance from Austen was the sensible thing. "I would have thought you were smart enough not to let that happen."

Austen laughed without humor. "So would I. Suzanna, please, let's go someplace where we can sit and talk."

If you go, you'll be walking into a field of land

131

mines, her smart side screamed. But the pleading in his eyes melted her heart. "All right, but just dinner. Don't get any other ideas."

He smiled, and she heard those land mines exploding.

Chapter Nineteen

Haley paced across her suite. She'd taken a chance showing up without Austen's knowledge, but she had no choice. She needed to leave New York fast. When Brad discovered what she'd done, he'd be furious. Haley snorted. She wasn't about to allow him and that woman to leave her high and dry. She paused in front of the sliding doors leading onto the balcony. The view of the beach and ocean beyond was spectacular.

She narrowed her eyes. She was convinced that once enough time had passed, Austen, upon seeing her, wouldn't be able to resist her. If Brad hadn't returned to his office and ruined her plan, she was certain Austen's resistance would have crumbled. A catlike smile spread across her face. Men didn't dump her. When she was good and ready, she dumped them. She'd trapped Austen once. She'd do it again. She needed to convince him Brad had threatened her, and she was afraid to go back.

A flyer for the conference caught her eye. What were the chances Suzanna would also be here? Well, that little nobody wasn't going to stand in her way. No matter what she had to do, Austen would be hers.

****

Suzanna was about to close the store when a group of women came in. "Sorry, could you tell us where the Sand Bar restaurant is located?" an attractive redhead asked.

"It's at the other end of the shops," Suzanna replied.

"Ellyn, look, she has Austen Kincaid's books," a tall blonde said.

"He's so handsome," a brunette added.

Never one to overlook a sale, Suzanna smiled. "I'll be happy to ring those up for you."

Each of the ladies grabbed a copy of *Backlash*.

"Are you aware Austen is here for the Association of Mystery Writers' conference?" Suzanna asked.

"No," the one named Ellyn said.

"Can we still get tickets?" the blonde asked.

"Not for the conference," Suzanna replied. "But some of the attendees will be on the sunset cruise Friday night, and Austen will be there. You can check and see if they still have tickets."

Ellyn laughed. "We're a happy-hour group, and that sounds perfect."

After the women left, Suzanna locked up and hesitated next to her car. Suzanna had chosen The Porches for dinner. Located on the beach, it was a popular restaurant, and there wouldn't be a chance of them being alone.

But did that really matter? she thought. *He'll be sitting across from you. How do you plan on keeping your feelings from showing? Ever since you laid eyes on him, your emotions have fluctuated from wanting to throttle him to wanting to throw yourself into his arms. Suzanna, get a grip. When your thoughts turn to kissing him, think of Haley. That will definitely dampen your lustful thoughts.*

When she arrived at the restaurant, Austen was

waiting near the entrance, wearing jeans that fit him way too well and a polo shirt that set off the blue of his eyes. When he smiled, Suzanna's heart skipped a beat. *I'm in deep trouble,* she thought as she approached.

"This is nice," Austen said, after they'd been seated.

Suzanna's nerves were strung so tight, she found it hard to relax. *I'll listen to what he has to say, then politely leave.* "The food is good. Especially the shrimp and crab cakes."

The waiter arrived for their drink order. Austen asked for a beer and, without checking, ordered Suzanna a glass of cabernet.

"See, I haven't forgotten what you like," Austen said after the waiter left.

I should tell the confident ass I've switched to white wine. Instead, she asked, "Have you been to Hilton Head before?"

"Years ago. A college friend of mine's parents live here." He indicated the tiki hut, visible from where they sat. "We spent most of our time there."

"It's fun, and they usually have a good band."

"How about going there for a couple of drinks after dinner?"

Suzanna's internal alarm went off like a siren. "Austen, this is not a date. I'm here to listen to what you have to say, nothing else. Besides, I have to get up early. The rest of the conference attendees arrive tomorrow. Were you aware JJ Jackson and Melinda Pearce are also coming?"

He shook his head. "Have you heard I'm no longer with H&H?"

She nodded. "You were lucky Miller and James

signed you."

"Tell me about it. I was truly afraid my career was over."

"I guess you should have considered that before starting the affair."

Austen winced. "Suzanna, I did not have an affair with Haley. Allowing her to trap me is a mistake I'll regret for the rest of my life. And the incident in Brad's office wasn't what it seemed. Haley set it up for us to get caught. I told her to stay away from me, and I wanted nothing to do with her, but she wouldn't listen. Please, you must believe me."

"If none of it was true, why didn't you defend yourself against all the awful publicity?"

"I tried. It was my word against Brad's. When I left his office, Haley was crying, telling him I seduced her and how sorry she was. The entire situation made me sick. I went into hiding and wallowed in self-pity."

The pain and remorse showed in his eyes. The barrier she'd erected against her feelings started to crumble. In fear of her own emotions, she changed the subject. "Now that Haley is here, all that's missing is Brad and Clarice."

Confusion crossed Austen's face before he replied, "I can't imagine any reason either of them would show up."

"Yes, well, it's all a little déjà vu."

He reached across and took her hand. "We could go to my room and pretend we're still on the ship."

Suzanna slipped her hand from his and shook her head. "How does the saying go? That ship has sailed."

"Good one." Austen leaned close and lowered his voice. "The ship might have sailed, but our memories and what happened between us will never leave."

Tears prickled behind Suzanna's eyes. "Austen, you can't just show up, say a few sweet words, and expect me to forget the hurt you put me through." No longer able to control her tears and not wanting to make a spectacle of herself, she pushed back her chair. "Oh, God, I can't do this." She hurried from the restaurant. The beach was the closest, so she headed in that direction. She lived in Sea Pines, and it was a ways away, but she'd walk miles before she'd turn back. Besides, he had to pay the check. By that time, she'd be far enough Austen wouldn't find her.

She slipped off her sandals and ran. She jogged as often as she could, so hopefully she'd leave Austen behind. Why, why, why did he have to come here? She'd moved on with her life. Seeing him did nothing but bring all her conflicting emotions to the surface. Tears streaked down her cheeks. The painful truth was she still loved him, and deep inside, she wanted him to also love her. "Damn you, Austen Kincaid," she said aloud through gritted teeth.

"Baby, I'm so sorry."

Startled, Suzanna turned her head to find a slightly out of breath Austen following her.

Puffs of sand flew behind her as she increased her speed. "Go away."

"Suzanna, I can't change what I did, but I can promise you I'll never hurt you again."

Suzanna skirted around children building sandcastles, sunbathers, and empty beach chairs, Austen right on her heels. "How can I ever trust you?"

"Let me prove it to you."

Suzanna swallowed, then on a shaky breath asked,

"If you hadn't found me here, would you have ever called me?"

"I picked up my phone a hundred times, but I couldn't come up with the right words to tell you how sorry I was. And I wasn't sure how to make right the wrong I did. I intended on stopping in Charlotte on my way home hoping you'd see me. Suzanna, will you please stop so we can talk?"

Suzanna slowed. Waves crashed at their feet, and the sky above turned pink, blue, and orange as the sun met the water. They stood staring into each other's eyes.

"Austen, I want to believe you, but I'm scared. I can't and I won't go through that hurt again."

He took her in his arms and kissed the moisture from her cheeks. "Baby, don't be scared. Please believe me when I tell you I'm so, so sorry. I was a fool, Suzanna. Please don't cry," he whispered. "Forgive me." He cupped her face and gently kissed her. "I love you," he murmured. "I've always loved you." He covered her mouth with a searing kiss.

He loved her. Suzanna's world stood still. When his lips touched hers, all her misgivings fled. She wrapped her arms around his neck and hungrily kissed him back.

He held her tight. When he broke their kiss, his love for her was etched on his face.

"Austen, do you truly mean it?"

"I want us to try and rebuild what we had. I want you to be in my life and be able to trust me."

"That's not going to be easy. Once trust is gone, it's hard to get back."

"I promise you I'll never give you a reason to

doubt me. Suzanna, I honestly believe fate has brought us together again. We can't let it slip away."

The tears flowing over her cheeks were now happy ones. "Austen, I love you so much."

A smile spread across his face. He let out a loud whoop and twirled her around. People nearby clapped and cheered.

Unaware they'd had an audience witnessing their tableau, Suzanna, her cheeks pink with embarrassment, buried her face in Austen's chest.

Laughing, his arm around her, Austen headed for the restaurant. "I left my wallet so they'd know I'd be back to pay the bill. You know, suddenly I'm starving. Let's finish dinner." He bent to whisper in her ear. "Then I can get us a bottle of champagne, and we can go to my hotel to get reacquainted."

The heat in his eyes sent tingles of anticipation over Suzanna's skin. "You read my mind, but my place is closer."

Chapter Twenty

After a delicious meal, Austen drove behind Suzanna through the Sea Pines gate. When he'd told her he loved her, the words had come out without a second thought. It wasn't until that minute he'd realized they'd always been true. What an idiot he'd been. He'd known Haley was trouble but had ignored his conscience. He wouldn't have blamed Suzanna if she'd told him to go to hell. He'd be eternally grateful to the gods, stars, fate, or whatever entity intervened to give him another chance.

Austen parked next to Suzanna and came around to the hunter-green front door. He stepped into the small entry. "This is nice." To his left, a galley kitchen with an L-shaped bar divided the living area. To his right, a short hall led to a bathroom and, he supposed, her bedroom. Straight ahead, sliding doors opened to a screened-in porch overlooking the woods. "This is exactly the type of place I'd like to rent after the conference is over."

"Not a place on the beach?"

"I imagine that would be pretty costly."

"I wouldn't have thought money would be an issue."

Austen snorted. "Think again."

An orange tiger cat yawned and sat up from where it had been sleeping on the sofa.

"You have a cat," Austen said, bending to scratch behind its ears.

"That's Citrus," Suzanna replied. "I took her in as a stray."

"I love cats. We always had them on the farm. They liked being around the horses."

"Growing up, I asked for a kitten, but my mother said it would scratch the furniture and shed all over. My neighbor is nice enough to keep an eye on Citrus for me while I'm at the conference."

Austen moved to where a painting of the beach at dawn hung above a fireplace. "This is nice."

"Thanks. My cousin Shannon painted it. I don't have champagne, but there's wine."

"Wine will work." He stood in front of a cabinet which held an array of animals and sea creatures. "These are great. How long have you been collecting blown glass?"

"I started when I was twelve. My family went to the aquarium. I bought that dolphin when we were on Santa Maya."

"I like the smiling frog." He took the drink Suzanna handed him. "Let's sit out on the porch." He stepped out onto the tiled floor. A curved wicker sofa ran along two walls, with a small two-person table along the third. "This is nice and private back here."

Suzanna took a seat on the sofa. "Yes, and it's perfect. We get a lot of tourists during the summer, and this is away from all the busier areas."

He sat next to her and sipped his wine. "Mentally, I feel as if I've just come down from a huge adrenaline rush. I suppose it was my anxiety over your reaction and fear you wouldn't want me in your life anymore."

Suzanna let out a long sigh. "Me, too. It's as if my anger and hurt have all vanished. I'm relaxed for the first time in months. Dealing with my mother over leaving Charlotte to open the bookstore hasn't exactly been stress-free."

"And I added to your stress."

Suzanna smiled. "Yes, you did."

He placed his wineglass on the coffee table and took Suzanna's from her. "Since I added to your stress, let's see if I can relieve some of it for you."

When his arms went around her and his lips found hers, Suzanna melted into his embrace.

All the hurt, all the tears, all the lonely nights she'd longed for him, slipped away. Austen was here, he loved her, and nothing else mattered.

Without breaking their kiss, he eased her back onto the sofa. His hand ran up her leg and under her sundress.

"I love these dresses you wear." He slid her panties off. "It makes getting to you so much easier."

Suzanna gasped as his fingers stroked her wet heat.

"See what I mean?"

Within seconds, Suzanna's climax burst through her, and she cried his name. "Austen, now," she demanded, reaching for his zipper.

While tremors of her orgasm still consumed her, his thick shaft entered her. "Austen!" Suzanna exclaimed as the thrilling sensations only he could give her coursed through her body.

"Sweet Suzanna," he murmured as they moved as one.

The throbbing ache between her legs grew in intensity. Suzanna tugged at the hair at the base of his neck. "Whatever you do, Austen, don't you dare stop," she said, gasping each word. "Sweet heaven," she cried, arching her back.

"Suzanna." He thrust hard and deep, and she shattered.

When her world stopped spinning, Suzanna buried her face in his damp neck and smiled. "I needed that."

Austen chuckled. His voice low and raspy, he said, "You and me both, darlin'. Damn, Suzanna, you about did me in."

She stroked his back. "That's too bad. I was going to suggest I show you the view from my bedroom."

"I said you about did me in." He rose and lifted her in his arms. "Not that I didn't have enough energy for another round."

The next morning, seated on her porch, Suzanna and Austen were drinking coffee and eating omelets. "My friend Amy and I are going to take turns between the conference and the bookstore," Suzanna said. "This morning I'll be working at the registration table. Then throughout the weekend, I'll help where I'm needed. The editors and agents fly in today. I understand the conference is full, so you'll have a nice audience for your speech Saturday night."

Austen made a sour face. "I do okay talking to people one-on-one, but standing in front of a crowd freaks me out."

"I'm sure you'll be fine. Like they say, pretend they're in their underwear."

He grinned. "The only one I want to picture in her underwear is you."

Suzanna rolled her eyes. "Yes, well, as I was saying, tomorrow is the dress-up welcome party on the sunset cruise."

He gave her a mischievous grin. "You and I back on the water sounds fun."

"Yes, well, we'll be surrounded by people, so don't get any ideas."

"Did you say dress-up party?"

"The mystery writers' group thought it would be fun for everyone to dress as their favorite mystery author or character. I'd love to go as Miss Marple, but I'm too young. So, I'll be Nancy Drew."

"You'll make a cute Nancy Drew. But I don't have any kind of costume." He grinned. "I always liked Shaggy."

"From the cartoon?"

He nodded. "Too bad I don't have clothes from the '70s."

"We have a number of clothing consignment stores on the island. Perhaps you could find something."

"I have time this morning. I'll see what I can do. On Saturday, do I speak before or after dinner?"

"After."

"Good. That gives everyone a chance to get drunk, and they won't pay attention to me."

"I'm sure you'll do fine. And there's dancing afterward."

"Nice. Will you save me a dance?"

Suzanna pursed her lips. "I'll think about it. My dance card is pretty full."

He lowered his voice, and the sex appeal in his eyes had ripples of delight skipping over her skin. "If that's the case, you'd better save the last dance for me, because, darlin', I'll be taking you home."

The images that conjured made Suzanna's toes

curl. She knew if she didn't leave for work that minute, they'd be back in bed. She cleared her throat. "I'll make sure of it. Now, I must go. Amy is going to wonder what happened to me." Suzanna grabbed her purse and headed for the door.

On the wall, a framed drawing caught Austen's attention. "You kept it." He indicated the sketch of the two of them on the ship.

"I almost didn't," Suzanna replied. "At one point, I thought about using it for a dartboard."

Austen winced. "Ouch." He sighed. "I can't say I'd blame you. Why didn't you take it down?"

"Because I wanted to be reminded what a fool I'd been. And I'd never let it happen again."

Austen took her in his arms and lifted the gold heart charm she wore. "I'm surprised you kept this."

"This is the first I've had it on since I learned about you and Haley. I almost threw it into the trash, but I couldn't."

He lightly kissed her. "I'm glad you didn't. Suzanna, if it takes the rest of my life, I'll prove to you how much I love you, and I'll never again cause you that kind of pain."

"Good. Because if you do, I'll use you as a dartboard."

"I'll remember that." They stepped outside. "Can we meet for lunch?"

"Sure. Registration is from ten to one, but there are other volunteers. There's a nice poolside dining area at the hotel."

"Great, I'll be there, say, around twelve thirty."

He held her close for a long sexy kiss. "Until next time."

Suzanna sat in her car as he drove away. If her relationship with Austen blew up in her face, she had no one to blame but herself. At least this time, she was going in with open eyes. At the slightest sign he wasn't being sincere, she'd walk away, her pride intact but her heart in shreds.

"Oh, my God, what happened with you and Austen?" Amy grabbed Suzanna's arm as she stepped through the bookstore door. "I've been going crazy not knowing if you killed him or made up."

"I can guarantee he's not dead," Suzanna said, skirting around her friend.

"Wait a minute." Amy followed right on her heels. "Peg said you went to dinner with him. The last I knew, you'd left him and Haley at the airport and didn't care if you ever saw him again."

Suzanna placed her purse behind the counter. "Well, we kind of made up."

"What?"

Suzanna let out a long sigh. It was useless to try to hide anything from Amy. "He spent the night, and he told me he loved me."

Amy gaped. "Are you serious? What about his affair with Haley?"

Suzanna repeated Austen's explanation.

"Do you believe him?"

Suzanna nodded. "I still don't trust him one hundred percent, but I think he's sincere when he says he loves me. We have a way to go to restore our relationship, but, Amy, I'm so happy."

Chapter Twenty-One

Austen reentered the hotel and headed for the check-in desk. Hopefully Haley was gone, and he could get into his own room. "Good morning," he said to the young woman behind the counter. "Can you tell me if Mrs. Henderson has checked out of room 312?"

"No, she hasn't," she replied.

Austen thanked her and headed for the elevators. With irritation, he stabbed the button for the third floor. His tenuous relationship with Suzanna could crumble if she discovered Haley hadn't left. He'd be damned if he'd allow her to come between them again.

He knocked on room 312 and impatiently waited for her to answer. When she opened the door, Austen brushed past her. "Haley, why the hell haven't you gone?"

"Well, good morning to you too," she snapped as she closed the door. "I haven't been able to find a flight."

Austen narrowed his eyes. "Bullshit. You're stalling, and it isn't going to work." He pulled out his cell phone. "I'll check the flights."

"No, Austen, wait," Haley stammered. "I can't go back to New York."

"Why not?"

Tears formed in her eyes. "I'm convinced Brad has a girlfriend, and when I confronted him, he went crazy and hit me. I'm afraid to go anywhere near him."

"Brad hit you?" Austen asked with astonishment.

"Yes."

He studied Haley's face. She put on a convincing show, but he didn't believe a word she said. "I've never seen anyone as angry as Brad was when he found us in his office. If he didn't become violent then, I can't see any other circumstance when he would."

"Are you saying I'm lying?"

"I'm saying I wouldn't put anything past you. But, if it's true, then go to one of your friends, but leave."

"I don't understand how you can be so cruel." Haley sniffed. "You don't care if Brad kills me."

Austen let out an exasperated breath. "I doubt Brad wants to kill you. If that were true, he would have done it a long time ago. I can't help you. I want a relationship with Suzanna, and your presence makes the situation extremely uncomfortable."

Anger flashed in Haley's eyes. "I honestly don't care how uncomfortable Suzanna is. My life is at stake."

Austen's patience was at an end. When Haley wanted something bad enough, nothing would stop her. "I don't care where you go, but I want you out of my room."

"Who the hell do you think you are, giving me orders? I'll stay wherever I damn well please."

"Haley, I'm done arguing with you. These rooms are reserved for conference attendees. People should start arriving this morning at ten. There are plenty of other hotels on the island for you to choose from. I'm going to go clean up, pack, and check out of the room I used yesterday. Then, I'm going to come here, and I expect you to be gone." Not allowing her another word, he left.

Haley reached for the first thing at hand and threw it. The empty ice bucket clanged against the door and fell to the carpet. Her hands balled into fists. She stomped her foot. "Fuck you, Austen Kincaid," she spat through gritted teeth. "I don't lose. You might want that little nobody Suzanna, but you're not going to have her."

Haley went into the adjoining bedroom and jerked open her suitcase. She'd leave this room, but she wasn't leaving the hotel. This was the last place Brad would look for her. Thankfully, years ago she was smart enough to open her own bank account under her maiden name. By now he'd have discovered she cleaned out their joint account and the apartment safe. *See if his little girlfriend Clarice stays with him now that he's broke.* Brad's outrage at her sleeping with Austen made her blood boil. The hypocrite. Who knew how long he'd been with Clarice right under her nose? No one made a fool out of her, including Austen. She glanced at the clock. Nine-thirty. If she hurried, she'd check in before conference goers arrived.

In the lobby, Haley plastered a smile on her face and approached the reservation counter. "Hello, I signed up late for the conference and was hoping you had a room available."

"Sure, let me check," the young man behind the counter said.

Haley leaned slightly forward, giving him a nice view down her top. "I'd so appreciate that."

He stared at her cleavage, smiled, and punched keys on his computer. "You're extremely lucky, um,

Miss…?"

Haley hesitated before replying, "Beal." If Austen checked, he wouldn't realize it was her.

"Miss Beal. We had a cancellation from a non-conference guest. The room isn't a suite, but it has a view of the pool area. I think you'll find it satisfactory."

"I'll take it."

Key in hand, Haley rounded a corner to find three women next to a sign that read "Mystery Writers' Conference Registration."

She slipped behind a group of large potted plants to watch. Yes, Suzanna was one of the women. Austen must have known ahead of time she'd be here. Why else would he agree to be the conference speaker? What did he see in Suzanna anyway? She supposed she was pretty enough, but there was no flair, no style. All she wore was those silly dresses. She glanced at Suzanna's feet. Of course, sandals, not heels. The idea Austen preferred Suzanna over her was beyond belief. Haley tossed her head. She could please Austen in a way that little country girl couldn't imagine. All she needed to do was get him back into her bed, and she'd prove it to him.

"Skulking behind the foliage. Now whose wife could you be hiding from? Or spying on?"

Haley jumped and turned at the sound of the voice behind her. Melinda Pearce stood, in her black suit and pearls, as proper and starched as some old maid. "For heaven sakes, Melinda, you scared me half to death."

"Too bad it wasn't fatal."

Before Haley could form a scathing reply, Melinda continued. "I'm surprised to see you. I wouldn't have thought this type of conference would interest H&H."

Melinda cocked her head. "Or did Austen bring you to Hilton Head?"

"I'm not here representing H&H. Just a little vacation. I wasn't aware Austen was on the island."

Melinda snorted. "Considering the way you sneak around with men, that's kind of hard to believe."

Haley narrowed her eyes. "Speaking of men, did I ever tell you how your dear husband used to tell me sex with you was like screwing a dead fish?"

Melinda leaned closer to Haley. "You're a disgusting, filthy piece of trash. If it takes my last breath, I'm going to make sure the world knows just what a vile, backstabbing, two-faced sleaze the famous author really is."

Haley snorted. "You're a bitter rejected woman. Who do you think will believe you?"

"It's too bad that skit on the ship wasn't real, because I'd love to shove a knife in your heart." She turned on her heel and strolled away.

"Ugly cow," Haley mouthed to Melinda's retreating back. She gritted her teeth in frustration. Damn it. The last thing she needed was Melinda and her big mouth telling people she was here. This situation was getting worse by the minute. Furious for letting herself be seen, Haley cautiously made her way to the elevators. *I'll find my room and make my next plan, for I'm not going anywhere.*

The doors opened, and without paying attention to the elevator's other passenger, Haley pressed the button to her floor.

"I never expected to see you here," a male voice said.

Haley whipped around and, when she realized who

he was, smirked. "Mark. Who on earth invited you? I wouldn't have thought your piddly book sales could qualify you to be a guest author. Or are you here strictly as an attendee?" She cocked her head. "I know, you're here hoping to get tips on how to write something someone would want to read."

"And what about you? Are you here chasing after Austen? Rumor has it he realized what an evil whore you are and dumped you."

Haley tossed her head and scoffed. "No one dumps me. You should know that." The doors slid open, and she stepped out. "Oh, and consider your contract with H&H canceled." Laughing at the horror on his face, Haley strolled along the hall to her room. She hadn't any say in regard to his contract, but the loser didn't know that. She paused outside her door. If Mark ran into Austen, he'd no doubt tell him about their encounter, and Austen would know she hadn't left. She needed to change her appearance if her plan were to work.

Chapter Twenty-Two

"Hello, can I have your name?" Suzanna asked the next woman in line.

"Hi, I'm Sara with the Sea Pines Book Club."

"Welcome," Suzanna said with a smile. "I also live in Sea Pines. Here's your packet and schedule."

"Our group is looking forward to all the speakers, especially Austen Kincaid."

"I'm sure you'll enjoy the conference," Suzanna replied. "Don't forget to sign up for the costume welcome party tomorrow night aboard the sunset cruise."

By twelve-thirty, registration had slowed, and Suzanna's replacement arrived. Suzanna hurried to the poolside café to meet Austen. She found him seated at the outdoor bar. "Hi," she said, sitting next to him. "Were all the tables full?"

Austen nodded. "I put our name in. It should only be a few minutes. Would you like something to drink?"

"Iced tea, thanks. After I eat, I have to make sure the author swag table is organized. I forgot to ask, is your suite okay?"

Austen hesitated. Sighed, then began. "Suzanna, when I got back this morning, Haley was still in my room. I told her she needed to leave. When I went back later, she was gone, but I can't guarantee she's left the island."

At the sound of Haley's name, Suzanna's irritation spiked. "What was she doing in your room?"

He explained what had happened the day before. "At that point, it was easier to let her stay in my room, and I took a different one. When I got here this morning, I expected she'd be gone."

"You don't have any idea where she is?"

Austen shook his head.

"If she's still here, there's nothing we can do about it. But she'd better stay away from me. Because famous author or not, I'll tell her exactly what I think of her."

Austen took Suzanna's hand. "I did my best to make her understand I don't want anything to do with her. Haley doesn't take rejection well, so we may not have seen the last of her. I'm sorry I brought this upon us. When I came out of the airport, and you were standing there, I believed fate had stepped in and given us a second chance. Then she had to show up like the villain in a scary movie."

Suzanna squeezed his hand. "Villains usually get what they deserve, so hopefully she'll get hers. Let's move on to a nicer topic. What do you have planned for this afternoon? You're not scheduled for anything until cocktails on the rooftop patio at five."

Austen leaned closer and lowered his voice. "That's hours from now. How much time do you have before you're needed again?"

The promise in his eyes sent lust-filled images through her mind. "I have until two o'clock."

A slow grin spread across his face. "How hungry are you?"

"Not very."

"If memory serves me correctly, we had a similar

conversation on the ship."

Suzanna smiled. "It ended rather nicely."

"Shall we see if we can repeat the results?"

Suzanna licked her lips. "Perhaps we can make an even better ending."

Austen tossed a twenty on the bar and grabbed Suzanna's hand. "Darlin', I love a challenge."

Giggling like a little girl, Suzanna allowed him to lead her to the elevators, down the third-floor hall, and into his suite. "Very nice," she said when he closed the door. "I've never been in one of these rooms."

Along one wall was a wet bar, small refrigerator, coffee maker, and microwave. A table and two chairs sat across from a love seat and recliner.

Suzanna stepped to the sliding door leading onto the balcony. "Great view."

He stood behind her and unzipped her dress. "Not as nice as this."

She sighed as her dress fell to the floor.

An hour later, the distant sound of the ocean waves filled the room. Suzanna lay in Austen's arms. An occasional splash from the pool and children's laughter floated up on the warm breeze from the open sliding door. She smiled in contented bliss. Her fingers stroked his damp back. Her breasts, sensitive from his kisses, pressed into his thick chest hair. Each time she was with him, more of her defenses dropped away. And the pain that clenched at her heart loosened its grip. She wanted this man, and no other could take his place.

Austen kissed her cheek. "Penny for your thoughts?"

"I was thinking how nice it would be to stay right here forever."

"Hmm, let's see. We'd drink champagne, eat rich dark chocolate, dance on the balcony under the stars, and make love until dawn."

Suzanna chuckled. "Exactly. There's just one problem."

"What's that?"

"Who's going to pay for it all?"

"Oh, did I forget to say we'd win the lottery first?"

"Or inherit bundles of money."

"That would also work."

Suzanna wiggled out of his arms and reached for her clothes. "But until either of those happens, one of us has to earn a living."

"Right. You go ahead. I'll wait here." He yawned. "Bring food when you come back."

Suzanna rolled her eyes, bent over him, and lightly kissed his lips. "Poor baby, did I wear you out?"

He grinned, grabbed her around the waist, and rolled her beneath him. "You stepped right into my trap."

"Austen, let me up. You're wrinkling my dress."

"Then let's take it off."

Laughing, she pushed at his shoulders. "Stop it. I have to go."

His erection pressed against her. "Austen." Her protest trailed off when her panties slid down her legs.

Chapter Twenty-Three

At four o'clock, Amy arrived with a garment bag over one arm and a large tote in the other.

"Thank goodness," Suzanna said. "I need to clean up before the cocktail hour."

Amy took in Suzanna's slightly wrinkled dress and smudged makeup. "Austen?"

"Yes. He has a comfortable suite."

Amy grinned. "I can see that."

Suzanna took the bags from Amy. "It's a good thing we decided to take one of the rooms for changing."

"No kidding. Little did we know what we'd need it for. So, what should I do here? I'm all yours. Peg is closing the store, and I have a sitter for Violet."

"Authors are dropping off swag, and I've been trying to keep it organized. I'll be back as soon as I can."

Suzanna hurried to the elevator and pushed the button for the second floor just as JJ Jackson stepped inside. "Sorry, which floor?"

"Five, please." He stared at Suzanna. "Don't I know you from somewhere?"

"I was on the mystery cruise last year."

"Of course. You were with Austen Kincaid." He cleared his throat. "Sorry. That was a nasty business with H&H. Unfortunately, Haley only cares about herself. It doesn't matter who she hurts or who she stabs in the back."

Suzanna wasn't sure how to reply, so she blurted, "Austen's the keynote."

He nodded. "I understand Haley is also here. As long as she doesn't cause trouble and keeps her distance, Austen should do fine."

"She followed him here, and he told her to leave, but we're not sure she did."

JJ snorted. "Since when does Haley do what she's told? I wouldn't put it past her to be lurking behind some corner."

The elevator door opened. "It was nice seeing you," Suzanna said as she stepped from the elevator. "Enjoy the conference." She hurried down the hallway. Her mind went back to the conversation she'd overheard between Melinda and JJ on the ship. It was obvious neither of them cared for Haley, but what had she done to make them dislike her so? She'd ask Austen if he knew.

"I can't wait to meet Austen," Amy was saying as she and Suzanna entered the rooftop bar and made their way around the crowd.

"There he is." Suzanna pointed.

"Wow, he's even hunkier in person than on his book jacket," Amy said. "No wonder he knocks your socks off."

Suzanna laughed. "My socks and everything else. Come on. I'll introduce you."

Austen, handsome in khaki pants and a navy short-sleeve shirt, was engaged in conversation with a group of admirers when Suzanna and Amy stopped next to him.

"Oh, Mr. Kincaid, it's wonderful to meet you," one of the girls was saying. "My name is Tana. Would you please sign my book?"

"Sure, I'd be happy to."

If Suzanna didn't step in, he'd be signing books all night. "Hello," she said with a smile. "Mr. Kincaid will be selling and signing books Saturday afternoon. I'm sorry, but I need to take him away. There are people he must speak to."

The girls frowned at Suzanna but reluctantly left.

"Thank you," Austen said. "I wasn't sure how to manage that situation."

"Surrounded by pretty girls? I'm sure you would have come up with something," Suzanna teased. "Austen, I'd like you to meet my friend Amy Karr. Amy, Austen Kincaid."

"I've heard a lot about you," Amy said.

"I'm sure more bad than good lately," Austen replied.

Amy grinned. "Until now, yes."

"I hope to change that."

"You'd better."

Suzanna rolled her eyes. "Okay, that's enough. Amy's kind of protective of me."

"That's what best friends are for," Austen said.

"I'm nothing compared to Suzanna's cousin Jenn. Take my advice, and don't let her find out if you hurt her again."

"Okay, okay, enough." Suzanna slipped her arm through Austen's. "Let's get a drink."

They maneuvered their way past groups of chattering conference attendees until they reached the bar. At the far end, Suzanna spotted Melinda and JJ in conversation. She tugged on Austen's arm and lowered her voice. "Do you know why those two dislike Haley so much?"

Austen glanced down the bar. "Yes, but let's go somewhere a little less crowded."

Drinks in hand, the three of them made their way to an empty table.

"Okay, spill it," Suzanna said.

Austen sipped his beer. "I'm not sure of all the details, but JJ Jackson was Haley's agent when she first started out. She received a number of rejections, but he stood by her. When she finally got a contract, and her books took off, she dropped him for a more well-known agent."

"Nice," Amy said.

"It doesn't surprise me," Suzanna said. She told them about her encounter in the elevator with JJ.

"It doesn't help that Haley trashed him as an agent," Austen added, "blaming him for her earlier rejections. She almost cost him his career."

"What about Melinda?" Suzanna asked.

"She claims Haley is responsible for her divorce. When she discovered the affair, she had some kind of breakdown. I was told she needed therapy."

Suzanna understood Melinda's pain. "Then why in the world does she still work for H&H? If it were me, I'd never want to see Haley again."

"Loyalty, I suppose. I understand she's been with Brad since the beginning," Austen said.

"Did she ever remarry?" Amy asked.

"Not that I'm aware of," Austen replied. "Everything I told you is secondhand gossip."

"I don't understand why Haley's husband put up

with her for this long," Amy said.

Austen smiled. "You and a number of people."

Suzanna sipped her wine, replaying Melinda's warning in Costa Maya. "Austen, remember the skit on the ship and how convincing the acting was?"

"Yeah, why?"

"I'm not sure it was all acting. I'm starting to wonder if they all hate Haley as much as they pretended."

"I wouldn't be surprised. I really hope she's left the island, or one of them might actually murder her."

"Wait a minute," Amy interjected. "Everything you've talked about happened in the past. Could any of them still hold that kind of grudge?"

Austen shrugged. "It's hard to say. Emotions can run deep. Haley tends to burn her bridges. She'll use anyone or do anything to get what she wants." He rose. "I need another beer. How about you two?"

Both Suzanna and Amy shook their heads. "Did you get the feeling that talking about Haley was making Austen uncomfortable?" Amy asked after Austen left.

Suzanna nodded. "She's still a touchy subject between us. I'm not good at hiding how much I despise that woman. At the airport when she grabbed Austen and kissed him, it took everything I had not to knock her on her ass."

Amy smiled. "There's enough material for Austen to write a good murder mystery."

Suzanna grinned back. "Good idea. I'd love to help him write the murder scene."

"What's so funny?" Austen asked, returning to the table with an attractive thirty-something man in tow.

"Girl talk," Suzanna replied.

Austen indicated the man standing next to him. "Suzanna, Amy, this is Mark Gray, a fellow author I met at H&H."

"It's nice to meet you," Suzanna and Amy said as one.

"I loved your first book," Amy added.

Mark pulled out a chair. "Thanks. I hope my latest one does as well."

"Suzanna and Amy own the local bookstore," Austen said. "They're also helping out with the conference."

"I recall seeing your name listed in the program," Mark responded. "I'll have to check out your store while I'm here."

"Have you been to Hilton Head before?" Amy asked.

Amy's interest in Mark was clear to see, and Suzanna allowed the conversation to swirl around her. Her attention strayed to an adjacent table where Melinda and JJ had taken seats. Suzanna's interest piqued. Tears trickled down Melinda's cheeks, and JJ's face was furious as he placed his arm around her shoulders to comfort her. *I wonder what that's all about. They seem so suited for each other. I hope there's a romance blooming.*

Suzanna was drawn back to the conversation when Mark said, "I'm scheduled to be on a few panels, but perhaps we can work out a time when you can show me around the island."

Amy hesitated, but Suzanna, knowing her friend, knew she wanted to say yes. "We aren't scheduled to help on Sunday," Suzanna interjected.

"I'd have to see about getting a sitter for Violet,"

Amy said.

While Mark asked Amy about Violet, Austen leaned toward Suzanna. "I'd like to check out some rental properties on Sunday, and I hoped you'd go with me."

Suzanna frowned in puzzlement. "You're not staying with me?"

"I didn't want to assume you'd invite me."

Suzanna laughed and bent to kiss him. "Perhaps I should wait and see how well you behave."

A group of women approached the table. "Excuse me, Mr. Kincaid. We wanted to tell you how much we enjoyed your latest book."

Austen glanced at her name tag and smiled. "Thanks, Linda."

"We're looking forward to hearing you speak Saturday night."

"Don't forget all the authors will be signing their books on Saturday afternoon," Suzanna added.

"We'll be there."

"I think you're going to do well in sales," Suzanna continued after the women moved off.

"This conference could be a blessing in disguise," Austen said. "It might be the boost my career needed."

"I have an idea," Suzanna interjected. "Since tomorrow is the welcome party on the sunset cruise, we could all meet for dinner at the Lands' End Tavern, on South Beach. The boat is docked there, so we can make sure to get a seat on the upper deck."

Amy smiled at Mark. "Perfect. Do you have a costume?"

Mark nodded.

"Wonderful," Amy replied. "And it's a full moon,

so that will make the trip even better."

In a far corner, wearing a large hat and oversized sunglasses, Haley seethed. There they all were enjoying themselves, while she had to hide like some criminal. Dumpy Melinda wasn't bad enough. That loser JJ Jackson was here as well. There they sat, all cuddled up. Well, they deserved each other. Her attention strayed to Austen and Suzanna, and her anger burned. It should be her he looked at with such love in his eyes, not Suzanna.

When she noticed the other man at the table, she adjusted her hat lower on her forehead. *Damn it to hell, what's he doing with them?* All she needed was for him to tell Austen about their encounter in the elevator. *The attendance at this little conference is becoming quite interesting. They should rename the event: The Writing World Rejects.* She sipped her drink. *I wonder if I need a better disguise.*

"Excuse me," a female voice said.

Startled, Haley jumped. With her attention on Austen and the others, she hadn't heard the woman approach. Haley glanced up into the no-nonsense face of a gray-haired woman. "I see you're not wearing your conference ID. You might not be aware that this gathering is reserved for conference attendees only."

Indignation ignited Haley's temper. Who did this bitch think she was talking to? Haley opened her mouth to inform the stick-up-her-ass woman she was Haley Henderson, and she had more of a right to be part of this conference than Austen Kincaid, but stopped herself in time. Instead, she smiled. "I'm so sorry, I must have left my ID in my room."

"In your welcome packet, it's very clear. You must

wear your ID at all conference functions."

Wanting to tell the woman where she could stuff her ID, Haley rose. "I'll go get it."

Chapter Twenty-Four

"I don't know about the rest of you, but I'm getting hungry," Austen said.

"How about San Miquels," Amy suggested.

"If you like Mexican food, you'll love it," Suzanna said. "We can eat outside near the marina, and the sunsets are fantastic."

"Sounds great," Mark added.

"I'll drive," Amy said. "I've only had one glass of wine."

As they skirted past the bar, Suzanna spotted two ladies talking. One woman wearing a big hat and large sunglasses had her face in shadow, so Suzanna didn't have a clear view, but something about her seemed familiar. She wanted to point her out to Austen, but he had stopped to speak to Rhonda Penders from Wild Rose Press. By the time they'd finished, the woman was gone.

Austen took her hand. "Is something wrong?"

"No, it doesn't matter. Let's go. I'm starving."

They arrived at the restaurant and were able to get seats in the covered outdoor dining area. Sailboats glided across the water, while pelicans dove for their dinner. The sun slipped lower in the sky, and a warm breeze stirred the salty air.

"I can see why you enjoy living here," Mark said. "It's beautiful."

"It's our little paradise," Suzanna said.

"I could live here," Austen added. "I have to say I love New York, but this is more laidback."

"Mark, are you from New York?" Amy asked.

"No. I grew up in Ann Arbor, Michigan. I moved to New York four years ago. And I agree with Austen. The city is becoming too stressful."

The tightening of Mark's mouth piqued Suzanna's curiosity as to what he meant. A group of ladies at the next table distracted her from her thoughts. They wore conference badges and were having a fun time. Suzanna smiled at them, and they smiled and waved back. The one closest to their table leaned forward.

"Sorry to bother you, but I'm Elaine, and we're the Beach Book Club from Long Cove. Mr. Kincaid, we just finished reading your last book, and we loved it."

All the ladies clapped and cheered.

Austen grinned. "Thanks, I appreciate that. Do you really meet on the beach?"

"Yes, the last Thursday of the month, if you'd like to join us," a lady whose name tag read *Kitty* replied.

"Sounds great," Amy added. "My friend and I"— she indicated Suzanna—"own Beachside Books. You'll have to stop in. We give discounts to book clubs."

"We'll be there," Maggie interjected.

"We hope to see all of you at the book signing on Saturday afternoon," Suzanna said.

"We have our books for Mr. Kincaid to sign," Fran added.

The ladies' food and more drinks arrived. "Enjoy yourselves," Suzanna said with a smile as their own waitress took their order.

Four men wearing Hilton Head Golf Club shirts

passed their table. Mark gestured in their direction. "Austen, do you golf?"

"Let's put it this way, I try."

"I'm going in the morning; would you like to join me?"

Austen hesitated and turned to Suzanna. "Do you know if I'm scheduled for anything tomorrow?"

Suzanna reached for her purse and pulled out a folded paper. "I don't see you listed until Saturday, and Mark isn't on a panel until three o'clock. If you go early enough, there shouldn't be a problem."

"Great," Mark said. "I'll see about getting us a tee time."

They finished their dinner as the sun slid into the water, and stars twinkled in the darkening sky.

"I have to get home," Amy said. "I'll drop all of you off at the hotel."

When they arrived at the Huntington, Mark hung back, talking to Amy, while Austen and Suzanna made their way inside.

"How about a nightcap on my balcony?" Austen asked.

"Only a nightcap?"

Austen wrapped his arm around her shoulders and grinned. "We can start with that, then end with breakfast in bed."

"Sounds wonderful, but I have to work tomorrow, and you're going golfing."

"True. So, I guess we skip the nightcap."

****

Dawn had barely touched the morning sky as Austen and Mark sipped coffee, waiting their turn to tee up.

"What a perfect way to begin the day," Austen said. "This would be easy to get used to."

Mark nodded. "No kidding." He cleared his throat. "There's something I wanted to talk to you about."

"This sounds serious."

"It's more awkward than anything." Mark sipped his coffee. "It has to do with Haley."

"Let me guess. You also got caught up in the black widow's web."

Mark laughed without humor. "You got it."

"When did it happen?"

"I was her victim before you, and before I'd signed with H&H. I hadn't read any of her books, so when she came on to me, I didn't know who she was. We were at a Christmas party with a number of people from publishing houses, along with editors and agents. She was a little drunk, and so was I. She's attractive and likes to show off her body." Mark shrugged. "What's a guy supposed to do? She dumped me pretty quick when I signed with H&H. And she threatened to ruin me if I told anyone about our affair."

"She's a royal bitch," Austen said. "She threatened me as well, but I told her to give it her best shot. Do you still have a contract with H&H?"

"I did until yesterday." Mark filled him in on his conversation with Haley. "I imagine they'll let me go."

"First, Haley can't fire you; that would be up to Brad. Considering they're not speaking, I doubt she'll say anything to anyone. She wanted to scare you, that's all."

Mark's eyes narrowed in anger. "I wasn't sure how much power she had with the company."

"If she and Brad were getting along, she could

cause trouble, but don't worry. As for you seeing Haley, do you recall what time it was?"

"Just before eleven. I was on my way to my room, and she stepped onto the elevator."

"Did you notice what floor she got off on?"

Mark shook his head. "I was so pissed, I didn't pay any attention. Why?"

"Because she was supposed to have left the hotel. Damn. I'll have to ask at the desk and see if she's registered."

"I believe she had luggage, but I was so surprised to see her, I can't be sure."

Austen nodded. "I understand."

Mark hesitated. "I do have a new manuscript, and I'd like to try another publisher. Do you have any suggestions?"

"Let me talk to my editor. Perhaps Miller and James will be interested."

Mark smiled with relief. "That would be great. My first book did all right, but it didn't take off like yours. I honestly want to get as far away from H&H and Haley as possible."

Austen shook his head in disgust. "One of these times, Haley is going to mess with the wrong person."

"Why doesn't Brad throw her out on her ass?"

"He did."

Mark's brows rose. "Really? When?"

Austen explained why Haley arrived on Hilton Head. "Hopefully, she's gone off to screw up someone else's life and will leave us alone."

Mark grinned. "Right on."

****

Haley stood in front of her hotel room mirror and

admired her new shoulder-length deep-brown wig and tinted glasses. Perfect. She reached for the bright pink blouse covered with smiling tropical fish and matching pink Bermuda shorts and shuddered. Flip-flops and a large floppy hat completed her outfit. No one who knew her would ever recognize her dressed like this. She grabbed her non-designer straw bag and headed for the poolside restaurant, intending to put her disguise to the test.

Haley spotted Melinda Pearce seated at the outdoor bar and took a nearby seat. When Melinda glanced her way, Haley held her breath. When Melinda gave her a friendly smile, Haley almost laughed. If she spoke, she might give herself away, so she smiled back.

Thankfully, a group of chattering women joined them at the bar, cutting off any conversation Melinda might have begun. Haley spotted their hotel name tags. *I wonder if they're part of the conference.*

"We have to get tickets for the sunset cruise," the one whose tag read *Angela* said.

"I made reservations, so we're all set," Heidi said.

Sudden inspiration struck Haley. She smiled at the woman whose tag read *Patty*. "Excuse me. I just got here; is the cruise you're referring to part of the conference?"

"Yes," she replied. "You can reserve a spot when you check in at the registration desk."

"But you don't have to be part of the conference in order to go," Laurie added.

Lilly nodded. "That's right. My boyfriend is meeting me there."

"Thank you, you've been very helpful," Haley said.

"No problem," Angela replied. "We work here at the hotel spa. So, if you need your hair done, or any other pampering, stop in."

Haley thanked them again and went to see about getting a ticket.

Chapter Twenty-Five

A short distance away at the Island Sands Hotel, Brad Henderson paced across his fourth-floor suite. "I know damn well the conniving bitch is here with Austen Kincaid. Did she honestly think I wouldn't find them?"

Clarice Abbot, seated on the sofa, sighed. "Just because Austen is attending this conference, doesn't mean Haley's here as well. But, if she is, what are you going to do about it?"

"I'm going to get my fucking money back, then make sure neither she nor Austen ever publishes another book."

"You should call the police and your attorney and let them deal with Haley and the money. As for Austen, according to what I learned, he was a last-minute replacement for the conference's keynote speaker. I don't see how they could have planned to meet here."

"You're just saying that because you have a soft spot for Kincaid." Brad snorted.

"I have a soft spot for him because he's a hell of a writer, and I'm sorry to see him leave H&H. His involvement with Haley was unwise, to say the least. But I believe he realizes his mistake, and I can't see him taking another chance on ruining his career over her. As for Haley, she doesn't like rejection. So, after you tossed her out, I wouldn't put it past her to try and get Austen back."

"I should have thrown her out years ago. It's too bad that skit on the ship wasn't real. Then we'd be done with her."

"I said from the beginning, that entire performance was Haley's little taunt," Clarice said with disgust. "She knew we all hated her and would love to plunge a knife into her."

"I loved the expression on her face when JJ called her a bitch," Brad said, smiling. "That definitely wasn't in the skit." He shook his head. "At one point, I actually considered pushing her overboard."

Clarice laughed. "I'm surprised someone didn't."

Brad refilled both their coffee cups. "Back to our problem at hand. I still think Austen is my best means of tracking Haley down. I had no idea how many hotels were on this island."

"The conference goers are staying next door at the Huntington, but that doesn't mean Haley also is. I picked up a conference itinerary, and there's a costume welcome party on a sunset cruise tonight. I can see if the boat is booked for conference goers only. If not, we can try to get a ticket. If Haley is still here, she won't be able to resist such a gathering. And, if she's still after Austen, she'll be there."

Brad paused in his pacing. "Costumes, how convenient. I sure as hell don't want to tip my hand until I can get her alone."

Clarice glanced over the paper she held. "We're supposed to dress as a mystery character or detective." She tapped her pen against her chin. "We'd need something simple."

"I'd imagine Sherlock Holmes would be a popular

costume. That would be fairly easy, and I'd blend in."

Clarice nodded. "I'll check on tickets, then go and see what I can find." As she placed the pamphlet on the table, a name jumped out at her. "Damn it to hell."

"What is it now?" Brad asked.

"There's a list of conference attendees. JJ Jackson and Melinda Pearce are both here."

Brad swore colorfully. "The last thing we need is for those two to see us."

"They're not exactly fans of Haley. They'd most likely be on your side."

"Yes, well, I don't need the entire publishing world to know I was stupid enough to allow Haley to clean me out. There's already speculation on whether H&H is going under."

Clarice's eyes glittered in anger. "And I wouldn't put it past Haley for starting that rumor."

Brad, hands in his pockets, stared out the sliding door and didn't reply.

"It is a rumor, isn't it? H&H is doing fine, right?"

He ran his fingers across his forehead. "I'm not going to lie. Haley took a substantial amount of money. I was an idiot for not clearing out the account myself. Besides, you know as well as me, the brick-and-mortar publishing houses lately have taken a hit. We have top-selling authors who bring us a nice income, but they can't sustain us forever. We're bringing on new authors, but it will take a while for them to show a decent profit. I hate to admit it, but losing Austen hurt us. I'd beg in the streets though before I'd bring him back."

"As long as we're being honest," Clarice continued. "Quite a few of our authors have left because of Haley. She's either hateful to the women or comes on to the men. Honestly, Brad, what in hell do you see in that woman?"

A flush crept up Brad's cheeks. "I can tell you one thing: I'm done playing her stooge. I'll do whatever it takes to get her out of my life."

Clarice rose and went to stand next to Brad. She placed her hand on his arm. "Don't you think it's time you told me the truth? What has she been holding over you for all these years?"

Brad gazed into Clarice's eyes, took a deep breath, and slowly exhaled. "I should have shared this with you a long time ago. It happened in college. Before I opened the publishing house, I made a lot of money off a series of books under a pseudonym."

Clarice's brows rose in surprise. "I didn't know you could write."

Brad laughed without humor. "I can't, but Clay Parks could."

"Who?"

"Let's sit." He led Clarice to a chair and took the sofa across from her. "In college, my roommate's name was Clay Parks, a quiet guy who spent most of his time on his computer. I spent my time with friends partying and didn't pay much attention to him. All I knew is he was from Ohio, and his only family was a grandmother. When she passed away, Clay was on his way back to Ohio when a drunk driver killed him. I really felt awful for ignoring him the way I had, so I offered to pack up his belongings for the school. In a large plastic tote in his closet, I found thick envelopes of manuscripts. I suppose Clay had intended to send them off to a publisher, but for some reason never had. I started to read the one on top and couldn't put it down. I'd tried my hand at writing, but I was crap. Now here I had a thrilling story right in front of me." Brad shook his head. "I still can't believe what I did. I sent the first manuscript off and was offered a contract. I didn't want anyone to question me about writing the book, so I chose a different name."

"How did Haley find out?" Clarice asked in a quiet voice.

"When the guilt threatened to eat me alive, I erased everything I could about my fictional author from the internet, which wasn't much. My mistake was keeping copies of all the published books. Haley came upon them and read one. She liked it so much, she tried to research the author. When she found nothing, her curiosity led her to dig deeper. Remember, this all happened before the big-name online booksellers. And fortunately for me, the publishing house had folded. I thought I was in the clear, until Haley found a manuscript in the bottom of a box I'd forgotten about. The manuscript had Clay's name but notes in my handwriting. She confronted me, and like a fool, I told her the truth. My only excuse is that this happened before I realized what a conniving, backstabbing, evil person she is."

Tears formed in Clarice's eyes, and she wrapped her arms around Brad. "She truly is a despicable human being."

Brad held Clarice close. "If there was a way to right the wrong I did, I would. Years ago, I anonymously donated the money I made from the sales of the books to a charity, in Clay's name."

Clarice kissed his cheek. "Haley's hurt too many

people for too long, and it's time it stopped."

Fiery anger burned in Brad's eyes. "And it's time for us to stop hiding our love. Let Haley do her worst. I don't give a damn anymore."

Chapter Twenty-Six

Morning sunlight peeked through the tall sea pines as Suzanna kissed Austen and left the hotel. She'd go home, shower, then make sure she had all she needed for her costume. As soon as the consignment shop, the Hidden Closet, opened, she'd try and find something for Austen.

She'd just finished getting dressed when her cell chimed. Expecting Amy, she smiled in delight to see the call was from her cousin Jenn.

"Hey, hi, this is a pleasant surprise," Suzanna said. "I thought you were traveling."

"I am," Jenn replied. "I wanted to see how things were going with the conference, and if everything is okay with the hotel?"

"The Huntington is perfect, thanks to you. As far as the conference, so far so good."

"And?"

"And what?"

"Suzanna, I can tell by your voice you're dying to tell me something."

Suzanna laughed. "Okay, promise you'll hear me out before you start shouting."

"If you have to say that, this is not good."

"Actually, it is. Austen's here."

"What? Don't tell me you've fallen for more of his bullshit."

"He said it was all a mistake. Haley was waiting for him in his room, and he told her to leave. Then he passed out. She staged the pictures. Jenn, he pleaded with me to believe him."

"And do you?"

"Yes. Haley is devious enough to fake something like that."

"Suzanna, be careful. I don't want you to get hurt again."

"I won't. I'm not as naïve as I once was. He said he loves me, and I believe he's sincere."

"So, did you have mind-blowing makeup sex?"

Suzanna grinned. "Did we ever."

"Good for you. I'm also calling to tell you the news. I'm supposed to wait, but I can't."

"What?"

"I've just left the ranch, and Diana's pregnant."

"Really? That's wonderful. I'll bet they're both ecstatic."

"Dillon's already a basket case. Ever since Diana learned to ride, he can't keep her off Flora. He's freaked out she's going to get hurt."

"Flora's a good horse. Diana will be fine. I'm so excited for them. I thought about taking Austen to the ranch."

"Bring him for the Labor Day get-together. We can all give him the third degree."

"On the other hand, perhaps not."

"Oh, come on, we won't be too rough on him." Jenn paused. "What about your mother? Does Aunt Augusta know about your relationship?"

"Thankfully, no. I wanted to tell her all about the cruise and how I fell in love, but thank goodness I was smart enough not to. She'd be relishing the fact that she warned me about girls alone on cruises and men who take advantage of them."

"Eventually you'll have to introduce Austen to her, and she'll ask how you met."

"I'll deal with that when it happens, which won't be soon. So, what's going on with you?"

"I'm on my way home to Chapel Hill. There's a rumor the Huntington purchased an old hotel in Charleston and plans to restore it. They want to open a line of boutique hotels. I'd love to be part of starting that up."

"Tell them."

"I'm pretty low on the managerial chain."

"Jenn, you've been with that company for years. You'd do a wonderful job."

"Yes, well, we'll see. There's a rest area coming up, and I have to pee. Keep me updated on you and Austen. Love you."

"Love you, too." Suzanna disconnected the call and smiled. Among all her McCoy cousins, she was closest to Jenn. How many hours had Jenn stayed on the phone listening to her cry over Austen? Suzanna gnawed on her lower lip. Perhaps taking him to meet her family wasn't such a good idea. Hard telling what Jenn might say to him. Suzanna picked up her purse. September was a couple of months away. She'd worry about it then.

At nine sharp, Suzanna unlocked the door to Beachside Books. Minutes later, Amy came in, Peg right on her heels.

"Good morning," Suzanna said. "Amy, I didn't expect to see you until later."

"I dropped Violet off at preschool and decided to come on in," Amy replied. "I can help you at the conference, if you need me."

"Don't you girls worry about a thing," Peg said. "I'll take care of the store and meet you later on the boat."

Suzanna didn't miss the fact Amy had taken extra care with her appearance. Her short, curly blonde hair shone, her makeup was perfect, and her short skirt and top showed off her trim legs and nice figure. If Suzanna wasn't mistaken, Mark Gray was the reason. She inwardly smiled. "Great. I need to run over to the Hidden Closet. I'll meet you at the hotel around eleven."

Amy nodded. "What time do you think the boys will get done golfing?"

"Maybe around noon or so. I can text Austen and see if they'd like to meet us for lunch."

Amy's eyes sparkled. "Sure."

As hard as she tried, Suzanna was unable to hold back her smile.

"What?" Amy asked.

"Nothing."

"Come on, what is it?"

Suzanna chuckled. "Okay, you're terrible when it comes to hiding your feelings."

Amy sighed. "Am I that obvious?"

"Yes, but it's because I know you so well. Besides, Mark seems like a nice guy."

"He is. And he's not turned off by Violet like most guys are."

Suzanna's heart broke a little for her friend. A weekend fling, and Amy found herself pregnant. The guy, an executive at the advertising company Amy worked for, wasn't interested in being a father, so Amy had raised her three-year-old daughter on her own.

Amy gnawed on her lower lip. "The relationship may not develop into anything, but he's the first man I've been this attracted to in a long time. I just hope I'm not reading him wrong."

"He seemed awfully interested in you last night. And, once he sees you in that killer outfit, he'll melt like butter in your hands."

Amy smiled. "That's the plan."

Suzanna gave Amy a quick hug. "I'm off to find Austen a costume for tonight. I'll see you later."

The Hidden Closet was a popular upscale secondhand store owned by Suzanna's tennis friend Maryanne. She entered the store to find it packed. She made her way to the back, where men's clothes were kept. Instantly she spotted a tan trench coat. Visions of Sam Spade popped into her head, and she hurried to where it hung. As she reached for the coat, it was snatched from her hands.

Suzanna blinked. Clarice Abbot stood there holding the coat. Her cheeks were flushed, and she nervously glanced around.

"Miss Abbot, this is a surprise. I didn't know you were attending the conference."

"What?" she stammered.

"The mystery writers' conference. I assume that's why you're here on Hilton Head."

Clarice shook her head. "Oh, no…" She stared at Suzanna and hesitated. Recognition dawned in her eyes. "Um, have we met?"

"On the Who Done It? cruise. I'm Suzanna Shay, a

friend of Austen Kincaid."

"Oh, yes."

"Austen's here. He's the conference keynote speaker."

"Really. Since he left H&H, I haven't kept track of him." She gave a shaky laugh. "This is quite a coincidence. I own a time-share in Sea Pines, and this is my week."

"I also live in Sea Pines," Suzanna said. "Where is your time-share located?"

Clarice hesitated. "Um, near Harbor Town."

"How nice. My friend and I own Beachside Books. If you get a chance while you're here, please stop by." She indicated the coat Clarice still held. "Tonight is the conference welcome party on the sunset cruise boat. Everyone is supposed to dress as their favorite detective or mystery writer. Austen needs a costume, and that coat would make a great Sam Spade."

Clarice gazed at the coat as if it might bite her. She handed it to Suzanna. "Here, you take it. I thought my friend would like it, but it's too small." She turned to go. "It was nice seeing you again." She plunged into the crowd and was gone.

Suzanna frowned. What a strange encounter. For someone supposedly on vacation, Clarice acted awfully tense. *Time-share week, my ass.* It was obvious she scrambled to come up with a location. *Wait until Austen hears another member of the murder cruise is in town.* Suzanna, thrilled she had the trench coat, went to find a fedora. Three consignment shops later, she found what she needed. A bit worn, the hat would work nicely.

As she slipped into her car, her cell rang. She frowned when her mother's name was displayed.

"Hello, Mama," Suzanna said.

"Suzanna, I haven't heard from you and wondered if you're all right."

Before Suzanna could respond, her mother continued. "All types of awful things can happen to girls living alone, surrounded by who knows what kind of people. I still don't understand why you had to move. You could have opened your little bookshop here in Charlotte."

Suzanna gritted her teeth. Little bookshop indeed. "Mama, I told you I live in a very safe community. The island is full of happy vacationers who want nothing more than to enjoy themselves."

"And men who want nothing more than to take advantage of innocent girls."

Visions of her and Austen making love made Suzanna grin. If her mother only knew. "Mama, I'm very busy with the conference, and I can't talk right now."

"That's nice. You don't have time for your mother, after you and your sister leave me all alone."

Resigned, Suzanna sighed. "Why don't you visit Grandma and Grandpa at the ranch? Did you hear Diana is pregnant?"

"Mama and Daddy are off again. Honestly, at their age, one of them could have a heart attack or stroke. Then what would they do? What did you say about Diana?"

Suzanna repeated what Jenn had told her. "It sounds as if Dillon and Diana are both thrilled."

"No, I hadn't heard, but no one tells me anything anyway." She sniffed. "Another one of my brothers is going to be a grandparent before me."

Suzanna tapped her fingers on the steering wheel in frustration. One minute her mother thought every man Suzanna dated would either harm her or was a lazy bum, the next complaining she didn't have grandchildren. Suzanna changed the subject. "How is your book club going?"

"Fine, I suppose. The last book was a thriller by a new author, Austen Kincaid. Cheryl chose the book. I didn't care for it at all. It had way too much violence for my taste."

Suzanna had to stifle a laugh.

"Suzanna, are you all right? You sound as if you're choking."

"I'm fine, Mama, but I really have to go. I'll call soon. Love you." Suzanna disconnected the call before her mother could respond. *Good grief.* She laughed. Wait until she told Austen her mother's opinion of his book.

When she returned to the hotel, Austen was heading for the elevator. "Austen," she called.

He stopped and waited for her. "Hi," he said. "This is perfect timing. I've been working out. Let me wash up, and I'll meet you outside."

"I'll ride up with you. I want you to see what I bought, and I have something to tell you."

When the elevator doors closed, Austen took her in his arms and kissed her. "Perhaps Amy and Mark can start lunch without us."

Suzanna grinned and stepped from his embrace. "As nice as that sounds, I haven't time, and you need a shower. Besides, I'm starving."

Austen gave her an exaggerated sad face, and Suzanna burst out laughing. "Poor boy. You're so sexually deprived."

"That's right. It's been at least five hours."

"Take your mind off sex and focus on the fact that Clarice Abbot is on the island."

Austen paused, the room key in his hand. "Seriously?"

Suzanna explained about meeting Clarice. "She said she's here because it's her time-share week, but that's quite a coincidence."

"I agree. But what does it mean?"

"I don't know, but all the players in Haley's skit are here. I can't help but feel something bad is going to happen."

"All that's missing is Brad. If he shows up, and Haley is still here, that could be trouble."

Suzanna nodded. "We'd better keep our eyes open."

Once in his room, Suzanna opened her bag. "Wait until you see what I found for you to wear." She extracted the coat and hat. "Welcome, Mr. Sam Spade."

Austen grinned. "Perfect. Where's my Maltese Falcon?"

"I almost bought a stuffed crow, but decided it wasn't quite right. Now, let me tell you about my conversation with my mother."

When she'd finished, Austen grinned. "That's too funny. I'm on her disapproval list before I've even met her. I suppose you can't please everyone."

"Trust me, no one can please my mother."

He held her close and kissed her. "I love you."

She scrunched up her nose. "I love you too, but you really need a shower."

He stepped back. "Sorry. How about I clean up and

spend the afternoon making love to you?"

"That's a wonderful idea, but we can't. I have conference duties." She kissed him lightly. "How about instead of this afternoon, we switch to all night?"

"It's a date."

****

Clarice Abbot, seated at The Low Country Backyard, took a long sip of her gin and tonic. Her nerves rattled, she'd stopped at the first outdoor bar she found. What were the chances she'd come face-to-face with Suzanna? Talk about her heart almost stopping. Brad would be furious if he knew she'd been discovered. With any luck, Suzanna would believe her story about the time-share. Did she and Brad dare go on the sunset cruise? *Damn it to hell,* she silently swore. This was all Haley's fault. That woman did nothing but cause trouble. *I'm tired of playing second fiddle to her. Brad had better follow through with his threat and finally divorce the sleazebag. One way or another, I want her out of our lives.* In the meantime, what to do about tonight? No matter the risk, they needed to discover if Haley was here, which meant their costumes must be good enough to conceal their identities.

Chapter Twenty-Seven

That evening, at the South Beach marina, Suzanna as Nancy Drew, Austen as Sam Spade, Mark as Shaggy, and Amy as Daphne Blake, sat in the Island Pirate Restaurant eating hamburgers.

"I love your cloche hat," Amy said. "I'm glad you decided to do an original Nancy."

"I'm afraid most won't realize who I'm supposed to be," Suzanna replied. "As for you two, how in the world did you manage to get '70s hippy clothes?"

"Mark brought his," Amy said. "And my aunt gave me some of her old clothes for a Halloween party I went to a few years ago."

"My bell-bottoms and tie-dyed shirt are compliments of my cousin who still dresses like it's 1969," Mark said.

Austen raised his beer and grinned. "Here's to rock and roll. I told Suzanna that Shaggy is my favorite sleuth."

"Did you boys have fun playing golf?" Suzanna asked.

Mark cleared his throat. "I did."

"He kicked my ass," Austen replied.

"Like I did on the ship," Suzanna teased.

Austen scowled. "Yeah, well, whatever."

Suzanna didn't try to conceal her smile as she glanced out the window to where the boat was docked.

"We'd better hurry so we can get seats on the upper deck."

Painted white, *The Sundown* was a two-deck double-hull catamaran which could hold seventy-five passengers, with Captain Phil Smith at the helm.

As they boarded, Captain Phil greeted them. A friend of Suzanna's, she hugged him warmly. "Hello. Are you ready for an onslaught of dressed up mystery lovers?"

Captain Phil chuckled. "As long as no one is murdered, we'll be fine."

"I'd like to introduce you to my friends Austen and Mark, and you know Amy."

He shook both men's hands and gave Amy a hug. "You'd better hurry and get a seat. There's already a large group gathered on the upper deck."

On their way up, they encountered Sherlock Holmes, Dick Tracy, Hercule Poirot, Miss Marple, Columbo, Charlie Chan, Miss Fisher, Lord Peter, and others Suzanna wasn't sure of. She sighed in relief when they were able to grab the last table near the rail. "I'm afraid it's going to be wall-to-wall people."

"How long is the ride, and where do we go?" Mark asked.

"It takes about an hour and a half," Suzanna replied. "This is Calibogue Sound. When we leave, you'll see the Harbor Town lighthouse in the distance. We'll pass Dafuskie Island, then we'll enter the May River."

"The sky is perfect. We should have a wonderful sunset and a beautiful full moon," Amy said. "And we usually see dolphins."

Austen rose. "Mark, why don't we go get drinks

before the crowd gets worse?"

"Sure. What would you ladies like?"

"You seem happier than I've seen you in a long time," Suzanna said after the men had left.

Amy smiled. "I am. Even though Mark and I just met, there's a connection between us I can't explain."

"Here we are, attracted to two men who live hundreds of miles away."

"Mark has wanted to leave New York for quite a while. He told me he's going to try and get a contract with Miller and James. He said Austen is going to put in a good word for him."

"That's great," Suzanna said. "Has he mentioned living here?"

Amy shook her head. "He said he really likes the island. Whether he'd move here, who knows."

As Austen and Mark returned with their drinks, the boat edged away from the dock.

"Talk about a crush at the bar," Austen said. "You can hardly move."

Mark nodded. "I've counted ten Sherlock Holmes."

"I swear I even saw Inspector Clouseau," Austen added.

Just then, two women dressed as cats passed their table. Around their necks, tags read *Mrs. Murphy*.

"I love it," Amy said with a grin.

"There's Harbor Town." Suzanna indicated the red-and-white-striped lighthouse. "We'll have to take you boys there before you leave."

"I understand there's parasailing," Austen said. "Suzanna, we should try it."

"Are you crazy?" Suzanna replied with a shudder. "It was bad enough on that slide in Costa Maya.

Dangling in the air on a kite isn't happening."

"Okay, how about a jet ski ride?"

"Remember what I told you about me and oceans? There are large fish out there who want to sting or eat you. You'll not catch me on anything that might tip over."

Austen rolled his eyes. "Sailboat?"

"A really big one."

They all laughed, and Suzanna smiled. The breeze was warm but pleasant. Summertime music played from the speakers, and the man she loved was seated across from her. She sipped her wine. Yes, life was good. She was about to point out Daufuskie Island, when someone shouted, "Dolphins."

People instantly hurried to the rail to see. Suzanna and the others rose as well. The dolphins, as if they knew they were being watched, splashed, leaped, and chattered, putting on quite a show. Suzanna was jostled back and forth. Everyone clapped and tried to take pictures. Bodies pressed close, and Suzanna, wanting to see better, stepped up to stand on the bench where the life jackets were stored. Suddenly, as she leaned out over the rail, she was shoved from behind, lifting her up and over the rail.

A scream lodged in her throat, as she plunged into the cold water. Instinct took over, and she kicked her way to the surface. She brushed the wet hair from her face as shouts and cries came to her from the boat. "Man overboard!" Captain Phil immediately reacted, slowing the boat nearly to a dead stop. The crew members grabbed life preservers and ran to the rails.

The full impact of what had happened pierced her shock. She glanced up as Austen was about to jump in after her. "No, Austen, don't. Throw me a life jacket."

An orange vest sailed through the air, landing a few feet away. Her dress clinging to her legs, Suzanna struggled to swim toward it. Then, the full realization of where she was hit. Oh, my God. She glanced around. The dolphins were still there, but what lay in the depths beneath her? *Suzanna, don't panic. Remain calm. The boat is turning back, and they'll have you on board soon.* She grabbed the life vest and lay across it, lifting her legs to keep them from dangling in the water.

When something brushed against her, fear threatened to consume her. *Not a shark. Not a shark. Please, not a shark.* Her heart thumped wildly in her chest, and her breath came in shallow gasps. As a sleek gray body surfaced, Suzanna let out a sob of relief. "Hello," she said through chattering teeth. "You're supposed to be friendly."

The dolphin circled her, then nudged her arm with his nose. Tentatively Suzanna held out her hand and stroked the smooth skin. "Nice Flipper."

With her attention on the dolphin, she hadn't noticed she was drifting farther from the boat. Shouts from the passengers brought her back to her surroundings. Mind-numbing panic engulfed her. The riptides were quite strong here. It could sweep her away in minutes. Without a second thought, Suzanna reached out and wrapped her arm around the dolphin. *Buddy, be my hero, and stay above the water and keep me safe.*

Trembling, frightened more than she'd ever been, Suzanna blinked back the tears that burned the back of her eyes. *Concentrate on anything but where you are, and you'll be fine. There probably isn't a shark for miles.* The dolphin stayed by her side, and she'd never loved anything as much as she did this large mammal.

The boat glided slowly up beside her, and a ladder was dropped over the side. Suzanna let go of her rescuer. "Thank you," she called as he dove under and swam away.

Austen, Amy, and Mark stood on the lower deck as she was helped on board.

Suzanna collapsed into Austen's arms. "Christ, Suzanna, what happened?" he gasped as he crushed her to his chest. "You scared about ten years off my life."

Suzanna, shivering uncontrollably, pressed her face into his shoulder and let her tears flow. "Austen, I was so scared."

He tightened his hold. "It's all right. I have you," he murmured. "You're safe." Austen guided her to an empty seat. "Sit down, and I'll get you some hot coffee."

Suzanna gulped back her sobs. "Put some Kahlua in it."

A soft-spoken woman with a kind smile handed Suzanna a thick beach towel. "I'm Darla, and I'm a nurse. I wanted to make sure you were all right."

"I'm a little shaky."

"That's understandable. I imagine you're in shock. Do you mind if I take your pulse?"

Suzanna shook her head. "No."

Darla held Suzanna's wrist. "It's a little fast but stronger than I expected. Did you hit your head on the rail as you fell?"

"No. I kind of dove right over."

"I'd suggest if you start to feel confused or unable to calm down, call your physician."

"Thank you so much," Suzanna said.

Darla stepped away, and Amy sat and hugged Suzanna. "How in the world did you end up in the water?"

"I'd like to know the same thing," Captain Phil said, kneeling in front of Suzanna.

"Tell me what happened?"

For the first time since the accident, Suzanna replayed the sequence of events leading to her fall. She stared in wide-eyed horror into Captain Phil's troubled face. "I was pushed."

Incredulity was clear in his voice. "Are you sure?"

"Yes." She explained that the people were crowded next to the railing, and how she'd stood on the built-in seat. "I leaned out to get a better look at the dolphins, and someone kind of lifted me up and shoved me over." Her voice broke. She hunched forward and willed her trembling to stop. "I'm terrified of sharks. If it hadn't been for the dolphin, I would have lost my mind."

"That was the most incredible thing I've ever seen," Mark said, sitting next to Amy. "You hear of instances where animals help humans, but never expect to witness it."

"No one was more surprised than me," Suzanna replied. "When he nudged my leg, I was convinced it was a shark."

Austen returned with her coffee, and Suzanna gratefully sipped the hot liquid.

"This is a serious matter," Captain Phil continued. "If you honestly believe you were pushed, I'll need to report the incident. I can also ask the passengers if anyone witnessed it."

Austen gaped. "Pushed. Suzanna, are you serious?"

She nodded.

Austen jumped to his feet. "Son of a bitch. I'll throw the bastard over myself."

Captain Phil stood. "Wait a minute. There will be none of that. I'll take care of this myself. Starting with all of you. So, who saw what?"

"Unfortunately, we weren't near Suzanna, so didn't see anything," Amy said.

"The crowd was packed in so tight, I ended up down the rail from her," Austen added. "I didn't even see her go over."

The coffee warming her and her mind clearing from her ordeal, Suzanna took in the people around her. Some stared, concern on their faces. But most went back to enjoying themselves. Who would have pushed her, and why? She tried to picture the faces of those standing close before she went over, but it was all a blur.

"Do you want to go back on the upper deck?" Austen asked.

Suzanna shook her head. "I'm not moving from this spot. Austen, why would someone push me?"

He took her hand. "Baby, I don't know. I've been thinking. With most in costume, I'm wondering if you were mistaken for someone else."

"I thought the same thing," Amy said. "Who in the world would want Suzanna hurt?"

****

In the small bathroom, Haley gulped in air, hoping to calm her jangled nerves. Had anyone seen her? Probably not. There were too many people pressed close together. She'd stepped around a large man, and there in front of her stood Suzanna. When she leaned over the rail, Haley reacted before she thought of the consequences. As Suzanna fell and people shouted, Haley eased away as quickly as possible. Now, the boat had stopped. They must have rescued Suzanna. All she needed to do was blend into the crowd until the boat docked.

"Hey, are you all right in there?" someone called from the other side of the bathroom door.

"Yes, coming." Haley glanced at herself in the tiny mirror, made sure her hat and wig were on straight, and unlocked the door. She kept her head down, then gasped when she collided with another person.

"Woah, watch," a male voice said.

Haley, her sunglasses knocked askew, gazed with horror into JJ Jackson's face. "Excuse me," she murmured as she adjusted her sunglasses and fled through a group of people.

Chapter Twenty-Eight

Suzanna, Austen, Amy, and Mark were seated around a table on the lower deck when the boat arrived at the marina. "Captain Phil said we need to wait until everyone is off so we can explain to the Coast Guard what happened," Austen said.

"I can't imagine they'll ever find out who pushed me," Suzanna said. "Perhaps it was truly an accident. People were crushed together. Someone from behind may have pressed closer to see the dolphins and pushed too hard, and we all went forward."

"You said you were sure you'd been shoved," Amy said. "Why are you changing your mind now?"

Suzanna sighed. "It all happened so fast. I don't want to cause a big to-do if I'm mistaken."

"Don't second-guess yourself," Austen said. "Your first reaction is most likely the truth."

Before Suzanna could reply, JJ Jackson and Melinda Pearse stopped in front of them.

"Suzanna, are you all right?" Melinda asked.

"Yes, thanks," Suzanna replied.

"People are saying you were pushed," JJ said. "Is that true?"

Suzanna nodded.

"I might be mistaken, but I think Haley is on this boat," JJ added.

Suzanna gaped, and Austen narrowed his eyes.

"What makes you say that?" Austen asked.

JJ explained his mishap with the woman at the bathrooms. "I didn't get a clear look at her face, and she lowered her voice, but there was something about her that reminded me of Haley."

"Son of a bitch," Austen swore. "If I discover it was her who shoved you, I'll kill her."

"Austen, don't say such a thing," Suzanna said. "Even if it was Haley, we have no proof she was the one."

Melinda snorted. "I wouldn't put anything past her." She cocked her head. "In fact, when I ran into her yesterday in the hotel lobby, she was hiding behind a potted plant. When I went to sign in for the conference, I noticed the plants were adjacent to the table where you were working."

"What time was this?" Austen asked.

"Before eleven," Melinda replied.

"Did you see where she went?"

"No. She said some ugly things that made me so mad I had to walk away before I punched her."

Again, Austen swore. "JJ, I need to tell Captain Phil you might have seen her. What was she wearing?"

JJ shook his head. "All I noticed was the big hat and huge sunglasses. She was swallowed up by the crowd pretty quickly."

"That describes half the women on the boat," Mark said.

"It's too bad it wasn't Haley who went overboard," JJ stated. "I would have enjoyed seeing her eaten by a shark."

Melinda grinned. "A shark eating a shark, how perfect."

Austen cleared his throat. "I'm going to stand near the ramp where everyone is getting off. If she's here, I'll spot her."

Mark pointed. "You might be too late. The line to debark is already moving."

Haley maneuvered herself until she was near the head of the line leaving the boat. Not much farther, and she'd be off. Her stomach fell, and her throat tightened when the Coast Guard officer asked the person in front of her for identification. She'd booked her ticket under her maiden name with a credit card Brad knew nothing about. She had to bluff her way through this, or her ass was cooked. When the officer asked her for ID, she gave him a dazzling smile. "I'm sorry, but all I have is a credit card with my name on it. I didn't drive, so I didn't bring my wallet."

"Where are you staying?" the officer asked.

"The Island Sands," Haley replied. It didn't matter if they eventually checked. They didn't know her real name.

As she waited for the officer to speak, Haley's palms grew damp, and her heart threatened to pound out of her chest. *Come on.* Why was he staring at her? When her fear was about to overtake her, the officer nodded. "Give your current address to the young woman seated at the end of the dock."

Relief washed over her. As rapidly as possible, Haley hurried away.

Austen excused himself as he worked his way through the mass of people to the rail. He was dismayed when he realized how many had already gotten off. He scanned the long dock, hoping to see a woman in a big hat that resembled Haley, but at least a dozen large hats filled the area. His eye was caught by a flash of bright orange. From the back she reminded him of Haley, but she would never have worn an outfit like that.

"Do you see her?" Mark asked as he, Amy, and Suzanna joined him at the rail.

Austen shook his head. "Too many people."

"If she's still at the hotel, we can confront her there," Suzanna said.

"I thought of that as well," Austen said. "Let's go. I don't want to give her a chance to get away."

Amy touched Suzanna's arm. "Did Captain Phil say it was okay for you to leave, or does the Coast Guard officer have more questions?"

"I believe I'm done. I gave them all my information. Besides, I'm freezing in these wet clothes."

Austen took Suzanna's hand. "Okay, then let's go."

"After you change, we'll meet in my room," Austen said when they arrived at the hotel.

Suzanna nodded as she and Amy headed for the elevator.

Austen and Mark went to the front desk.

"Hi," Austen said to the young woman behind the counter. "Can you tell me if Haley Henderson is staying here?"

"Sure," she replied with a smile as she tapped her computer keys. "I'm sorry, there's no one registered under that name."

Austen thanked her, and he and Mark moved away. Austen's brows drew together in puzzlement.

"Now what?" Mark asked.

"Just because she's not staying here, doesn't mean she's left the island. If JJ thought he saw her, and knowing how devious she can be, I wouldn't put it past her to still be here. And I'm convinced she's the one who pushed Suzanna."

"Okay, so what do we do?"

"Keep our eyes open and stay alert. If Haley is crazy enough to push Suzanna off a moving boat, she's capable of anything. She doesn't like rejection, and she was mad as hell when I told her to leave."

****

In her hotel room, Haley, her nerves still rattled, removed her wig and clothes. Talk about a narrow escape. Perhaps it would be wise to move to another hotel. There were too many staying here that could give her away. She slipped on her silk nightgown and sat on the edge of the bed.

No. As long as Austen is here, I'm not leaving. He has to realize it's me he loves, not that drab bookstore owner. That boat was the perfect opportunity to get rid of Suzanna. If only she'd drowned or been eaten by a shark... I need a foolproof plan to make sure she's out of Austen's life for good.

She paced the floor. *But I have to make sure no one suspects me. Should I change my appearance once again?* She glanced at the garish shorts and top with disgust. *What if I change from being a tacky tourist to a businesswoman? With my wig and tinted glasses, no one would recognize me in a conservative suit and pearls. I'd be able to sit in the lobby and watch for my chance to get Suzanna alone.* She tapped a bloodred fingernail against her cheek. *Whatever I do, it must appear as an accident, but how?*

Ideas swarmed in Haley's head. *Yes, that's it.* A smile spread across her face. Laughing aloud, she opened the sliding door and stepped onto her balcony. A light breeze ruffled the silk of her gown. Below, a couple stood on the beach in a loving embrace. Visions of Suzanna and Austen filled her mind, and she seethed with hatred. *My plan has to work, and Austen will be mine.*

Chapter Twenty-Nine

Saturday morning, Suzanna awoke in Austen's arms. She'd tossed and turned for most of the night dreaming of sharks as her mind replayed her fall from the boat. Did Haley truly hate her enough to try and hurt her? What did she think she'd gain? *Was she crazy enough to believe Austen would want her if I were gone?* Suzanna frowned. What if it was all a mistake? What if, in the midst of the crowd, with so many in costume, whoever pushed her mistook her for someone else?

"Austen, wake up." Suzanna gently shook him.

"No." He burrowed into the blanket.

"Austen, listen. We might be making a huge mistake."

Austen groaned and opened his eyes. "About what?"

Suzanna explained her thoughts. "You see, it may not have been me that was meant to go overboard."

Austen yawned and sat up. "I need coffee before my brain will function."

"I'll make some." Suzanna got up and went to the coffee maker. "The more I think about it, the more I believe I'm right. What would Haley accomplish by hurting me? You told her your relationship was over, so it would be pointless."

Austen sipped the hot brew. "I keep telling

everyone, Haley doesn't take no for an answer. And if there's something or someone she wants badly enough, she doesn't give up."

Suzanna's exuberance left her face. "You honestly believe she hates me that much?"

Austen placed his cup on the side table and took Suzanna in his arms. "She's ruthless and capable of anything. Sometimes I wonder if she's mentally off."

"Austen, you're scaring me. What should I do?"

"Make sure you're never alone. Even if she's left the hotel, that doesn't mean she's left the island. If JJ is right, she's wearing a disguise and will be harder to spot. What's your schedule today?"

"I'm to help direct people to the different workshops and author pitch sessions."

"Good, someone will always be near you. I can help out until two o'clock when I have to be on a panel. Then the author signing is at three."

"The predinner cocktails begin at six," Suzanna said. "Amy and I plan on getting ready around five."

Austen frowned. "I forgot about having to speak tonight. I suppose I should work on what I'm going to say."

Suzanna kissed his cheek. "Be your charming self, and you'll be fine."

After Suzanna left, Austen sat at the desk and wrote some talking points for that night's event. His thoughts kept wandering offtrack, so he gave up. *I need to find out if Haley is still here.* He glanced at the clock, and his stomach growled. *It's early enough. Perhaps if I sit in the restaurant, I'll spot her.*

Minutes later, Austen was seated at a table where he had a view of the elevators and most of the lobby.

His waiter, who Austen took for a college student, placed a pot of coffee on the table and took his order. People passed wearing conference badges, but none resembled Haley. When he spotted JJ and Melinda, an idea formed. He stood and caught their attention.

"Good morning," Austen said. "Would you join me? I want to talk to you about Haley."

JJ and Melinda glanced at each other, then nodded. Once they were seated, and cups of coffee were poured, Austen began.

"I'm convinced Haley pushed Suzanna off the boat last night, and I'm determined to find her and confront her. Can either of you recall anything that might help?"

"Melinda and I have gone over what we saw, and it isn't much," JJ said. "When the woman I believe to be Haley ran into me, I thought about following her, but I'd had two beers, and I was on my way to the gents."

"I was a way down the rail from Suzanna when she fell into the water," Melinda continued. "Everyone's attention was focused on her, so Haley could have easily slipped away."

JJ nodded. "If Haley did push Suzanna overboard, she's truly unhinged and, as far as I'm concerned, extremely dangerous. If I were you, I'd make sure Suzanna is with someone at all times."

Austen let out a long breath. "My thoughts exactly. I wish there were a way to discover if Haley was still here at the hotel or on the island." He frowned. "I suppose I could begin by calling all the hotels, asking if she's registered."

Melinda hesitated. "This may not be of any importance, and I'm not sure it was him, but as we were leaving the dock area, I thought I spotted Brad

Henderson getting into a rental car."

Austen threw up his hands and let them fall. "So, who's surprised. This entire situation is becoming too weird. Suzanna ran into Clarice Abbot at a consignment shop. She said she was here for her time-share week, but Suzanna doesn't believe it."

Melinda nodded. "If Clarice is here, then that was Brad I saw. They don't think anyone knows they've been having an affair for years. Most believe the reason he stays with Haley is because she has something over him. The toxic atmosphere at H&H lately is why I've decided to leave. Besides, I'm quite sure Brad is in financial difficulty, and Haley is most likely to blame. I tell you, if Haley had been the one pushed overboard, I'd guarantee either Brad or Clarice would have done it."

JJ took Melinda's hand in his. "Add me to that list. That woman is pure evil, and a number of people would be thrilled to have her out of their lives for good."

"Including me," Austen said. "How I allowed that woman to pull me into her web is beyond me. Because of my stupidity, I almost lost the most important person in my life."

JJ and Melinda rose to leave. "Now that we know Haley is wearing a disguise, we'll keep our eyes open," JJ said.

****

Clarice lifted the pot and poured herself and Brad more coffee. "If you're right, we need to notify the police."

Brad ran his hand through his hair. "I know it was her. I don't care what kind of getup she's wearing, she has a mole on the back of her knee that was visible when she leaned forward and pushed that young woman."

Clarice buttered her toast. "Her name is Suzanna, and again I'll repeat, call the police."

"What am I supposed to say? 'I believe my unhinged wife, wearing a disguise, pushed an innocent person off a boat.' "

"We should have told the Coast Guard last night. With your description, they might have caught her."

"Then we'd be involved, and I still don't want Haley to know I'm here. We need to find out where she's staying."

"I've been thinking about that. If she's disguising herself, wouldn't she also use a different name?"

Brad scoffed. "What, Bonnie Parker?"

Clarice smiled. "It fits, but perhaps something a little more like her own. What's her maiden name?"

"Beal."

Clarice reached for her phone. After searching hotel listings, she punched in the number for the Huntington. "Yes, I believe my friend is staying there, Beal. Could you please check for me?" She paused, said thank you, and ended the call. "She's there."

Brad narrowed his eyes. "Excellent. Now we can make our plan."

Chapter Thirty

At ten that morning, Suzanna positioned herself at the top of the stairs on the mezzanine level, around the corner from the elevators leading to the rooftop bar and the exercise room.

She read over her schedule. Her third group passed by, and there wasn't another due for thirty minutes. Her body slightly ached from her fall from the boat, and she wouldn't mind sitting for a while. She glanced around. To her right was the guest business center. Seated at a table outside the door was a dark-haired woman in a suit who appeared to be in deep concentration with her phone. Not wanting to disturb her, Suzanna leaned against the rail overlooking the lobby. Below was an arrangement of comfortable couches and chairs on a thick rug. Deciding she'd hurry down and relax for a few minutes, she stepped to the top of the stairs.

Haley cautiously peered from her phone to Suzanna. This was the moment she'd waited for. She checked to make sure no one was in sight. Suzanna was close enough to the top of the stairs; all it would take was one little push. Haley smiled to herself. *See if you survive falling down a flight of marble steps.* Haley rose and took two steps, when the sound of tapping heels grew closer.

"Suzanna, wait," Amy called, coming up behind her. "We have problems. Some of the editors have gone over their allotted time for author pitches, and everything is backing up. They need help shifting authors around, so they asked me to come get you."

"What about directing authors from here?" Suzanna asked.

"I'll take your place. I could use a break from all the chaos."

"Is it that bad?"

Amy rolled her eyes. "Yes."

"Great." Suzanna headed toward the rooms set aside for author pitches. As she passed her, the woman seated at the table turned away and held her phone to her ear. *I wonder if she's one of the agents*, Suzanna thought. She started to ask if she needed assistance when the woman rose and headed for the elevators.

Haley cursed fluently under her breath. A perfect opportunity lost. Desperation clawed at her chest. Time was running out. Her last chance to get rid of Suzanna was tonight. Once she and Austen left the hotel, he'd be out of her life for good.

Suzanna, relieved of her afternoon duties, slipped into the room where Austen was seated at a table signing books. He was surrounded by smiling women of all ages, with a line extending halfway across the room. *If he doesn't hurry up, he'll be late for the predinner cocktail hour.* Suzanna spotted Amy and motioned for her.

"I know we're running late," Amy said when she reached Suzanna. "I've been trying to move the ladies along, but they keep stalling."

Suzanna, a mischievous glint in her eye, took a notebook from her bag and wrote, "I'm not wearing any panties - S." She folded the paper and handed it to

Amy. "Give this to him and no one else."

Amy grinned and did as she asked.

Suzanna stifled her laugh as Austen's face turned red, and he refolded the paper. He glanced over the crowd until he saw her. The unspoken *I'll get you for this* was clear in his eyes.

Suzanna blew him a kiss and scurried out the door.

In the hotel room she shared with Amy, Suzanna took a quick shower, reapplied her makeup, and curled her hair. She slipped on the little black dress she'd worn on the ship. Recalling what she and Austen had done the last time she'd had it on made her knees weak. She dabbed on Austen's favorite perfume, when a knock sounded at the door.

Suzanna opened it to see Austen, wearing tan slacks with a light-blue shirt and navy sport coat, looking as handsome as he'd done on the cruise. She smiled. "This is a little déjà vu." She cocked her head. "But you've forgotten the pizza?"

"It's in my room." He stepped through the door and closed it behind him. He backed Suzanna against the wall.

"Austen, what are you doing?"

"You make me crazy in that dress. Do you remember what happened last time you had it on?" He lifted her dress, revealing the black thong she wore. "I thought you said you weren't wearing panties."

She batted his hand away. "Stop that. You'll wrinkle my dress."

"Oh, no, darlin', you don't tease me like that and get away with it. I had to hide my hard-on under that table."

Suzanna laughed, unable to hold back her mirth.

"The expression on your face was priceless."

He gave her a slow grin. "Let's see if I can change your amusement to cries of pleasure." He cupped her chin in his palm and brought his mouth down on hers.

Suzanna's body was reacting to his demanding kisses when the door opened, and Amy came in.

"Whoops, sorry."

Suzanna broke their kiss and, tugging down her dress, stepped from Austen's embrace. "It's okay. We were just leaving."

"Sure, you were," Amy replied with a grin. "You two look fabulous. I'm supposed to meet Mark in the lobby, so I need to hurry."

Suzanna glanced at the digital clock. "You've got twenty minutes. We'll see you downstairs."

"Do you really have a pizza in your room?" Suzanna asked as they stepped into the elevator.

"Yes. My plan was to bribe you with food, then have my way with you."

"We don't have time for you to seduce me, nor are you going to mess up my hair, but I didn't have lunch, and I'm starving. I really don't want to drink on an empty stomach, so let's stop long enough to eat a couple of slices."

"I already beat you to it. It smelled so good, I couldn't resist." He opened the door to his suite, and Suzanna stepped in.

The pizza box lay on the table near the window. Suzanna took a piece and groaned in delight as she bit into the hot cheese and spicy pepperoni.

"You keep making noises like that, and I won't care about your hair or dress."

"Sorry, but this is so good. We were crazy busy all

day. The schedule was thrown off early, which screwed everything up. Did you work on your speech for tonight?"

Austen frowned. "I suppose it's as good as it's going to get. I did have an interesting conversation with JJ and Melinda." He filled her in on what they'd told him.

"Wow. If that's all true, there's more than just us looking for Haley."

Austen narrowed his eyes. "And I want to be the one who finds her first."

"We'd better go," Suzanna said. "I hope I can enjoy myself, wondering if Haley is lurking in the shadows."

They made their way to the lobby, where the cocktail party was in full swing. "The more they drink, the better my speech will sound," Austen said.

"Speaking of," Suzanna said, "I'd love a glass of wine."

"Come with me to the bar. I don't want to leave you here alone."

Suzanna took in the happy smiling people around them, and fear of the unknown crept up her spine. Was there someone in this room who wanted to cause her harm? She took Austen's arm. "Don't worry. I'm not leaving your side."

Chapter Thirty-One

The lobby of the Huntington, one of the high-end hotels on the island, was covered with mosaic tiles of aqua, turquoise, and white. Crystal magnolia-shaped lights hung beneath a sky-blue ceiling, and potted palms were placed among the seating areas.

Austen handed Suzanna her glass of red wine and frowned. "I suppose we should mingle."

Suzanna grinned. "Don't overflow with excitement."

"The idea of being among all these people makes me nervous."

"Austen, no one is going to hurt me with everyone looking on."

"But we don't know what Haley is wearing. She could sneak up behind you, and we won't realize it's her."

"How about if we stay on the perimeter?"

Austen nodded.

"There's Amy and Mark." Suzanna pointed. "They can help us keep an eye out."

Amy and Mark joined them. "Everyone looks fabulous," Amy said. "I love dressing up."

"Me too," Suzanna replied. "Austen is concerned Haley is lurking in the shadows."

Amy's eyes grew large. "Do you honestly think so?"

Austen shrugged. "I might be paranoid over nothing, but it's better to be alert than let our guard down."

"I agree," Mark added.

"They're going into dinner," Suzanna said. "Let's find our table."

They made their way along the deep-blue carpeted hallway to the ballroom. Flickering light from hurricane lamps reflected off sparkling wine glasses sitting on white cloth-draped tables. Bamboo fans stirred the air, and French doors led out onto the stone patio.

"Here we are," Suzanna said, spotting their place cards.

"Who else is sitting with us?" Mark asked.

Suzanna glanced at the other names. "My goodness, it's JJ and Melinda and two people I don't recognize."

At that moment, an older woman with short salt-and-pepper hair, wearing a colorful flower-print dress, stopped at their table. "Hello. I'm Ann, and I'm with the *Hilton Head News*."

"Welcome, I'm Suzanna." She proceeded to introduce the others. "Are you here covering the conference?"

"That's right." She turned her attention toward Austen. "I'd love an interview, and I promise no questions about your trouble with H&H."

Austen nodded. "I appreciate that. I'm not leaving the island for a while, so we can set up a time."

"Perfect," Ann replied, reaching in her handbag. "Here's my card. Call me when you're free."

JJ and Melinda, along with their last table companion, joined them. She turned out to be an attractive African American woman named Eve, a bookstore owner from Savannah.

"Don't we all look festive," Amy said after they all introduced themselves.

"I love an excuse to dress up," Eve said.

"Melinda, I meant to tell you on the cruise how pretty your pearl choker is," Suzanna said.

Melinda smiled, and JJ took her hand. "Thank you. It was a gift. I hardly ever take it off."

"I'm looking forward to hearing you speak," Eve said to Austen.

Austen gave her a polite smile. "I have to admit, public speaking isn't my favorite thing."

"Then why did you agree to be the keynote speaker?" Ann asked.

"The Mystery Writers were nice enough to invite me, so I'm here. Besides, selling books is all about marketing yourself."

Ann nodded. Her attention turned to Suzanna. "Are you also an author?"

"No. Amy and I own Beachside Books here on the island."

"Nice store. I've been there." Ann cocked her head. "I know this is prying, but are you and Austen an item?"

Austen didn't miss a beat. "That's right."

The curiosity on Ann's face was clear to see. "Perhaps I should interview you both."

Suzanna sipped her wine. *The publicity would be great for the store. But I wonder if information about Haley is her real goal?* Suzanna smiled. "We'd love to, thanks."

Their conversation was interrupted by the arrival of

their salads. They ate in silence, until Ann nonchalantly said, "A friend of mine claims she saw Haley Henderson at the airport. Is she also scheduled to speak?"

Everyone except Eve froze as if in a tableau. Amy was the first to find her voice. "No. Haley isn't supposed to be here at all."

Eve frowned. "It's odd that you say that. A couple of years ago, Haley did a book signing at our store, and I became well acquainted with her. I could have sworn a woman resembling Haley stood next to me this morning at the drugstore trying on dark-framed sunglasses. I didn't speak to her because I wasn't sure it was actually her."

"What was she wearing?" Austen asked.

"That's where it really becomes odd. Her hair was dark and pulled back in a bun. She had on a severe dark suit and a high-necked white blouse."

"Not exactly Haley's style," Melinda stated.

"But a perfect disguise," JJ added.

Ann's attention flickered from one person to the other. "Okay, people. There's not a chance in hell I'm going to sit here and not ask what's going on."

They were temporarily saved from answering by the arrival of the main course. Although, seeing the determined set to Ann's jaw, Suzanna didn't think this reprieve would last long, and she was right. As soon as the waiter left, Ann continued. "I said I wouldn't ask Austen questions in regard to H&H, and I won't. I have to admit I did research on the publisher when the—" She hesitated. "—trouble broke. There are rumors Haley and Brad's marriage has been rocky for years. There's also talk the publisher is in financial difficulties. And a friend of mine at the *Times* texted me to say Brad Henderson left New York in a hurry. So, this leads me to ask, why does Haley need a disguise, and why, after Eve's revelations, do all of you look as if a parade of dancing elephants just passed by?"

Suzanna surreptitiously glanced at Austen, who had developed a keen interest in his water glass. Seeming to come to a decision, Austen cleared his throat.

"None of what I'm about to tell you is a secret, just a sequence of events that led up to someone pushing Suzanna off the sunset cruise boat last night. We suspect it was Haley." He sipped his wine and explained in more detail.

Ann's attention hung on every word. When he'd finished, her expression reminded Suzanna of someone who'd been handed an unexpected prize. Her reporter's radar was on full alert.

"Austen, you're telling me you believe Haley Henderson, the mystery diva, is out to harm Suzanna because you refused to have an affair with her?"

"I said we suspect Haley. I don't have any proof."

"Haley is a cruel, vindictive woman," Melinda said. "Those who know her well wouldn't be surprised at anything she does."

"I question her mental stability," JJ added.

Ann's brows rose. "These are some serious accusations."

"We're telling you this in confidence," Austen said.

Ann nodded. "I'll agree to stay quiet as long as I'm the first to hear how this all ends."

"I hope it ends with Haley being confronted and

made to answer for her actions," Austen replied.

Suzanna, temporarily forgetting about their other table companion, turned to where a wide-eyed Eve sat.

"I won't say anything either," she said in a quiet voice.

Austen smiled. "I really appreciate that."

At that moment, the head of the Southeast Association of Mystery Writers took the stage. "May I have everyone's attention. I hope you've all enjoyed the wonderful food and are ready to hear our keynote speaker, Austen Kincaid. We're going to take a short ten-minute break before we hear from Austen."

"Here we go," Austen murmured so only Suzanna heard. "I need to see a man. I'll be right back." He stood and headed for the entrance.

"I believe I'll visit the ladies'," Ann said.

"I'll join you." Eve also rose.

Without a word, Mark smiled and left his seat, followed by JJ and Melinda. Amy slid into Austen's vacated seat. "I might have seen Haley in her disguise."

Suzanna leaned close. "When, where?"

"This afternoon when I changed places with you on the mezzanine. I swear Haley was seated at the table outside the business center."

"Oh, my God." Suzanna gasped. "You're right. I saw her too. I thought she might be an agent, and I started to ask her if she needed help, but she hurried away before I had a chance."

"What was she doing there?"

Suzanna pictured the flight of marble stairs, and her blood ran cold. "Christ, Amy, there were times when the hallway was empty, and I was alone. Haley may have been sitting there for a while, and I didn't notice her. My attention was either on directing authors or watching people in the lobby below."

Amy's voice quivered when she replied, "She pushed you off a boat. What if she planned to push you down the stairs?"

Suzanna's stomach turned. She swallowed back the bile rising in her throat. *I will not throw up. I will not throw up,* she repeated to herself.

"Are you all right?" Amy asked. "Your face is the color of chalk."

Suzanna took a deep breath and sipped her water. As her nausea eased, her fear changed to anger. "I'm sick and tired of Haley and her crazy behavior. From now on, I'll be alert to everyone around me. If I spot anyone I believe is Haley, I'm going to get in her face and put an end to this for good. Amy, we can't tell Austen any of this until later. It's going to upset him, and he's already wound up about his talk."

"Sure. Here they all come."

The rest took their seats, while Austen stood next to Suzanna. "Wish me luck," he whispered.

Suzanna smiled. "Just be your charming self, and you'll do fine."

Chapter Thirty-Two

Austen's talk ended with loud applause. He stepped off the stage and stopped to chat with people as he made his way back to their table.

"You were great," Amy said when he'd taken his seat.

"Yes," the others agreed.

Suzanna squeezed his hand. "What did I tell you? You knocked their socks off."

Austen rolled his eyes. "I'm glad it's over. And now hand me the wine."

"They'll be starting the dancing soon," Amy said.

"That's my cue to say good night," Ann said. "Loud music gives me an awful headache." She shook her head. "I can hear my mother telling the teenage me to turn that screaming noise down. Now I sound like her."

Melinda laughed. "Isn't that the truth."

"There are some ladies from Savannah motioning for me to join them," Eve said. "It was so nice meeting all of you."

"We're going to call it a night as well," JJ said. "A quiet nightcap on our balcony is more our speed."

Ann stood. "Don't forget about our interview."

"I'll be in touch," Austen replied.

"I'm ready to dance," Amy said.

"Me too," Suzanna added.

Austen pushed the bottle of wine toward Mark. "I guess that means we have to stay."

"Oh, stop it," Suzanna said. "You enjoy dancing as much as I do."

Austen grinned. "Especially if you dirty-dance with me like you did on the ship."

"Suzanna, dirty-dancing?" Amy asked with disbelief.

Suzanna flapped her hands. "Yes, well, there was drinking involved."

"Here's the band," Mark said. "I believe they're the same guys who play at the tiki hut."

Amy smiled in delight. "They're great."

"We're going to need more wine," Austen said. "I'll be right back."

"Amy, let's go to the ladies' before the music begins," Suzanna said.

Austen, standing in line at the bar, studied those around him. Was Haley hiding in plain sight? If Eve was right and Haley was wearing a disguise, how unhinged had she become? *If I do see Brad, I'll tell him to find his crazy wife and take her back to New York.* Scenes from a stalker movie he'd seen years ago flashed in his mind, and dread crept over him. Haley couldn't be that insane, could she? *Damn it to hell, if I'd shown more self-control with Haley, we wouldn't be in this mess. If she hurts Suzanna, there isn't anyone to blame but myself. The conference is over tomorrow. After that, it will be much harder for Haley to get near Suzanna.* He just had to keep her safe for one more night.

Austen returned with the wine, as the band took the stage.

"Our first song will get everyone moving," the guitar player said. "So come on up and two-step."

"Don't look at me," Austen said. "I can't do that."

"Neither can I," Mark added.

Suzanna stood. "Come on, Amy, let's show them how this is done." They linked arms and joined the dance. Austen's concern for her safety turned to desire as her little black dress swayed, showing off her sexy long legs.

"They're the prettiest ones up there," Mark said, interrupting Austen's lustful thoughts.

"That they are."

Mark cleared his throat. "The babysitter is going to stay all night with Violet, so Amy doesn't have to worry about driving home. I'm hoping to persuade her not to use the room she and Suzanna have here, and instead stay with me."

Austen grinned. "Good luck, buddy."

"I'm thinking a few slow dances and a moonlit walk on the beach might send her thoughts in the right direction."

"Sounds like a plan. Suzanna and I may do the same, but we'll stay out of your space."

The band switched to a slow song, and Austen and Mark both rose. "Good luck," Austen said as Mark headed toward Amy.

Suzanna wrapped her arms around Austen's neck. "I hoped you'd join me. This is one of my favorite songs."

Austen held her close, softly singing the words, as they glided across the dance floor.

Suzanna laid her head on his shoulder. "I love when you sing to me."

Austen changed the words and sang about what he'd like to do to her.

Suzanna lifted her head, her cheeks pink. "Stop that."

"I thought you liked it when I did those things to you."

The band switched to a fast song, and Suzanna stepped from his embrace. "You can do all those things to me later, but now…" She moved with the beat. "Dance with me."

For every step Suzanna took, Austen kept right with her. They were so in tune with one another, people backed away, giving them the floor. When the song ended, Austen lifted Suzanna off her feet and twirled her around to loud applause.

Both laughing, hand in hand, they left the floor. "I'm dying of thirst," Suzanna said when they arrived at their table. She lifted her wineglass and emptied it. "That's better."

"It's stifling in here," Austen said. "Let's get some fresh air."

"Sure. Grab the wine, and I'll tell Amy we're going outside." Suzanna scanned the room. "Austen, I don't see her anywhere."

"Um. She's probably with Mark."

"Well, yes, but where are they? It's not like her not to tell me she's leaving." Suzanna cocked her head. "Okay, what's up? You have that *I got caught with my hand in the cookie jar* expression."

Austen sighed and explained Mark's plan. "I'd say, so far it's working."

Suzanna snorted. "Are you serious? Let me enlighten you. It will most likely be Amy who seduces him, not the other way around."

Austen shrugged. "Good for them. Now let's go."

Chapter Thirty-Three

Doors from the banquet room opened onto the patio next to the pool. Tiny lights strung in the trees lit the night with a soft glow, and a sultry breeze surrounded them.

"This is certainly a popular place," Austen said as they maneuvered around groups of people standing near the outdoor bar.

Suzanna scanned their surroundings. "We might not find an empty table."

They were passing the pool, searching for a place to sit, when Suzanna's attention was caught by women singing, "Bunco, Bunco, Bunco."

Suzanna, laughing, spotted the group of women. "Austen, come with me. I'd like you to meet my friends. We play Bunco together."

Austen's brows rose. "You play what?"

"It's a dice game. Come on."

"Hello, ladies," Suzanna said when they reached their table. "What are y'all doing here?"

"Girls' night out," Ellis replied. "Don't you remember?"

Sara smiled. "Now we know why you couldn't join us. Who's this handsome guy?"

"This is Austen Kincaid. He's part of the conference."

"I think he's more than part of the conference,"

Linda said.

Austen grinned. "I'm trying my best."

"Oh, I don't think you're going to have to try too hard." Val chuckled.

Suzanna rolled her eyes. "Okay, enough."

"So, did you two just meet?" Catherine asked.

Austen gave Suzanna a quizzical look before saying, "No, on a mystery cruise."

"Suzanna, you went on that months ago, and you didn't tell us about Austen?" Dee said reproachfully.

Uncomfortable with the direction the conversation was going, Suzanna smiled and tried to change the subject. "Are you girls having fun?"

"When there's food and alcohol involved, we always have a good time," Lynne said.

"I haven't seen your car at the condo. Have you been staying here?" Monica asked.

"Amy and I decided to get a room, so we wouldn't be driving back and forth."

All eyes turned to Austen. "That's convenient," Jane said.

"Austen, will you be on the island long?" Barbara asked.

"As long as Suzanna will put up with me."

"In that case," Debbie said, "I'm sure you'll have a nice long stay."

Suzanna took Austen's arm. Her friends were enjoying her discomfort, and before things became much worse, she needed to escape. No doubt her email would be full tomorrow with a flood of questions. "Okay, well, I'll see all of you next month at Bunco. Stay out of trouble."

"I think you're going to get into more trouble than

we are," Genie called.

Their laughter followed them as Suzanna hurried away. "They seem fun," Austen said.

"They are."

"You didn't tell them about us."

Suzanna hung her purse on the back of a chair and set her wine on the empty table. "When I moved here, there wasn't an 'us'."

Austen, quiet for a moment, reached out and took her into his arms. "There is an 'us' now."

"Yes, there is."

From somewhere close by came the sound of a slow blues number. "Now, this is more like it." They swayed to the music, and Austen nibbled on her earlobe.

Suzanna giggled. "Stop that. It tickles."

"How about if I work my way down?"

"Austen."

Haley stood in a shadowed corner of the patio, concealed from the others by thick foliage, her fists clenched. Glaring through the clear lenses of her dark-framed glasses, she seethed with anger and self-pity. In front of her, Austen held Suzanna, rubbing his hand seductively along her back. Bitter hatred roiled in Haley's stomach at the realization Austen would never be hers. *He won't leave that little nobody for me.*

Haley's mouth formed a thin line. *Talk about a nobody. Austen Kincaid wouldn't be here today if it weren't for me. I was the one who made sure H&H's marketing department went all out publicizing his books.* She narrowed her eyes. It should have been her as the keynote speaker at this so-called conference, not Austen. *I'm the famous author who has books in five different languages. Well, if I can't have Austen, I'll make sure he can't have his little country frump.*

A sudden gust of wind tugged at her dark wig, and she reached up to secure it. Out of the darkness behind her, someone spoke, and Haley jumped.

"Dressing like a proper lady won't disguise the whore inside."

Haley stiffened. It was a voice she knew all too well. She slowly turned. The malevolent smile on her visitor's face sent both a shiver of unease and a wave of anger through her.

"Hello, Haley, surprised to see me?"

"How did you find me?"

"You aren't as clever as you think. I expected you to show up tonight. I kept an eye out for someone skulking in the bushes, and here you are."

"What do you want?"

"I decided it was time for you to stop destroying other people's lives. You're an evil, vindictive bitch who needs to leave this world."

"And you're going to stop me?" Haley snorted. "Well, I'm not going anywhere, so you can just go to hell."

The steel blade of the knife gleamed in the moonlight. "Oh, but you're wrong. It's not me who's going to hell."

Haley held out her arms and opened her mouth to scream.

"Don't bother," her visitor said. "Between the music and the crowd around the bar and pool, no one will hear you."

Run, Haley's mind shouted.

****

Suzanna sighed in pure contentment. *I'm happier right now than I've ever been,* she thought as Austen twirled them to the music. When her stiletto heels sank into the sand, she gasped in surprise. "Austen, my shoes. What are you doing?"

"Kick them off. This is more romantic."

Laughing in delight, Suzanna did as he asked. He twirled her around and around until water lapped at their feet.

"Let's go skinny-dipping," he said, nuzzling her neck.

"No, are you crazy? There are people everywhere."

"They're not paying attention to us," he persisted.

"Austen, we are not taking our clothes off here on the beach."

"Does that mean making love in the dunes is out as well?"

"Yes."

"Then I suggest we go to our room before I pick you up and carry you into the water. Once you're wet, you'll have to take your dress off."

"You wouldn't dare."

He gave her a mischievous smile, and Suzanna broke away. She grabbed her shoes and ran toward the hotel with Austen right behind.

Tipsy enough not to care, Suzanna entered the lobby and sped across the floor heading for the elevator. When the doors slid shut, she and Austen bent over laughing.

"I can't imagine how many people had their phones out, and that's now been recorded," Suzanna said.

Austen snorted. "Who knows; it might increase my

sales." He unlocked his hotel room door, took Suzanna's hand, and pulled her inside. He closed and locked the door, tossed his jacket on a chair, then grinned. Now I'm going to do something I've wanted to do all night." He backed her against the wall.

Suzanna licked her lips. Austen's expression reminded her of an animal who's just cornered his prey. "Austen, I'm not sure about this."

"Trust me, darlin'." He slid his hand under her dress and slid her lace thong down her legs. "Put your stilettos back on, then spread your legs."

Her breath coming in shallow gasps, Suzanna did as he asked. "Oh, sweet heaven," she cried as he fell to his knees, lifted her dress, and put his mouth on her. Suzanna placed her palms against the wall to help keep her upright as Austen's tongue brought an orgasm slamming through her.

"You have the sweetest tasting little…"

"Austen," Suzanna cried as her body reacted to her second explosion.

Austen rose and, in one swift move, thrust his hard shaft in deep.

"Wrap your legs around me," he demanded.

Suzanna held his shoulders tight, as his rhythm increased.

"It's my turn." His voice was a low growl with his own release. "That's it, darlin', give me one more."

"Austen," Suzanna screamed as she came for the third time.

"I'm not sure I'm capable of walking," Suzanna said when her feet touched the floor.

"You and me both, darlin'," Austen replied on a ragged breath. He grinned. "I hope there wasn't anyone on the other side of that wall."

Pink stained Suzanna's cheeks. Chuckling, he led her to the bed. "I think it's your turn to be on top."

Chapter Thirty-Four

A couple of hours later, Suzanna awoke with a pounding headache and her mouth as dry as cotton. *Oh,* she silently groaned. *How much wine did we drink?* She squinted at the clock which read two-fifteen. *I need about a dozen aspirin.* She eased out of bed, hoping not to wake Austen, and stumbled to the bathroom. When her reflection in the mirror came into focus, Suzanna gasped. Her once meticulously styled hair resembled a fright wig. Her smudged mascara made her look like a racoon, and her lips were swollen from Austen's kisses. Good grief. Talk about the morning after.

She glanced over the sink, looking for her brush and makeup remover. Then her alcohol-saturated brain remembered this was Austen's room, not hers. Where was her purse? She searched the rest of the suite, but it wasn't there. Both her room key and cell were in it. *Come on, Suzanna, think. You had it when you left the dinner banquet. You stopped to talk to the girls, then.* "Damn it to hell," she swore. *I hung it on the back of a chair by the pool bar. Maybe someone found it and turned it in at the front desk.* She headed for the door, then realized she had on nothing but Austen's shirt. *I could go to my room and wake up Amy, but what if she and Mark are there and not in his room?*

She had no choice but to put her wrinkled dress back on. She retraced her steps to the bathroom, laying the shirt across the end of the bed. She washed her face, rinsed out her mouth with toothpaste. Finding Austen's brush, she tried to untangle her hair. After slipping her dress on, she picked up Austen's room key from the dresser, then let herself out.

In the lobby, she stopped at the front desk, thankful there weren't many people around. "Hi," she said to the older man working the night shift. "Do you know if anyone has turned in a black beaded evening bag?"

His polite smile gave no indication her disheveled appearance was anything unusual. "No, miss, but I'll check." He returned minutes later. "I'm sorry, we don't have anything matching that description."

Suzanna thanked him and headed for the doors leading to the pool bar. Once outside, the night was eerily quiet. No distant voices or music playing. Just the ebb and flow of the waves on the beach. A sense of unease came over her. Should she go back and awaken Austen? *Suzanna, get a grip. The patio isn't far.* She quickened her steps. The tapping of her heels echoed as she took the path that wound around flowering shrubs toward the dimly lit pool. She paused, scanning the tables, hoping to spot her bag. She sighed in relief when she noticed the gold chain sparkling in the moonlight. As she headed in that direction, a movement to her left caught her attention.

****

Austen rolled over in bed and put his arm out for Suzanna. There was nothing but smooth sheets. He opened his eyes and rose up on one elbow.

"Suzanna?" he called. When she didn't answer, he got up and went to the bathroom. Finding it empty, he headed for the sitting area, but still no Suzanna. He peeked out onto the balcony. Nothing. Then he noticed his shirt on the bed and that her dress was gone. What the hell? Why would she leave? Disquiet niggled at the edges of his mind.

His cell lay on the desk, and he picked it up. When her phone rang and rang, eventually going to voice mail, his concern grew. *All right, don't panic. Think clearly.* He went into the bathroom and splashed water on his face. He dressed in jeans and a T-shirt and slipped on running shoes. He grabbed a bottle of water from the mini fridge and chugged it. He'd start with her room, but what if that's where Mark and Amy ended up? *I'll check out the lobby first.* He searched for his room key, but it was gone. Okay, Suzanna must have it, meaning she intended to come back. He headed out the door.

Once in the almost deserted lobby, Austen paused. The bars and restaurants were all closed. In a far corner, a few people were seated in a grouping of sofas and chairs. He started their way to ask if they'd seen Suzanna, when someone called his name.

Austen paused to see one of the other authors he'd been on a panel with. "Hey, so I'm not the only one still up. I meant to tell you your talk earlier was great."

"Thanks. You haven't by chance seen a redhead in a black dress, have you?"

He laughed. "Christ, don't tell me you lost her."

Austen smiled. "I hope not."

"Wait a minute. I believe I did see her going out to the pool." He chuckled. "Perhaps she decided to take a midnight swim."

Austen thanked him and hurried as fast as he could without drawing attention to himself. Once outside, he ran. As he approached the tables and chairs, he slowed. The shape lying on the ground made his blood run cold. *No, please, no.* His legs heavy as lead, he eased closer to where Suzanna lay in a crumpled heap.

He knelt next to her and touched her cheek. "Suzanna, can you hear me?" An ambulance. He needed to call for help. He patted his pockets. "Fuck." He'd left his phone in the room.

With trembling fingers, he placed them on Suzanna's neck. Tears of relief pricked his eyes. There was a pulse. "Suzanna, can you hear me?"

He should go for help, but he didn't want to leave her. "Suzanna," he said louder.

Her eyes fluttered open. "Austen." Her voice was barely above a whisper.

"Yes, darlin', it's me. Where are you hurt?"

She attempted to sit up and winced. "What happened? Where am I?"

"You're outdoors near the hotel pool."

"What? Why?" She tenderly touched the side of her head above her ear and cried out. "Oh."

Austen leaned closer and gently ran his fingers where she indicated. "There's a good-sized lump." He silently cursed when his fingers showed red from her blood. "Suzanna, I need to call 911, but I don't have my phone."

"Austen, please don't leave me."

"Suzanna, you need a medic."

"I feel scraped and bruised, but I don't think anything is broken."

"Move your arms and legs slowly to make sure."

Suzanna did as he asked. "Other than my head hurting, I'm fine. Help me sit up. My bag is hanging on a chair. My cell is inside."

"Damn it, Suzanna, is that why you came out here alone?" Fear for her life caused his words to sound sharper than he intended.

Tears streamed down her cheeks. "Austen, I'm sorry. I realized my bag was missing and came to find it."

"It's all right. Don't cry. Will you be okay while I get your bag?"

She nodded, then winced. "Hurry."

Austen rose and scanned the empty chairs. He wasn't sure if he was more relieved she was alive or pissed to the point he'd like to shake her until her teeth rattled. He spotted her bag and had almost reached the chair when something in the dim light caught his eye. He froze as ice ran down his spine. He cautiously took in their surroundings. Across the top of the tables, he could make out the bar, where someone sat, hunched over.

"Austen, did you find it?" Suzanna called.

He didn't want to scare Suzanna any more than she already was, but every nerve in his body told him something definitely was wrong. "Don't move."

"Why? What's going on?"

"Suzanna, stay where you are. There's someone else here."

"What? Who? Austen, I'm frightened."

"Just stay put." Austen carefully approached the figure. As he got closer, he made out the form of a woman. He swallowed hard. Her arms lay folded on the bar, and the dark wig she wore was askew, revealing short hair beneath. The lifeless eyes staring at him through dark-rimmed glasses were ones he knew well.

He bent closer, and the knife protruding from her chest was clear to see.

"Austen, where are you?"

"I'm right here." He grabbed Suzanna's purse and hurried to her.

"What do you mean someone's here?"

Austen ran his hand over his face and told her what he'd found.

"No, Austen. Not Haley."

"There's no doubt. She's wearing the dark suit and glasses she was spotted in."

"Do you think she was the one who hit me?"

"No."

"Then who?" Realization dawned, and the color drained from her face. "It was the murderer, wasn't it?"

Austen's voice shook. "Christ almighty, Suzanna, you could have also been killed."

Suzanna held her stomach and bent over. "I'm going to be sick."

"It's okay. Calm down and take deep breaths."

"Austen, what does this remind you of?" By the light from a nearby post, Suzanna's eyes appeared huge in her pale face.

"Son of a bitch," Austen swore. "The cruise."

Suzanna nodded. "And all the participants in the skit are here."

Austen let out a long breath. "Right." He held out her purse. "Give me your phone. It's time to call the police."

Chapter Thirty-Five

Austen disconnected the call. "The police and paramedics are on their way. After they deal with Haley, they can check you over."

Suzanna, now seated in a chair, gingerly touched the side of her head. "I don't think that's necessary."

"You could have a concussion. You were unconscious. Better have it looked at." Austen paced back and forth. "Do you realize how lucky you were? Whoever killed Haley must have hit you, then ran off. Why in the hell didn't you wake me up to come with you?"

Suzanna sighed. "You're right. It was a stupid thing to do. I woke up with the headache from hell and wanted aspirin. That's when I realized my purse was missing. Austen, my phone and room key were in that bag. I wasn't thinking about the danger, only retrieving my bag and having to go out looking like the walk of shame."

"What?"

"Nothing. You wouldn't understand." She rubbed her temples. If only the drum solo in her head would stop. "How are we going to explain all of this to the police? I mean once we tell them about the skit, we'll implicate Melinda and JJ."

"Don't forget Brad."

"But I like Melinda and JJ."

"Yes, well, they both had motives."

"I would imagine out of all of them, Brad's motive is the strongest."

Austen shrugged. "Who knows what would drive someone to commit murder."

"Perhaps there's someone else here who hated her that we're not aware of."

"Possibly, but I doubt it. This is so Haley. She can't even die without drama. Now, she's dragged us into this."

"Actually, I dragged us into this by being in the wrong place at the wrong time. If I'd stayed upstairs, someone else would have discovered her."

Austen glanced at Haley's body. "I suppose for Haley's sake, it's better we found her instead of a stranger."

The hotel doors opened, and two men came toward them.

"Are you Mr. Kincaid?" the taller of the two asked.

Austen nodded. "And this is my friend, Suzanna Shay."

"I'm Detective Michael Kline, and this is my partner, Sergeant Scott."

"You should know someone struck Suzanna on the side of the head, and I found her lying here just before discovering Haley."

Kline's gaze took in Suzanna. "Miss, do you need medical attention?"

"I don't think so," Suzanna replied. "I just have a bump on my head."

"It's a good-sized lump, and there was blood," Austen added.

"If you change your mind, I'll have a paramedic

take a look. Now, Mr. Kincaid, tell me what led up to you discovering the body."

Austen explained waking up and Suzanna being gone. And how searching for her led him to the pool area.

"And you, Miss Shay?" Kline asked.

"I came looking for my purse, which I left out here last night. The last thing I remember is seeing someone out of the corner of my eye before I was struck."

Scott, who had been examining Haley, said, "Definitely homicide. There's a knife sticking out of her chest."

"Call it in," Kline said. "And inform the hotel manager we'll be sealing off this entire area."

"They're going to love that," Scott said as he headed back inside the hotel.

Kline turned back to Austen and Suzanna. "I need statements from you both. Along with any information you can give me about the victim." His gaze landed on Austen. "You referred to her as Haley. I assume this means you knew her?"

Here we go, Austen thought. "Yes. Her name is Haley Henderson."

"I noticed the poster in the lobby indicating there's some type of writers' conference going on. Was Miss Henderson part of that?"

Austen shook his head and sighed. "She's here because of me."

The detective's brows rose. "Let's sit." He indicated a nearby table. "And you can tell me about it. Beginning with where you're from and why you're here."

"I live in New York City, and Suzanna lives here

on the island," Austen said.

Kline paused from taking notes. "Austen Kincaid. The one who writes thriller novels?"

"That's right," Austen replied.

"I like your books. Please continue."

"Thanks." Austen took a deep breath. "I'm here because I was asked to be the keynote speaker at the conference." He paused. "There was a recent situation involving Haley and myself." He related the incident in Brad's office, reiterating that the entire thing was blown out of proportion by the media. He decided to leave out Haley's attempt to blackmail him for sex. "H&H let me go," he continued, "and I hadn't seen Haley until she followed me here to Hilton Head. When she confronted me at the airport, I told her over and over again to leave, but she wouldn't listen. I honestly wasn't sure if she was still here, until a fellow conference participant saw her in her disguise."

"She's wearing a disguise?"

Again, Austen nodded. "Supposedly she had more than one."

"How do you know this?"

Beneath the table, Suzanna squeezed Austen's hand. He gave her a reassuring squeeze in return. He had no choice but to tell Kline about JJ's encounter with Haley on the sunset cruise boat.

"Is Mr. Jackson staying here at the Huntington?" Kline asked after Austen finished.

"Yes, both he and Melinda Pearce are here."

"Along with Haley's husband Brad and Clarice Abbot," Suzanna said. "But we don't know where they're staying."

Kline cocked his head. "I have a feeling there's

more to this story than you're telling me. Let's begin again. Who are all these people, and how were they involved with Miss Henderson?"

Austen gave Suzanna an *it's all yours* look, and she cleared her throat. "You see we were all on a Who Done It cruise almost a year ago." She described the murder skit but hesitated before going into detail on each person's animosity toward Haley.

"Are you saying you believe this skit was once again played out, ending with Miss Henderson's death?" Kline asked with incredulity.

"Yes," Austen replied.

"What proof do you have?"

Austen shrugged. "None. Just knowledge of Haley and how she's left hurt and destruction in her wake."

Before Kline could continue, Scott arrived with paramedics and crime scene techs.

"The medical examiner should be here shortly," Scott said, coming up to their table. "The night clerk contacted the hotel manager. She's on her way and isn't happy a dead body was found on her property."

Kline scowled. "I would imagine Miss Henderson wishes she wasn't here either."

"There's the ME," Scott said as a balding fiftysomething man wearing jeans and a Georgia Bull Dogs T-shirt headed their way. He pulled on white coveralls and blue booties before approaching the body.

A sour-faced woman rounded the bend in the path and hurried in their direction.

Scott sighed. "I suppose that's Deirdre Cloud, the hotel manager. Lucky me," he murmured as he went to greet her.

"When do you think we can leave?" Suzanna asked

Austen. "It must be close to four in the morning. I'm exhausted, and I ache all over."

"Soon, I hope. Kline is going to want our contact information first."

"Besides, I want to go somewhere we can talk in private."

Austen nodded. "I know. I have a thousand questions swirling around in my head."

"Unless there's someone here we don't know about, the list of suspects is pretty short."

"Yes, but which one of them and how?"

"The how is obvious. There's a knife in her chest."

Austen frowned. "But how did she end up at the pool bar?"

Suzanna opened her mouth to reply when Austen, spotting Kline coming their way, motioned her to stop.

Kline resumed his seat. "The ME is going to be taking the body away. I need to notify her next of kin. You have no idea where her husband is staying?"

Both Austen and Suzanna shook their heads.

Letting out a long sigh, Kline rose. "Give your cell numbers to Scott, and don't leave the island without notifying my office." He glowered at Austen. "Just because you're a good thriller writer, don't get any ideas about interfering in this case. If you discover any helpful information, notify me or Scott. Am I clear?"

"Sure, no problem," Austen replied.

Chapter Thirty-Six

"I have to get this dress off and take a shower to wash the blood out of my hair," Suzanna said as she and Austen stepped into the elevator. "I wish I knew if Amy and Mark are in our room or his."

"You can take a shower in my room and put on one of my shirts for the time being. By then the kitchen will be open so we can order a pot of coffee and breakfast."

Suzanna yawned. "Okay. Even though I'm exhausted, I'm too wound up to sleep."

"Tell me about it." He gave Suzanna a mischievous grin. "Speaking of the shower, I could use one myself."

Suzanna narrowed her eyes. "You can't be serious thinking about sex after what we've been through."

His grin widened. "Darlin', I'm always thinking about sex."

"Well, get over it. Put your mind to better uses, like who's our murderer." She picked up his shirt, which still lay across the bed, and shut the bathroom door with a decisive click.

Austen made them each a cup of coffee from the room's small coffee maker, then opened his laptop and brought up a blank Word document titling the page, "Who killed Haley?"
Suspects:
Brad Henderson
Melinda Pearce

JJ Jackson

"What are you doing?" Suzanna asked, coming up behind him and peering over his shoulder.

"I thought it would be helpful if we wrote down who our suspects are and their motives for killing Haley."

"Don't forget to add Clarice Abbot."

Austen added Clarice's name and sighed. "I can't imagine any of these people actually shoving a knife into Haley's chest."

"If not them, who?"

"There might be an unknown person who has a motive we know nothing about."

"Then that person had to have been on the cruise. Otherwise, how would they know how the skit ended?"

Austen rubbed his forehead. "Okay, what if Haley's murder is all a weird coincidence?"

"Austen, in the skit she was killed with a knife in her heart sitting at a bar. Don't you think that's too much of a coincidence?"

"Probably. I need more coffee and food." He glanced at the clock. "It's after six. The restaurant should be open. Let's go down. Who knows, we might run into JJ and Melinda."

"Did you forget there's a Sunday brunch this morning for all the conference participants? We're supposed to meet Amy and Mark at ten o'clock."

Austen shook his head. "I'm hungry now. Let's get something light, and we can eat again later."

"Sounds good, but I need clothes."

Austen headed for the bathroom. "Call Amy and find out where they are while I take a quick shower."

Suzanna, not wanting to wake up Amy and Mark,

hesitated. While she debated what to do, her cell phone rang. When the digital display read Amy's name, Suzanna grabbed her phone. "Hey, Amy, I was just about to call you."

"Oh, good, you're up. I wanted to let you know I won't be joining you for the brunch."

"Why? Where are you?"

"I'm home with Violet."

"You're not with Mark? What happened?"

"I take it you haven't spoken to Mark."

"No. There's been a situation, but tell me what's happened first."

"Mark and I left the dance and were in his room, and things were moving along nicely when I got a call from the sitter. Violet had a fever and was crying for me. I'm sure it's her ear infection again. I'm taking her to the hospital this morning."

"What a bummer," Suzanna said. "Did Mark drive you home?"

"No, I told him to stay at the hotel, and I drove myself. So much for my romantic evening. So what situation are you talking about?"

Suzanna filled Amy in on their eventful morning. "So, here we are playing detective and writing down clues."

"How awful," Amy exclaimed. "Suzanna, it's a wonder you weren't also killed. I can't believe someone had the nerve to stab her out in the open. Are you sure you're all right?"

"I have a pretty good lump on my head, and I'm bruised, but I'll make it."

"Okay, I have to run. Violet is screaming again. Can you let Mark know I won't be there? When I left last night, I told him I wasn't sure what my morning would be like. I'll call you later."

"Let me know what the doctor says about Violet."

Suzanna disconnected and relayed what Amy had said when Austen came out of the bathroom. "It's such a shame," Suzanna continued. "Amy was so looking forward to her night alone with Mark."

Austen nodded. "I imagine Mark is disappointed as well. Are you ready?"

"I have to go to my room and change." She put her wrinkled blood-stained dress back on.

"I wonder if Kline has spoken with JJ and Melinda. And if he's located Brad," Suzanna said, as they made their way to the elevators. "If so, I'd love to know what they told him."

"If we see them, perhaps we can find out."

In her room, Suzanna changed into capri pants and a short-sleeved top. "Austen, something happened yesterday while I was helping out with the editor and agent pitches that I haven't had a chance to tell you about." She explained how she and Amy thought they might have seen Haley outside of the business center.

Austen swore colorfully. "She was probably planning on pushing you down those marble stairs."

"We're not sure it was her." Suzanna gnawed on her lower lip. "But she did resemble the woman Eve said she'd seen."

"We'll need to tell Kline."

"There's something else that's been bothering me since the cruise," Suzanna said, slipping on sandals.

"What's that?"

"If those who participated in the skit hated Haley so much, why did they agree to be a part of it?"

"I'd say for their feelings toward Brad and H&H. Besides, JJ and Melinda are the only two we know disliked Haley."

"Are you kidding? What about Brad?"

"I honestly don't know how he feels. She's been cheating on him for years, and he stays with her."

"But why? Is he that crazy in love with her, or is there a reason he doesn't divorce her?"

Back in the hall, Austen pushed the button for the elevator. "Good point." He hesitated. "Mark told me that after their affair she threatened him if he ever told anyone."

"What?" Suzanna squeaked. "Mark also had an affair with Haley?"

Austen winced. "I wasn't supposed to say anything. It was a while ago, so please don't tell Amy."

Suzanna's mouth formed a thin line. "What the hell is it about that trashy woman that men find irresistible?"

The elevator doors opened, and Austen steered Suzanna toward the restaurant. "Let's change the subject, okay?"

Suzanna glowered. "Good idea."

Chapter Thirty-Seven

They slid into a booth, and Austen glanced around. "I don't see anyone I recognize."

Suzanna pointed. "There's Mark." She waved, and he smiled and headed toward them.

"Good morning," he said. "I see you had the same idea, breakfast before brunch."

Suzanna stood and slid in next to Austen. "Have a seat."

"Thanks. I suppose you've spoken to Amy?"

Suzanna nodded. "She's taking Violet to the hospital this morning."

"I was signed up to go on the fishing trip, but I'm going to cancel. I thought I'd spend the day with Amy and Violet."

"She's supposed to call me when she gets home," Suzanna said. "Since you haven't mentioned it, I take it you haven't heard what's happened."

"No, what?"

"Haley was killed last night," Austen said.

Mark's eyes opened wide. "What? How?"

Austen explained the circumstances leading up to finding Haley. "The police want to speak to everyone who knew her."

Mark shook his head. "I'm having a tough time taking this all in. Haley made a lot of enemies, but actually kill her, who'd do that?"

"That's exactly what we're trying to figure out."

"This is all getting too weird," Mark said. "We're pretty sure Haley was the one who tried to drown Suzanna, but now she's the one who gets killed."

"And there's a good chance Suzanna encountered the killer," Austen added.

"Are you kidding me?" Mark exclaimed.

"Unfortunately, it's true," Suzanna said.

"Good God, Suzanna, it's a wonder you're not dead as well," Mark said after she'd explained.

Austen glared at Suzanna. "Tell me about it."

Suzanna rolled her eyes. "I'm fine. Can we please move on?"

"Who's your number one suspect?" Mark asked.

Suzanna's brows knitted together as she recalled the conversation she'd overheard in the elevator on the ship, along with the tableau she had witnessed at the adjoining table in the dining room. "From all I've learned about Brad and Haley's tumultuous relationship, I'd think he's definitely at the top of my list. And I wouldn't be surprised if he and Clarice aren't closer than people are led to believe."

"I have to agree," Mark said. "I happened to spot Clarice leaving an uptown hotel, and while I waited for a cab, Brad soon followed."

"I still don't understand; if neither Haley or Brad were happy in the marriage, why not divorce?" Suzanna asked.

Austen's shoulders rose and fell. "Money. Brad's a great businessman, and Haley's books bring in a nice profit. It's their personalities that are like honey and vinegar."

"You're saying it's easier to kill her than divorce

her?"

"Could be."

Mark cleared his throat. "My first choice is Clarice."

"Why is that?" Austen asked.

"As the saying goes, if looks could kill. And some I've seen Clarice give Haley should have dropped her on the spot."

"That brings us to JJ and Melinda," Austen said. "Neither of whom have any love lost for Haley."

"These people might have all hated Haley," Suzanna stated. "But to be filled with enough rage to shove a knife into her chest?"

Austen nodded. "That brings us right back to those who knew about the skit."

"What skit?" Mark asked.

While Austen filled Mark in, Suzanna spotted Kline leaving the elevator with JJ and Melinda. She nudged Austen, indicating the three with a nod of her head.

When Kline headed for the hotel entrance, JJ and Melinda entered the restaurant. Austen rose and waved.

As the two approached, the strain on their faces was clear to see.

"Please join us," Austen said.

Melinda hesitated and glanced at JJ who nodded. Her voice shook when she spoke. "We've been interrogated over that woman's death. Not that I wouldn't have wanted to shove a knife into her, but it wasn't me." She smiled. "But hats off to whoever had the guts to send her to hell where she belongs."

JJ placed his head in his hands and groaned. "Melinda, you can't talk like that. Do you not understand we're suspects in Haley's murder?"

"That's absurd. We were together all night. In fact, we went to bed early. I had a headache and took one of my sleeping pills," she stated. "It's ludicrous for anyone to suspect us."

Suzanna studied JJ as his eyes shifted away from Melinda. He nervously fiddled with the saltshaker. *Something's not right,* she thought, glancing back at Melinda who was still expressing her displeasure with Kline.

"He also had the nerve to tell us we couldn't leave the island. I told him if he wants to find Haley's murderer," Melinda continued, "he needs to find Brad and Clarice. If anyone has a motive to want her dead, it's those two. Clarice has wanted Brad to divorce Haley for years. I'm not sure when their affair began, but I do know she'd do about anything to be Mrs. Brad Henderson."

"Can you two think of anyone else besides Brad and Clarice who would have motive to kill her?" Austen asked.

Melinda snorted. "How long of a list would you like? That woman managed to piss off just about everyone she met."

"Kline described how she was found," JJ said. "It reminded me of the murder skit on the mystery cruise. If there's a connection, that would narrow the suspect list to those who were on the ship."

Austen nodded. "I agree. Which means unless there's someone here we aren't aware of, that list is pretty short."

Melinda's eyes grew wide, and JJ stared at the table as they realized Austen's meaning.

"You're not suggesting it's one of us?" Melinda exclaimed.

****

In their hotel room, Brad Henderson poured more coffee into his cup. He indicated the pot. "Would you like a refill?"

Clarice shook her head and frowned. "I still can't believe you cornered that woman last night and accused her of being Haley. She stared at you like you were crazy."

"She was fine once I apologized. Besides, you have to admit she did resemble Haley."

"More like a frumpy Miss Marple. Can you honestly picture Haley dressed like that?"

"We heard she was wearing a disguise. I can't think of a better one."

"We were lucky none of those women she was with recognized you. The last thing we need is to bring unwanted attention to ourselves."

"The pool area was packed with people. No one paid any attention to us. With my ball cap and flowered shirt and you in T-shirt and shorts, we resembled every other tourist." Brad sighed. "Although, none of it matters. It seems Haley outmaneuvered us."

"All may not be lost. The conference ends today. If Haley stays, it's going to be harder for her to blend in with a crowd."

"What do you suggest? Sit in the lobby of the Huntington hoping she passes by?"

"Do you have a better idea?"

As Brad opened his mouth to reply, a knock sounded on their hotel room door. They stared at each other, then Brad whispered, "Who could that be?"

Clarice tightened the belt on her robe and stood. "I'll see." She opened the door to find two men in suits standing in the hall. "Can I help you?"

"Are you Clarice Abbot?" the taller of the two asked.

Clarice nodded.

"I'm Detective Kline, and this is Sergeant Scott. Is Mr. Henderson here as well?"

Again, she nodded.

"We need to speak to you both. May we come in?"

Clarice stepped back, and the two men entered.

"I'm Brad Henderson," Brad said, standing. "What can we do for you?"

"Mr. Henderson, it's about your wife," Kline said. "Perhaps you should take a seat."

Brad glanced at Clarice who came to stand next to him. "Detective, what's happened?" Brad asked.

"I'm sorry to have to tell you your wife was killed last night," Kline said. "And we need to ask you some questions."

Brad stared in disbelief, and he swayed unsteadily.

"Brad, sit down before you fall," Clarice exclaimed. She helped him onto the sofa, then sat next to him and took his hand.

Brad's voice shook as he asked, "What do you mean she was killed?"

"Her body was discovered early this morning near the pool at the Huntington." Kline paused. "And it was murder."

Brad's face turned chalk white. "How?" he whispered.

"She was stabbed," Kline replied.

Brad shook his head. "I can't take this all in. How

did it happen?"

"That's what we're trying to find out," Kline continued. "She was found seated at the pool bar around three a.m. According to the medical examiner, she'd been killed at another location and moved."

"Moved, from where?" Brad asked.

"We discovered an area behind some tall shrubs near the pool where the ground is disturbed, and there are traces of blood."

Brad frowned. "How far from the bar is that?"

"It's not too far, but there are signs she was dragged."

Brad ran his hand over his face. "Who found her?"

"Austen Kincaid. We're also fairly sure his girlfriend Suzanna Shay was attacked by the same person who killed your wife."

Brad leapt to his feet. "There's your murderer, Detective. Austen Kincaid."

"Mr. Henderson, please sit down, and tell me why you think that?"

"Because he seduced my wife," Brad said, his eyes blazing with hatred. "And when she told him to stay away from her, he went berserk."

Clarice, brows raised, opened her mouth to speak, but at a stern glance from Brad, she cast her eyes downward.

"Can you be more specific?" Kline asked. "What exactly did Mr. Kincaid do?"

Brad hesitated as he ran his hand through his hair. "He wouldn't leave her alone. Calling all the time and showing up at the office. It got so bad, I had to release him from his contract."

Kline cocked his head. "I'm sorry this is a personal

question, but what was your reaction to your wife's affair?"

Brad's mouth formed a thin line. "Detective, that's none of your business."

"Mr. Henderson, someone killed your wife. You're here on the island, and you knew she had a relationship with Mr. Kincaid. I believe most men would show some type of emotion."

"What are you implying?"

Kline ignored Brad's question and asked, "Where were you two last night?"

"We went out to dinner, then came back up here."

Kline turned to Clarice. "Can you confirm this?"

Clarice, visibly shaken, replied, "Yes."

"What time did you return from dinner?"

"Around nine o'clock or so. The restaurant was packed, and we had to wait," Brad said.

"And neither of you left the hotel after you returned?"

Brad nodded. "That's correct."

"Mr. Henderson, do you have any idea, other than Mr. Kincaid, who might want to cause your wife harm?"

Clarice snorted.

"Miss Abbot, do you have something to add?" Kline asked.

Brad scowled, but Clarice ignored him and replied. "Detective, Haley Henderson had more enemies than she had friends."

"I understand there are similarities between Mrs. Henderson's death and a murder skit on a recent mystery cruise. It seems those who participated in the skit are all here on the island. Are you aware of this?"

When neither spoke, Kline continued. "Mr. Henderson, it's been brought to my attention that you and your wife were having marital difficulties, and you were wanting a divorce. Considering you're here with Miss Abbot, I'd have to conclude this is true. I find it hard to believe you didn't purposely come to Hilton Head looking for your wife. I also find it hard to believe you weren't aware of the others being here as well."

"All right, fine," Brad spat. "I did come looking for Haley. She cleaned out the house safe and our bank account. I wanted my money back, but by the time I discovered where she was staying, I never had an opportunity to confront her. So, Detective, you can take me off your suspect list. Why would I kill the woman before I found out what she'd done with all the money?" Brad's mouth formed a thin line. "Which means now that she's dead, I'm probably ruined."

Clarice narrowed her eyes. "You didn't tell me she also cleared out the safe."

Brad threw up his hands. "I was hoping to get it all back."

"Even though we're sure your wife was staying at the Huntington, when we checked the reservation list, she wasn't on it. Do you have any idea what name she might have used?" Kline asked.

"Her maiden name was Beal," Brad replied.

Kline rose. "That's all for now. Please don't leave the island."

"I need to get back to New York and try to save my business," Brad said. "How long do you expect this to take?"

"As long as it takes for me to discover who murdered your wife."

"Are you telling me the necklace is gone?" Clarice shouted after the detective left.

Brad slumped in the chair. "I'm afraid so."

"Are you sure she didn't take the paste copy she used in the skit?"

"Trust me, Haley would know the difference. She thought it was quite amusing to use the real diamond necklace on the ship instead of the fake."

Clarice gaped. "She brought the real one on the cruise?"

"I didn't know until we were getting ready for the skit."

"Brad, that's crazy."

Brad shrugged. "So, what's new?"

"And now she's dead, and we have no idea what she's done with the money and the necklace."

"That's about it."

Clarice's face turned red with fury. "Why in God's name didn't you tell me sooner?"

"How was I supposed to know it would be important?"

"Well, you sure as hell know now."

Chapter Thirty-Eight

"I need to pack up my room," Suzanna said as she and Austen finished their coffee in the hotel restaurant.

Earlier, Mark had headed for his own room to wait for Amy to call. Melinda said her head was pounding and planned on lying down, while JJ went off to check his email.

"I was thinking it might be a good idea to extend my stay here at the hotel," Austen said, signing the check. "I'll be close by in case there are any new developments."

Suzanna nodded. "Good idea. But I can't afford to stay."

"My suite will accommodate the both of us nicely."

"If that's an invitation, I accept. There's no way I'm going to let you snoop without me."

Austen laughed. "And what makes you think I plan on snooping?"

"We met on a mystery cruise, didn't we? Besides, how fun would it be if we were the ones to discover the murderer."

Austen grew serious. "Suzanna, whoever the murderer is shoved a knife into Haley's chest and left her body on display. This is a dangerous person. If we do discover any information, we'll go directly to Kline."

"Of course we will. Speaking of, here he comes."

Kline entered the restaurant. "Hello again. I have some information and more questions. Is there somewhere we can talk in private?"

Austen nodded. "We can go to my room."

Once upstairs, they got comfortable in the small seating area. "I wanted to let you know the medical examiner has determined Mrs. Henderson's body was moved after she was killed," Kline stated. "My men searched the outside area around the pool and discovered trampled foliage and blood stains."

"Wait a minute," Austen interrupted. "Haley wasn't heavy by any means, but someone would have had to either drag her or carry her to the outdoor bar. Not to mention hoisting her onto the barstool."

Kline nodded. "That's correct. We believe the body lay undiscovered until the area cleared of guests, then our murderer moved her."

"Wouldn't the murderer be taking a huge chance of getting caught?" Suzanna asked.

"The area where we believe the body lay was in a far corner of the patio where the shrubbery is quite dense. We also found the impression of a woman's high-heeled shoes. Our conclusion is Mrs. Henderson was standing observing the guests on the patio when someone approached her from behind."

"Do you know what time Haley was killed?" Austen asked.

"The medical examiner says between eleven p.m. and one a.m."

Suzanna's voice quivered when she said, "Austen and I were there. It became too hot in the ballroom where the conference party was going on, so we decided to step outside. What if Haley was watching us?"

Austen took Suzanna's hand and gave it a reassuring squeeze. "Detective, is your investigation turning more toward the murderer being a man?"

"Not necessarily. When needed, women can exert more strength than expected." He turned to Suzanna. "Miss Shay, were you and Mr. Kincaid together the entire night?"

"Except for later when I went looking for my purse," Suzanna replied.

"Could Mr. Kincaid have left the room while you slept?"

"What?" Suzanna asked with incredulity. "You can't suspect Austen."

"According to others, Mr. Kincaid pursued Mrs. Henderson after she broke off their affair."

Austen's mouth formed a thin line, as he held back his anger. "I imagine that's the story Haley fed her husband to save her ass, but it's a damned lie. The fact is the woman tried to blackmail me for sex." As soon as the words left his lips, Austen inwardly cursed. Next to him, Suzanna's body stiffened.

Kline's gaze sharpened. "What was she using to blackmail you, and how long did it last?"

Austen let out a long sigh. "She faked photos of her and me naked in bed and threatened to show Suzanna. As far as the blackmail, it didn't happen. I told her to go to hell."

"Was this what caused you to lose your contract with H&H?"

"Brad finding us in his office, which I remind you was another setup by Haley, is what cost me my contract."

"I imagine this made you awfully angry."

"Detective Kline, I did not kill Haley. Was I pissed? Yes. But shoving a knife in someone's chest isn't something I could conceivably ever do."

Kline's eyes locked with Austen's, and he nodded. He turned his attention to Suzanna.

"Miss Shay, do you recall anything out of the ordinary while on the patio?"

Austen took a surreptitious glance at Suzanna, and she glowered at him before replying.

"Nothing more than guests of the hotel and those attending the conference. The weather was perfect, and the area was packed."

Austen opened his mouth to speak, when Kline motioned for him to wait. "Miss Shay, have you remembered something?"

Suzanna hesitated. "I'm not sure. I hate to implicate someone if I'm not certain."

"That's okay. Even if it's a fleeting impression, it might lead us in another direction."

Suzanna took a deep breath. "When Austen and I left the ballroom and stepped onto the patio, I automatically scanned the crowd. There was a bunch of tourists at the bar, and I might have recognized one of them."

"Who?" Austen asked.

"Clarice Abbot."

Kline's eyes narrowed. "What makes you think it was her?"

"I ran into her a couple of days ago at a consignment shop. When she hurried away from me, I noticed a shell-shaped clip in the back of her hair. It's coral with tiny diamonds. I was with her in Costa Maya when she bought it. As I took in those seated around the bar, I thought I caught the clip sparkling."

"Is there anything else besides the clip which suggests to you it was Miss Abbot?"

"The woman's hair was thick and kind of curly, like Clarice's. That's probably why she wears the clip. But lots of women have thick curly hair and wear sparkly adornments. I truly didn't get a close look at her face."

"Did you see Brad with her?" Austen asked.

"Not that I recall. Honestly, I wouldn't have thought about it if the investigation hadn't brought that night back to my attention. It was one of those fleeting moments you don't realize your brain has registered."

Kline rose. "I understand this is the last day of the conference. I've asked those of interest not to leave."

"No problem," Austen said. "If there's availability, I plan on extending my stay here at the hotel."

"If you move somewhere else, please let me know."

Kline had no sooner left than Suzanna rounded on Austen. "When exactly were you going to tell me that witch tried to blackmail you for sex?"

Austen rubbed his temples. "Suzanna, having to face you with what happened in Brad's office was bad enough. I didn't want to make things worse."

"So, the answer is never."

"This is the type of situation I was trying to avoid." He stood and put his arms around her. "I'm sorry I didn't say anything, but I promise what I said is the truth. I didn't allow her to blackmail me."

For a few minutes, her body remained rigid, then she relaxed and sighed. "Okay. It's probably a good thing I was hit on the head. Otherwise I'd be the number one suspect for killing that woman."

"Yeah, well, I hope Kline has placed me at the bottom of the list," Austen replied. He glanced at the clock. "It's almost time to check out. I'd better go downstairs and see if this room is still available."

"Let me call Jenn and see if she can get you a discount."

Chapter Thirty-Nine

"You are not serious," Jenn exclaimed, after Suzanna filled her in on what had happened. "Christ, Suzanna, what were you thinking? You might have been killed."

"Calm down, Jenn, I'm tired but fine. And please don't tell the family. All I need is for my mother to find out."

Jenn laughed. "That would definitely not be good."

"Anyway, the other reason I'm calling is Austen decided to stay here at the hotel, and we were wondering if you can arrange a discount?"

Jenn snorted. "Austen is staying, not you?"

"Yes, me too."

"What a surprise. Hang tight, and let me see what I can do."

"Thanks. Have you heard any more about that Charleston job?"

"I got it. I head there next month."

"Congratulations. You'll have to keep me updated on how things go. In fact, if time works out, maybe I can bring Austen to meet you."

"Great. I can grill him before he meets the rest of the tribe."

Suzanna ended the call. "She said to give her a couple of minutes before you go down. I'm going to go to my room and pack my things, and Amy's. There isn't much, so it won't take me long."

As Suzanna placed items into the suitcases, her thoughts went over all that had happened since the conference began. The best being having Austen back in her life. And hopefully, a new relationship between Amy and Mark. And, as much as she hated to admit it, having Haley out of everyone's life.

As she folded her black dress, she paused, replaying the night of the murder. Mark didn't spend the night with Amy. Unease gripped her. How well did Austen know him? There certainly wasn't any love lost between Mark and Haley, but murder? And what about Clarice? *If I saw her at the pool bar, what was she doing there?*

She sat on the bed, the dress forgotten in her hands. *Then there's JJ, who became awfully fidgety when Melinda said they were together all night.* Suzanna, still seated, her thoughts swirling, jumped when someone knocked at her door.

"Yes," she called.

"Suzanna, it's me," Austen said.

She hurried to let him in.

"Everything is taken care of with the room," he said. "Jenn came through with a great discount." He glanced around at the unpacked suitcase. "I thought you'd be ready to go. Is something wrong?"

"I've been going over the night of the murder, and I've had some disquieting thoughts."

"Such as?"

"How well do you know Mark?"

Austen's brows rose. "I knew him from H&H. Why?"

"He wasn't with Amy that night, and he hated

Haley."

Austen sat next to her. "Are you saying you think Mark killed Haley?"

"It's a possibility."

Austen shook his head. "I can't picture him shoving a knife into her chest. Besides, when we told him of Haley's death, he genuinely seemed surprised."

Suzanna gnawed on her lower lip. "I don't think we can count him out. On the other hand, there's Clarice. What was she doing at the Huntington last night?"

"Kline said Haley was moved after she was killed. Clarice isn't that big. I can't see her being strong enough."

"But Brad is. Just because I didn't see him, doesn't mean he wasn't there as well. And the murderer could have gotten help to move Haley after everyone was gone. Then there's JJ. When Melinda was complaining about Kline's questions, he became fidgety. Did this have something to do with him or with Melinda?"

Austen rose and paced. "These are all valid points. Let's get you packed so we can go to my room and put all this in my laptop."

Soon they were seated at the desk in front of Austen's computer. He brought up the document he'd headed "Who Killed Haley?"

"Okay, let's start with Mark," Austen said. "I'd say we left the dance around eleven o'clock, just after Mark and Amy. If Kline is right, Haley was somewhere near the patio at that time."

"We don't know how long Mark and Amy were together before Amy received the call about Violet," Suzanna added.

"That's right. And how would Mark know Haley was there if he was in his room with Amy? Whoever killed Haley was somewhere on the patio."

Suzanna nodded. "Which brings us to Clarice. I know that was her seated at the bar."

"If only we could relive last night."

Suzanna's eyes widened. "Wait a minute. Austen, there might be pictures."

"What?"

"During the conference, I noticed someone taking pictures of all the events. What if photos were taken of the group on the patio?"

"Who was taking the pictures?"

"I don't know her name, but the conference heads would." Suzanna excitedly reached for her phone, then cursed when she realized the time. "Damn, the brunch isn't over yet." She leaped to her feet. "Which means the photographer is there."

They hurried to the elevator, where Suzanna impatiently stabbed the down button. "It's helpful that the banquet hall entrance is at the back so we can slip in."

They arrived just as Carolyn Long, the Association of Mystery Writers' president, was concluding her remarks by thanking everyone for coming.

Austen and Suzanna sat at an empty table in the rear of the room. Suzanna scanned the hall for the photographer. She grabbed Austen's arm. "There she is," she whispered as she spotted the flash.

Austen nodded. "I see her."

Everyone stood. Some headed for the exit, while others mingled. Suzanna rose. "Quick, let's catch her before she leaves."

They maneuvered past tables and groups of people until they approached a young woman with a camera strap around her neck.

"Excuse me," Suzanna said. "I'm Suzanna Shay, and this is Austen Kincaid. May we speak to you for a minute?"

She smiled. "Sure. I'm Gail Short. How can I help you?"

Suzanna made sure there wasn't anyone within earshot. "I suppose you've heard about the murder which took place on the patio last night."

Gail nodded. "How awful. Did you know her?"

"Yes," Austen said. "That's why we need your help."

"How is that?"

"Were you taking pictures of the ball?" Suzanna asked.

"Sure. I've been taking photos of all the events. Including your book signing, Mr. Kincaid. I'd be happy to show them to you."

"Thanks," Austen replied. "What we need to know is whether you took any photos on the patio after the ball?"

Gail paused in thought. "Yes. A number of guests wandered outside, and I took some random shots."

Excitement lit Suzanna's face. "Can we see them?"

"Sure, but I've been downloading each day's shots into my laptop."

"Let's go to my room," Austen said. "We'll have more privacy there."

Once upstairs, Gail hooked up her laptop and brought up the previous day's images.

"We specifically need the shots from the patio,"

Suzanna said.

Gail clicked through photo after photo, until Austen pointed. "Here they are."

"Please go slowly so we can study each one," Suzanna said.

Clusters of happy partygoers and vacationing tourists filled the screen until Suzanna pointed. "Wait. There's Clarice."

She was captured in profile, but it was definitely her.

Austen leaned in closer. "Yes, but I don't see Brad."

"Perhaps he's seated out of range of the shot, or in the bathroom," Suzanna suggested.

Austen frowned. "Could be."

"There's only a few more," Gail said. Her mouse clicked as images passed.

"Stop," Austen exclaimed. "Christ, Suzanna, do you see who I see?"

Chapter Forty

Suzanna's stomach clenched when there, in the far corner of the frame, was JJ Jackson.

Gail's gaze went from Suzanna to Austen. "I take it you see someone you weren't expecting."

"Yes," Austen said. "Is it possible to have a copy of the two pictures with people we recognize?"

Gail nodded. "I could email them to you."

Austen gave her his email address, and Gail stood. "I assume you'll share these with the police, and hopefully it will help them find the killer."

Suzanna and Austen thanked Gail. As soon as the door closed behind her, Suzanna asked, "What was JJ doing there?"

Austen shook his head. "This isn't good."

"Earlier when we were in the restaurant talking with Melinda and JJ, Melinda said she'd taken a sleeping pill and gone to bed. There's a chance she wouldn't have known if JJ had left."

"True. Now we have both JJ and Clarice at the scene. I suppose we should contact Kline."

"I wish we could speak to JJ first. I'd like to hear his explanation."

Austen ran his hand through his hair. "So would I, but it might be too dangerous. If JJ is the killer, and we let him know he was caught on film, he might take off before Kline has a chance to talk to him."

"I suppose you're right. And, if he does have a good explanation for being there, there's nothing to worry about. Besides, don't forget about Clarice. She's my number one suspect."

"Why's that?"

"If she's been in love with Brad for years, and the only way she'd have him is if Haley was out of the picture, she may have decided she's waited long enough. Love is a powerful motive."

"I've spent a lot of time with Clarice, and I have a hard time imagining her thrusting a knife into Haley." He sighed. "But I suppose her hatred could run that deep." He picked up his cell phone. "I'll call Kline."

A while later, when the knock came, Austen rose to answer. It was clear by the scowl on Kline's face he wasn't pleased.

"Let's sit, and you can show me the pictures. But first," Kline continued, "I thought I told you two not to play detective on your own. You should have informed me about the photographs before you approached the photographer."

"It all happened too fast," Suzanna said. "We wanted to catch her before she left the hotel."

Kline removed his notebook from his pocket. "What's her name, and does she live here on the island?"

"Her name is Gail Short, and we're not sure where she lives," Austen replied.

"Okay, let me see the photos."

Austen held out his cell phone. "Gail couldn't print them, so she emailed them to me."

Kline studied the first photo.

Suzanna pointed. "There's Clarice."

Austen brought up the next photo. "And there's JJ Jackson."

Kline's scowl deepened. "Send both photos to me. I can have prints made."

Austen did as he asked, and Kline stood. "We've temporarily sealed off Mrs. Henderson's room here at the hotel, so don't get any ideas of snooping around in there."

"Have you found any clues to her killer?" Suzanna excitedly asked.

"I'm not at liberty to discuss the case. Remember, this person killed in cold blood while others were close at hand. This tells me they were desperate and dangerous. We believe Mrs. Henderson was the target, but if cornered, our murderer might strike again. So, I'll tell you one more time, do not interfere in this investigation. If you learn anything else, contact me immediately."

Austen and Suzanna nodded, and Kline took his leave.

"I'd give anything to get into Haley's room," Suzanna said.

Austen rolled his eyes. "Did you not hear what the man said?"

"Oh, come on. You're as curious as I am."

"Yes, but we're not going clue hunting. This isn't a game on a cruise ship."

"I'm still concerned about JJ. Let's wait in the lobby for Kline to leave, then we can talk to JJ."

Austen glanced at the clock: three-fifteen. "Do you realize it's only been less than twenty-four hours since this all began? I'm hungry and exhausted. The restaurant is a good location to watch who comes and goes. We'll wait there, and I can get something to eat."

"Sounds good." Suzanna yawned. "I'm running out of steam as well."

Austen's hand was on the doorknob when a pounding came from the other side. Startled, he opened the door.

"They suspect JJ of killing that woman," a hysterical Melinda wailed, tears streaming down her cheeks.

"Melinda, come in." Suzanna guided her to the sofa. "Austen, get her some water."

"Here, drink this." Suzanna handed Melinda the glass. "Then tell us what happened."

Melinda's hand shook as she tried to sip the water. She took a ragged breath. "That detective came to our room and asked to speak to JJ. He told me I needed to wait out in the hall, but first he asked if I had taken a sleeping pill last night. I told him yes. One of my headaches was coming on, and if I didn't take something quickly, I wouldn't be able to sleep. He thanked me and asked me to step outside. There wasn't anyone else in the hall, so I pressed my ear to the door. At first, I didn't hear anything, then JJ yelled, 'Pictures, what pictures? Are you crazy? I didn't kill her.' That's when I realized that because I took a sleeping pill, he didn't have an alibi." Suzanna handed her a tissue, and she blew her nose. "I didn't have my key, so I couldn't go back in, so I came here."

"Melinda, you need to calm down," Suzanna gently said.

Melinda sniffed. "What pictures could that detective be talking about?"

Austen and Suzanna's eyes met, and Austen

sighed. "There's a photograph of JJ on the hotel patio near the pool after the ball ended. That's the estimated time the police believe Haley was killed."

Melinda's watery eyes opened wide. "What was JJ doing there?"

Suzanna took her hand. "That's what Kline is hoping to discover. If JJ has a convincing explanation, you have nothing to worry about."

Melinda's voice rose. "What if he doesn't believe him? JJ hated Haley, but he couldn't kill anyone."

"If it's any help, I can't see JJ being our murderer either," Suzanna said.

Melinda, her face splotchy from crying and her eye makeup smeared, gasped, "What if that detective doesn't believe him?"

Austen ran his fingers through his hair. "Melinda, we were about to go to the hotel restaurant. Come with us, and we'll be able to see when Kline leaves. Then you can find out what JJ has to say."

The expression Suzanna gave Austen clearly said, *don't think I won't be talking to JJ as well.* "Melinda, come, let's get your face washed, and you'll feel better."

Chapter Forty-One

As the three waited for the elevator, the door slid open, and JJ stood there. "JJ." Melinda sobbed and threw herself into his arms.

"Oh, JJ, I was so afraid that detective would arrest you. What were you doing on the pool patio last night?"

JJ, his face chalk white, held her close. "It will be all right."

"Let's go to my room," Austen said. "It's more private."

Once inside, Suzanna handed Melinda more tissues, as she and JJ sat on the sofa.

"What did Kline say?" Suzanna asked, also taking a seat.

JJ gave Melinda a reassuring hug. "He asked the same as Melinda. What was I doing there? I told him I couldn't sleep because of who I thought I saw."

"Who?" the three asked as one.

"Clarice. We'd left the ballroom and were headed for our room. I happened to glance across the lobby and caught a glimpse of a woman who reminded me of Clarice."

Suzanna leaned forward in her chair. "Where was she?"

"Heading for the doors that lead to the pool area. Like I said, I only caught a glimpse, but I couldn't get it off my mind. Curiosity got the better of me, and I decided to go take a look."

"Did you see her?" Austen asked.

JJ nodded. "She was seated at the bar. Even though she was surrounded by people, and wearing a T-shirt and shorts, it was her."

Melinda snorted. "Clarice Abbot would never dress like that. You must be mistaken."

"It was her, all right."

"Did you approach her?" Suzanna asked.

"I was about to, but she got up. I thought perhaps she was going to the ladies' room, so I waited, but she never came back."

Austen and Suzanna's eyes met, then he asked, "Did you see Brad?"

"No."

"But that doesn't mean he wasn't there," Melinda added.

"True," Suzanna said. "JJ, what did Kline say when you told him all this?"

JJ smiled. "Not to leave the island."

"Don't tell me he still suspects you," Melinda added.

JJ shrugged. "I don't know."

Melinda's mouth formed a thin line. "I said from the beginning my money is on Clarice for the killer."

"We need more proof," Austen said.

Suzanna stood and paced across the carpeted floor. "If only someone else had seen her later that night."

JJ and Melinda rose. "If we think of anything else, we'll let you know," JJ said.

After the two left, Suzanna and Austen yawned. "I'm about done," Austen said. "Let's order room service and go to bed."

"Sounds good," Suzanna replied. "Order us something while I call and check on Amy. If Violet's still sick, I'll have to open the bookstore in the morning."

"Hi, Amy," Suzanna said when Amy answered. "What's happening with Violet?"

"What a day," Amy replied. "After hours in the hospital, the doctors concluded Violet needs to have tubes put in her ears. I'm going to call tomorrow for an appointment with her pediatrician. She and I are both exhausted."

"I'm sorry to hear this. You two try and get some sleep, and I'll open the store in the morning."

"I'm dying to hear the latest on Haley's death, but it will have to wait."

"Is Mark still with you?"

"No, I haven't heard from him since this morning. I tried to get in touch with him a couple of times, but his phone went right to voice mail. I figured he changed his mind about sitting around in a hospital all day and tried to call me, but the reception in the hospital isn't good." Amy paused. "My brain is kind of mush. Are you saying you haven't seen him?"

Suzanna hesitated, a thousand thoughts swirling in her mind. "Last he told us, he was on his way to see you."

Amy's voice rose. "Then where is he?"

Suzanna did her best to keep her voice normal. "Amy, calm down. I'm sure there's a good explanation. Perhaps he was tired and fell asleep."

"All day?"

"I don't know. I'll send Austen to his room. If I learn anything, I'll call you."

"Suzanna, I have a bad feeling about this."
"I'll be in touch."

Chapter Forty-Two

"What's happened?" Austen asked as soon as Suzanna disconnected.

"Mark never showed up at the hospital." She filled him in on what Amy said. "Austen, my thoughts are going in a really bad direction."

Austen nodded. "Let's not think the worst until we have to. Do you know what his room number is?"

Suzanna shook her head. "Call down to the front desk and ask."

"They probably won't give it to me."

"I'll text Amy. Hopefully, she remembers." Seconds later, Suzanna's phone rang. "It's 405."

Austen headed for the door. "I'll be right back."

"I'm going with you."

When they reached Mark's room, Austen knocked. When there wasn't an answer, he knocked louder.

"Should we get a manager to let us in?" Suzanna asked.

"And our reason will be?"

"We're worried about him."

Austen ran his hand over his face. "Can this day get any more fucked-up? Come on."

"I know you're thinking what I'm thinking," Suzanna said as they waited for the elevator. "Mark is the killer."

"It doesn't make any sense. He wasn't on the

cruise. How would he know to place Haley's body at the bar?"

"Who knows. Perhaps the skit was talked about at H&H. Haley did write it, and she loved to brag on herself."

"It's just too far-fetched."

They'd reached the front desk, and Austen smiled at the young woman behind the counter. "Hi, Traci, we have a situation I was hoping you could help us with. We're concerned our friend isn't well and was wondering if we could be let into his room to check on him?"

"Oh, I don't have the authority for that. You'll need to speak with the manager."

"Are they here?" Austen asked.

"Yes, but I'm not sure where she is. Let me check."

Suzanna's nerves were stretched so tight she thought they might snap. *How could they all have been so wrong about Mark? He seemed such a nice and sincere guy. They said Ted Bundy was a nice guy too,* a voice in her head screamed. *What if he would have hurt Amy or Violet? Suzanna, get a grip. You're allowing your imagination to run out of control when the poor guy might be sick or injured.*

As they waited, a state trooper entered the lobby and approached the desk. He nodded at Austen and Suzanna. "Do you know if there's a manager working tonight?"

"That's what we're waiting on," Austen replied.

Soon a middle-aged woman stepped behind the counter. Her gaze went from the state trooper to Austen and Suzanna. "Can I help you?"

Austen motioned for the trooper to go first.

"I need to know if Mark Gray is staying here?" he asked.

Suzanna gasped, and the state trooper turned. "Do you know Mr. Gray?"

Before Suzanna could speak, Austen nodded. "He's our friend, and we were concerned something was wrong." Austen proceeded to explain about Mark's disappearance.

"Mr. Gray was in a car accident. We found a room key for this hotel among his personal items."

"Oh, no! Was he killed?" Suzanna asked, her voice trembling.

"No, miss, but he's in the hospital. The battery on his cell is dead, so we didn't know who to contact. That's why I'm here."

"Is he badly injured?" Austen asked.

"The air bags on the rental car released, but he's pretty banged up. He has a broken ankle and a concussion. Do you know whom we can notify?"

Austen shook his head. "He isn't able to tell you himself?"

"They had to operate on his ankle, and he's sedated."

"Can we see him?" Suzanna asked.

"I'd wait until tomorrow morning," the trooper suggested.

"How did the accident happen?" Austen asked.

"The other guy ran a red light. Mr. Gray was lucky. The situation could have been much worse."

"We'll be at the hospital in the morning," Austen said.

The trooper nodded and left. Relief and exhaustion washed over Suzanna. "Austen, I'm about to drop, and I need to call Amy."

"Tell me about it. Let's grab a couple of burgers here at the hotel, then go upstairs, and hopefully nothing else will happen."

They slid into a booth, and Suzanna made her call.

"How badly is he hurt?" Amy demanded, when Suzanna explained.

Suzanna filled her in on what the trooper had told them. "We're planning on heading over to the hospital in the morning. I'm going to ask Peg to open the store."

"I'll go over there as soon as I take Violet to the doctor. If his ankle is broken, he won't be able to travel, and he'll need a place to recover. If he's willing, I'm going to bring him here."

"Amy, that's a lot of responsibility. You already have Violet to take care of."

"I'll work it out. Suzanna, I believe Mark and I could have a future, and I want to help if I can."

"Okay, I'll call you tomorrow after we've seen him."

Suzanna disconnected as their food arrived. "I'm so ashamed of myself for even considering Mark as our killer."

Austen popped a French fry into his mouth. "I know, but our suspect list is pretty short."

"I honestly can't think about this anymore. Suddenly I'm so tired I don't know if I can stay awake to eat."

"Eat what you can, then hopefully we can go to bed."

Chapter Forty-Three

In their room at the Island Sands Hotel, Clarice and Brad stared at the photograph Kline held. "Miss Abbot, isn't that you?"

Clarice nodded.

"In your statement, you said you and Mr. Henderson went to dinner, then came back here. You neglected to mention your stop at the Huntington."

"The omission wasn't intentional," Brad stated. "The hotel is right next door, and we decided to stop for a nightcap."

"What time was this?"

"I don't recall," Brad said.

"Do you, Miss Abbot?"

Clarice shook her head.

"And neither of you encountered Mrs. Henderson?"

"That's right," Brad replied.

"What time did you leave?"

Brad frowned. "I have no idea. I don't believe it was late."

"Do you consider after eleven o'clock being late?"

"Detective, where is this going?"

"I don't appreciate people lying to me," Kline replied curtly. "So how about the truth. Why were you at the Huntington?"

"Oh, for heaven's sake, Brad, tell him," Clarice

snapped.

Brad rose and started to pace. "We went hoping to see Haley. I want the money she stole."

"Did you find her?"

"No. We spotted some people who could recognize us, so we left."

"Why didn't you want to be recognized?"

"I didn't want to have to explain why I was here."

"You said Mrs. Henderson cleaned out your bank account and safe," Kline continued. "What was in the safe?"

"Some of Haley's jewelry, but mostly pieces that belonged to my mother."

"Valuable pieces?"

Brad scoffed. "One necklace worth over five hundred thousand." Brad brightened. "Detective, have you been in Haley's hotel room? Did you find the jewelry?"

Kline rose. "We did search Mrs. Henderson's room, and there weren't any valuables found. We did find a deposit slip from a New York bank along with a safety deposit box key."

For a minute Brad looked confused, then he scowled in anger. "She must have opened a separate account from our joint one. Kline, that money belongs to me. And I'll bet the missing jewelry is in that deposit box."

"Perhaps, but this is still an ongoing investigation. Nothing will be released until we've concluded. Remember, don't either of you leave the island."

After Kline left, Clarice dropped onto the sofa and let out a long sigh. "All might not be lost. We just need to wait until Haley's effects are released to you."

"That may well be," Brad replied. "But there's still the little problem of Haley's murder."

****

Suzanna awoke from fitful dreams where shadowy figures were chasing her. She glanced at the clock: three a.m. Next to her, Austen slept peacefully. Unable to shake off the dreams, she rose. She slipped on a hotel robe and quietly opened the sliding door onto the balcony. The salty smell of the ocean and the warm breeze comforted her. She leaned on the railing and watched the lights of a ship passing in the distance. Visions of her and Austen on the cruise made her smile. *Perhaps that's a cruise ship, and two other strangers are falling in love.* She sighed. *If so, I hope their relationship isn't as tumultuous as mine and Austen's.*

Her attention was caught by a family of raccoons emerging from the bushes below. Her interest sharpened as a smaller one dragged something shiny from beneath a bush. Her thoughts went instantly to the area where Kline said Haley was standing. What if the murderer left a clue and the police missed it? Or an inquisitive animal thought it a great plaything. She glanced in the direction of the pool and patio. *I wonder if the crime tape is still up. I can't imagine they didn't cordon off the spot where Haley was killed.* She gnawed on her lower lip. *It wouldn't hurt to take a look.*

"What are you doing?"

Suzanna cried aloud and jumped. "Good grief, Austen, you scared me."

"Sorry. I woke up, and you were gone."

"I had awful dreams and came out here to clear my head."

Austen stood next to her. "It's a beautiful night."

"I've been watching a family of raccoons, and I had a thought."

Austen grinned. "I can't imagine what."

"Seriously, listen."

"You want to poke around the crime scene?" he exclaimed when she'd finished. "Tell me you weren't considering going there now alone in the middle of the night."

Suzanna made a shushing motion. "Keep your voice down. And to answer your question, no. I was hoping you'd go with me."

"Out of curiosity, what do you expect to find?"

"I don't know. Perhaps a small clue the police overlooked. Considering all the vegetation and the thick pine mulch, it could easily happen."

"Well, we're not going tonight. Besides the fact we don't have a flashlight, copperheads are nocturnal, and I have no intention of encountering one in the bushes."

Suzanna scrunched up her face. "Snakes, yuck. Neither do I. We can go in the morning."

Chapter Forty-Four

The next morning, as streaks of sunlight stabbed over the horizon, Suzanna stood behind a line of crime scene tape and frowned. Unable to get her idea of an overlooked clue from her mind, she'd given up on trying to sleep and quietly left their room. With any luck, she'd be back before Austen discovered she was gone.

Now she debated if she should take a chance and slip under the yellow tape. She glanced around and heard nothing but the singing of morning birds and the lapping of the ocean waves. No one was in sight as she bent beneath the tape. She stepped closer to the bushes and peered along the ground. If there was anything to be found here, the police would have seen it. She searched for a stick in order to poke deeper into the mulch. As she reached for a long branch, she noticed a path that wove through the trees.

Curious to see where it went, Suzanna slipped back under the tape. She made her way past palmetto palms, colorful magnolia trees, and a fragrant-smelling hedge. As she rounded a corner, a short distance away the edge of another pool and patio came into sight.

Suzanna halted. That must be the Island Sands Hotel. As her thoughts raced, a woman appeared heading in her direction. Suzanna's pulse quickened when she realized it was Clarice Abbot. Not wanting to be seen, Suzanna stepped behind a thicket of tall bamboo.

Clarice, her attention on the ground, started as two joggers approached. She ducked her head and hurried back in the direction she'd come from.

Suzanna waited until the joggers had passed, then stepped from the bamboo. What had Clarice been searching for? And why was she acting so skittish? Suzanna's brows knitted in thought. If Clarice and Brad were staying at the Island Sands, it would have been easy enough for one of them to kill Haley and escape using the path.

As a few more joggers appeared, Suzanna silently cursed. There wasn't any way she'd be able to poke around without drawing attention to herself. She'd tell Austen about Clarice and plan their next move.

When Suzanna returned to their room, Austen was awake and drinking coffee. By the scowl on his face, he wasn't pleased.

Suzanna smiled. "Good morning."

Without responding to her greeting, he replied, "Let me guess. You've been searching in the crime scene looking for clues."

"Actually, yes, and would you like to hear what I've discovered? Or do you want to sit there being an annoying ass?"

Austen snorted. "I suppose being an annoying ass isn't going to get me anywhere, so let's hear what you found."

Suzanna, deciding to keep him in suspense, went to the coffee maker and poured herself a cup. "Clarice and Brad are staying next door at the Island Sands Hotel, and there's a path leading from there to where Haley was killed." Smug satisfaction filled her face as Austen's jaw dropped.

She filled him in on seeing Clarice and her odd behavior. "So, I was right. She's afraid the police will find something to link either her or Brad to the murder. We just need to find it first."

Austen held up his hand. "Wait a minute. I agree Clarice's behavior is strange, but that doesn't mean she's a murderer."

"I'm telling you one of them did it, and I intend on proving it."

"How?"

"By flushing them out. I've been thinking. If they believe I found whatever Clarice was looking for, they might come after me. That's when we catch them."

"Have you lost your mind?"

Suzanna made a shushing motion. "Stop yelling. We need to come up with a good plan, that's all."

"By using you as bait?"

"Why not?"

"Because it's dangerous? These people could be stone-cold killers."

"We'll make sure there are steps put into place so nothing can go wrong."

Austen rolled his eyes. "I've heard that before."

"Do you have a better plan?"

"Yes, we let Kline know of our suspicions. Who knows, he may already be closing in on Brad and Clarice."

Suzanna scrunched up her nose. "What fun is there in that? Wouldn't it be thrilling if we solved the murder ourselves?"

"Suzanna, this isn't a skit on a who-done-it cruise.

I'll repeat, these people are dangerous."

"Okay, how about this? We'll check out the area around the crime scene. Then one way or another, we'll contact Kline."

Austen ran his hand through his hair. "When do you plan on doing this?"

"We'd look more suspicious after dark with flashlights. I'd honestly like to go now. I don't want Clarice to find whatever she was searching for before us."

"We still can't be seen on the other side of the crime scene tape."

"No, but if anyone asks, we can say I dropped something, and it rolled into the trees." She paused, a sudden dawning filling her eyes. "Austen, the trees."

"Yeah, there's quite a lot of them."

"No, listen. We're concentrating on the wrong path. Clarice wouldn't have taken Haley toward the hotel. She dragged her toward the patio and bar. So that's the area we need to search."

"That's still behind the yellow tape."

Suzanna gave a dismissive wave. "It's barely dawn. Most people are still sleeping."

"Like we should be doing," Austen mumbled.

"Fine, I'll go on my own."

"Don't you have to call Peg to open the store?"

"That's hours from now."

Austen threw up his hands in defeat.

"We have to go around this way," Suzanna said leading Austen toward the denser vegetation. "See, we're all alone." She slipped beneath the tape.

Austen followed, using the light on his phone as they cautiously stepped between tall shrubbery. "Watch where you step. Remember what I said about snakes."

"Austen, don't scare me."

"Trust me, I don't want to encounter one either. What exactly are we looking for?"

"Anything that shouldn't be here. Think about it. Clarice must have struggled pulling Haley's body. Perhaps an item she was wearing or in her pocket fell. Why else was she out this morning searching the ground? Do you see a stick or branch I can use to poke around under these bushes?"

Austen handed her a sturdy branch, as his cell rang.

"Austen," Suzanna hissed. "Turn it off."

"It's Mark. Hey buddy, how are you doing?"

Suzanna left Austen to talk to Mark and moved farther into the bushes. She cautiously stabbed the branch in the mulch and underbrush. She reached the spot where a tall sea pine left a gap in the hedge. She peered around the trunk of the tree. A few feet ahead was the Huntington's pool and patio. Suzanna's excitement grew. This must be the way the killer dragged Haley's body. She knelt, scraping away pine needles, sticks, and leaves, until something shiny caught her eye. Her breath held as she eased the object toward her. It was coated in dirt, and she couldn't make out what it was. Not wanting to touch the item with her hands, she checked her pockets for tissues. "Damn," she murmured. Empty. A rustling sound caught her attention. Not knowing what else to do, she removed her T-shirt, picked up her dirt-covered find, placed it in her pocket, and slipped her shirt back on.

"What are you doing?" Austen asked from behind her.

Suzanna flinched. "Austen, you scared me. I found

something."

"What?"

"I don't know. It might be nothing. Let's go to the room where we can see what it is in private."

"Okay, but Mark asked if I'd bring him clothes."

"Is he being released?"

"They said later this afternoon."

"That's great news. How are you going to get into his room?"

"He called the front desk, and they're going to let me in."

"I'd better call Amy and tell her what's happening."

"Mark has already spoken with her as well. She's going to the hospital after taking Violet to the doctor."

They reentered the hotel, and Austen headed toward the check-in counter. "I'll get Mark's key and get his clothes. I'm going to go ahead and take them to the hospital."

"Don't you want to see what I found?"

"I won't be long. If it's important, we'll need to call Kline."

"I'm going to call Peg and ask her to open the store."

Chapter Forty-Five

Suzanna entered Austen's room and grabbed some napkins from the coffee tray. She spread them out on the bar counter, removed the object from her pocket, and laid out her find. As she brushed the dirt away, disbelief and confusion filled her eyes as she realized what she'd found. *This can't be right. This is all wrong.* She rubbed her temples as past images swirled in her mind. As unbelievable as it was, she couldn't deny the truth. *I have to tell Austen before he leaves.* Suzanna rewrapped the pearls and placed them in her pocket. She opened the door and stifled a scream.

"Hello, Suzanna, going somewhere?"

Her voice slightly trembling, she replied, "Yes, I'm meeting Austen."

"I don't think so," Melinda said. "I believe you and I need to talk." She pushed Suzanna into the room and shut the door.

"Melinda, what are you doing?"

"I was really hoping it wouldn't come to this, but unfortunately I'm afraid you found my pearl choker."

Suzanna took a slight step back. "What are you talking about?"

"I was sitting on my balcony this morning when you and Austen passed below. You and Austen were asking a lot of questions, and I had a feeling you'd discovered something. So, I followed you. When you went toward the crime scene, I went around the opposite way. I arrived in time to see you pick my choker from the ground. I thought that's where I lost it, but I couldn't figure out how to search without getting caught." She shook her head. "I can't believe the police didn't discover it first."

Suzanna swallowed her fear. "It was covered with dirt and mulch. Melinda, this doesn't make any sense. JJ said you took a sleeping pill."

"That's what he thought, but that's not what happened."

"Then what did?"

"JJ spotted Clarice as we were leaving the ballroom. What he didn't see was Haley. Even with her disguise, I knew it was her seated with some tourists in the lobby. I told JJ I was going to take a pill and go to bed. He wanted to see what Clarice was up to, so he headed after her. I got onto the elevator, but instead of going to our room, I got off on the first floor and hurried to the elevator at the far end. I planned on going back to the lobby, but as I stepped off, Haley was heading outside near the far end of the dining area. I stayed behind her and followed as she snuck into those bushes which are behind the bar and pool patio."

Bile rose in Suzanna's throat at the matter-of-fact way Melinda was reciting her story.

"She was spying on you and Austen, so it was easy enough to sneak up on her." Melinda's expression turned ugly, and she snarled. "Even facing death, that bitch had the nerve to taunt me. My husband loved me, and she destroyed that love. I told her she was done ruining people's lives."

"So, you stabbed her?"

Melinda smiled and nodded. "Like I did in the skit, but this time it was for real. At the time, I wasn't sure what I was going to do, but as I passed a table where people had finished dining, I spotted a rather large steak knife." Her crazed smile widened. "How convenient. The bad part after she was dead, is I had to leave her lying there and hurry to our room. I needed to be in bed when JJ returned. I made it just in time."

"Does JJ know?"

Melinda let out a sigh. "Unfortunately, now he does. You see, I decided how fitting it would be for Haley also to be found seated at the bar as she wrote in the skit." Her eyes narrowed. "If it wasn't for my fondness for Brad, I would have never agreed to participate in that farce. That necklace she wore wasn't paste. Brad was furious when he realized she'd brought the real one, not the fake."

As Melinda rambled on, Suzanna eased toward where her cell phone lay near the end of the counter. Would she have time to tell Siri to call for help?

Melinda blinked, seeming to focus on her surroundings. She removed a gun from her pocket. "Suzanna, stop moving."

Suzanna's pulse quickened, and her hands grew damp. *Keep her talking. That's what they always say in detective novels.* "So how did JJ find out what you did?"

"I mistakenly thought he was asleep when I left the room to move Haley. I honestly don't think he ever suspected me. He truly thought it was either Brad or Clarice. I tried my best to point the detective in their direction. Then the idiot questioned JJ. I have to say that shook me up. I care dearly for JJ and wouldn't want him to go to jail for something he didn't do."

"But how did he find out?"

"I had a hell of a time dragging that woman through those bushes and trees. That's how I lost my choker." Melinda snorted. "She weighed a lot more than she pretended to. Anyway, I made it to the patio and was about to heave her onto the barstool when JJ showed up." She shook her head. "I really wish he'd stayed in our room."

"Did he help you put Haley on the stool?"

"I'm not saying any more. I want you to give me my choker. That was a present from my husband. Even though he broke my heart, I never stopped wearing it."

"What happens to me after I give you the choker?"

"You're going to write a suicide note, then you'll jump from the balcony."

Suzanna's blood went cold. "Melinda, no one will believe I killed myself."

"You'll say in your note that you couldn't get over Austen's affair with Haley, so you killed her and can't live with the guilt."

"Melinda, it won't work. I couldn't have killed Haley; I was with Austen when she died."

"It's his word against yours. You'll say he was covering for you."

Suzanna stared into Melinda's blank eyes. *She's insane.* "Was it you that hit me that night?"

"I am sorry about that, but I had no choice."

Anger replaced Suzanna's fear. "You could have killed me as well."

Melinda shrugged. "You were in the wrong place at the wrong time. Why were you there anyway?"

"I went to look for my purse."

"None of this matters now." She pointed the gun at Suzanna. "Sit at the desk and write the note."

"If JJ knows the truth, you won't get away with this." A chilling realization struck Suzanna. "Where is JJ?"

"He's sound asleep. I put some of my pills in his water bottle. He'll be out for hours."

"He'll eventually wake up."

"He's in love with me. He'll keep my secret. Now sit and start writing. I'll dictate what you'll say."

Suzanna took her seat, removed paper from the drawer, and wrote.

I no longer can deny killing Haley. If Austen says I didn't do it, he's not telling the truth. His affair with Haley broke my heart. I love him, and his betrayal is something I can never forgive or forget.

Melinda nodded in satisfaction. "That should do it. Get up and walk onto the balcony and stand against the railing."

Suzanna did as she was told.

From the shadow of the curtains, Melinda pointed the gun. "Now jump."

Suzanna pulled the choker from her pocket and held it over the railing. "Lower the gun, or I'll throw this. I have a good arm, and I'm sure I can reach that little pond. I'll bet the alligator who lives there will gobble it up."

Melinda screamed in rage and charged. The choker slipped from Suzanna's fingers as the two women struggled. Melinda's hands wrapped around Suzanna's throat as she bent her backward over the railing.

Suzanna, recalling wrestling with her male cousins, twisted in Melinda's grasp and stomped on her foot, throwing her off-balance. Using her own weight, Suzanna shoved Melinda. Her hands shaped like claws, Melinda grabbed for Suzanna as the door burst open, and Austen rushed in, followed by Kline.

Suzanna flung herself into Austen's arms as Kline subdued and cuffed a hysterical Melinda.

"Austen, thank God you're here."

Austen hugged her tight. "Are you all right?"

Her face pressed against his chest and trembling from head to toe, she nodded.

"I was in the parking lot on my way to the hospital when I realized I didn't have my car keys. I was in the lobby waiting for the elevator when Kline rushed in. He was passing below the balcony and saw what was happening. He said it looked like Melinda was trying to push you over the railing."

Suzanna brushed tears from her cheeks. "She was. Austen, how were we so fooled by her?"

"I don't know. She certainly put on a convincing act. What about JJ? Is he involved as well?"

"Not until the end. I think he helped her put Haley on the barstool."

Scott and state troopers arrived, and a sobbing Melinda was escorted out. Kline, scowling, turned to Austen and Suzanna. "Miss Shay, are you injured?"

"No, I'm fine."

Kline waved them to sit on the couch. "You two took a big risk. I thought I made myself clear, no interference."

Guilt clouded both Austen and Suzanna's faces. "We did intend on contacting you," Austen said.

"When? After you and Miss Shay disregarded the crime scene tape and trespassed?"

Suzanna opened her mouth to reply, but Kline held up his hand for her to wait. "Since the murder was discovered, I've had men watching the area. We found the pearl necklace but decided to leave it in place, expecting the person who lost it to return. We suspected this person to be our murderer, because an innocent person would have reported its loss." He turned his stern glance on Suzanna. "Those two joggers who passed you this morning were working for me. They also spotted Miss Abbot, who was on my suspect list. Imagine my surprise when it was reported to me that you two had discovered the necklace and removed it. I was on my way to speak with you both when I witnessed the incident on the balcony."

"We're incredibly sorry we caused all this trouble," Suzanna said.

Austen glared at Suzanna. "That's right. Tell me, Detective, did you also suspect Melinda? She sure had us fooled."

Kline gave a tight smile. "All of you were suspects. As for Miss Pearce, she was also spotted watching when you removed the necklace. I thought she tried awfully hard to place the blame on Miss Abbot."

"Will JJ be charged for helping her?" Suzanna asked.

"He participated in a crime. But I imagine a good attorney will get him off." Kline rose. "I'm sure you both will be called to testify."

Austen and Suzanna nodded.

"What will happen with Haley's body?" Austen asked.

"I'm on my way over to inform Mr. Henderson of the developments. I imagine he'll take care of the arrangements."

Again, Austen nodded.

Kline smiled. "You two stay out of trouble and keep your sleuthing to the pages of books."

Chapter Forty-Six

After Kline left, Austen let out a long sigh. "Thankfully, this is all over."

"Yes, and as nice as this hotel is, I'm ready to go home."

"I agree. How about we pack up, check out, then I'll take Mark his clothes. I'm surprised I haven't heard from him asking what's taking me so long."

"Perfect. I'm going to stop by the bookstore and make sure Peg doesn't need me. Mondays are usually our slow day."

A short time later, Suzanna pulled into her parking spot in front of her condo. When she opened her door, she was greeted by an extremely disgruntled feline.

"Meow."

"Hello, Citrus, baby."

This happy greeting was met with a baleful stare.

"Oh, what's wrong? Did you miss me?" Suzanna knelt and scratched behind her ears.

Citrus purred, then ran to stand in front of the cupboard where her treats were kept. "Meow."

Suzanna laughed. "Are you telling me, since I left you all alone, you deserve treats?"

"Meow."

"Okay, I suppose you're right." Suzanna placed the goodies on her place mat, freshened her water, and filled her food bowl. "That should keep you happy for a while."

Suzanna made a few trips to her car, unloading her belongings. She unpacked, sorted the laundry, and put away her toiletries. When her stomach growled, she glanced at the clock. What was taking Austen so long? She was about to call him when a knock came at the door.

"I was wondering where you've been," Suzanna said as Austen stepped in pulling his suitcase.

"Sorry, I had no idea how late it was. They released Mark, and I helped Amy get him settled in."

"How is he doing?"

"They have him pretty doped, but he's happy to be out of the hospital. I think he and Amy will be fine."

"And Violet?"

"You'll have to talk to Amy for the details, but the doctor gave her different medication to try."

"I'll do that. Are you hungry?"

"Starving."

"Me too. How about I call for something to be delivered?"

"Perfect. Where should I put my things?"

"There's an empty dresser and space in the guest room closet. Don't place anything on the bed. Citrus will lie on it. She's claimed that bed as hers."

The next morning, Austen awoke with Suzanna curled next to him. He smiled at his utter contentment. It was only a few days ago that he had thought his chances with Suzanna were over, but here he was back in her life. And he'd decided if she'd agree, they'd make it permanent.

"What are you smiling about?" Suzanna asked.

"How happy I am."

She snuggled closer. "Me too."

"Then let's get married."

Suzanna sat up. Her eyes opened wide. "What?"

"I said, let's get married."

"Isn't this a little sudden? We've just gotten back together."

"I love you and don't want to waste any more time. I want to spend the rest of my life with you. I'm not going back to New York. I can work fine from Hilton Head. I thought we could find a bigger place as soon as we get back from our honeymoon."

Speechless, Suzanna stared.

"How about getting married on the beach? I thought something small. Then we can rent a car and drive to North Carolina, and I'll meet your family. Afterward we can head for Kentucky, and I'll introduce you to mine. We can fly to New York from there, do some sightseeing, pack up my belongings, and send them here. Then, we get on the cruise ship for our honeymoon. What do you think?"

Suzanna gaped. She opened her mouth, but nothing came out. She swallowed. "That's quite a list. How long have you been planning this?"

"Since last night. I couldn't sleep, so I got up, and Citrus and I sat out on the screened-in porch. I think it's a great plan, and Citrus agrees."

Suzanna smiled. "Does she? I do have a job."

"Amy and Peg can handle it for a few weeks."

"Can I have time to digest all of this?"

Austen pulled her into his arms. "I'll give you one minute."

Epilogue

Austen drove the convertible up the winding road from Pine Bluff to the Lazy M Ranch.

"Now remember, my family can be kind of strange and a little loud," Suzanna said.

"Will you relax? Everything will be fine."

Suzanna gnawed on her lower lip. "My mother wasn't pleased I got married without her being there. She'll be sure to show her displeasure."

Austen grinned. "By the time we leave, your mother will be crazy about me."

Suzanna rolled her eyes. "Good luck." She pointed. "There's the ranch."

They stopped in front of a large two-story log house. "And there's Gran and Gramps on the porch."

Suzanna hurried to the steps and hugged her grandparents. "Gran, Gramps, this is my husband, Austen Kincaid. Austen, this is Ada and Chet McCoy."

Ada gave Austen a big hug, and Chet shook his hand. "Welcome to the family, young man."

"Thank you, sir," Austen replied.

"Who all is here?" Suzanna asked.

"Well, Dillon and Diana. You heard she's expecting?" Ada asked.

"Yes, that's wonderful."

"Sally and Sam. Jenn and your sister brought your mother," Ada continued.

Suzanna grimaced. "How mad is she?"

Ada patted Suzanna's shoulder. "She'll get over it."

"I think I'll take Austen to meet the rest before tackling Mother. Where is everyone?"

"They're at the guest cabin getting it ready for you two," Chet added.

"Oh, no. Hard telling what they're up to."

"Suzanna," chimed a chorus of voices.

Suzanna turned, and coming toward them were her cousins, mischievous expressions on all their faces. "It's about time you got here," Jenn said.

Introductions and hugs all around ensued. Dillon and Sam immediately took Austen to see the horses, while the women had to hear all about the wedding.

"He's absolutely gorgeous," Sally said.

"Lucky you," Savannah added.

Jenn frowned. "I suppose he seems nice enough."

"Except for me, I'd say it's time for drinks," Diana said.

"Definitely," Suzanna stated. "I'm going to need it before seeing Mother."

Savannah grinned. "That you will, sis."

That night after eating thick grilled steaks, baked potatoes, salad, and Ada's strawberry pie, the cousins gathered around the bonfire outside of the guest cabin.

"Austen, do you like ghost stories?" Sam asked.

"Oh, no," Jenn groaned. "Not again."

Suzanna laughed. "Sam loves telling the story of Wilhelmina, a ghost who supposedly walks these mountains."

"She is real," Diana said. "I actually saw her."

Dillon shook his head. "Darlin', you were scared

and half frozen. Your imagination was playing tricks on you."

Diana smiled. "Believe me or not, I know what I saw."

"Okay, you've got my attention," Austen said. "Tell me about Wilhelmina."

When Sam began, Suzanna rolled her eyes and poured herself more wine.

After a lively discussion of mountain legends, Austen and Suzanna said good night to the others and headed for the cabin and hot tub.

Suzanna smiled as she stepped from the bedroom onto the deck. Her cousins had surrounded the hot tub with candles and placed a bucket of champagne on the rim.

"Nice," Austen said, coming out behind her.

"I expect we'll find all kinds of surprises around the cabin."

Austen grinned. "There's some kind of lickable oil next to the bed."

"Really?"

He removed her robe. "Really."

****

"Austen, are you sure I look all right?" Suzanna asked as Austen drove through the tall gates of the Kincaid horse farm.

"Will you stop worrying?" Austen replied. "You're as beautiful as always."

Suzanna gave him a slight smile. "Thanks, but I'm still a nervous wreck."

"Trust me, my parents will love you."

Suzanna rolled her eyes and gazed at the pristine pastureland spreading out on either side of the long drive leading to the house. "How many acres belong to your family?"

Austen shrugged. "Two hundred or so."

When the two-story house came into view, Suzanna gasped. "Oh, my God, Austen, it looks like Tara."

Austen grinned. "Not quite."

Austen parked in the circular drive, and Suzanna stepped from the car. Six white columns stretched across the wide porch, and a stained-glass fanlight spread above the oak double front doors.

Suzanna swallowed hard and took Austen's hand as he led her up the steps. The doors were flung open, and a tall slim woman with short honey-brown hair rushed out.

"There you two are," she said with a smile as she hugged Austen. "And, Suzanna, welcome to our home." She engulfed Suzanna in a huge hug. "I'm so happy to meet you."

Suzanna instantly relaxed and hugged her back. "Mrs. Kincaid, it's so nice to meet you."

"None of that 'Mrs. Kincaid.' I'm Judith. And this is my husband, Bret."

Tall and muscular, Bret Kincaid was an older version of Austen. "Welcome to the Kincaid farm, little lady," he said, also hugging Suzanna. "Do you happen to like horses?"

Suzanna grinned. "As it happens, I grew up around them."

He slapped Austen's back. "Congratulations, son, she'll fit right in."

Judith took Suzanna's arm. "Come into the house and meet the rest of the family."

****

A week later, with the skyline of New York behind them, they stood on the deck of the cruise ship on their way to the Caribbean. "Ten days with nothing to do but enjoy the sunshine and make love," Austen said, hugging Suzanna.

"What about eating?"

"We'll find time for that as well." He kissed her. "I think our first meal should be champagne and pizza."

"I brought the little black dress."

Austen's smile was slow and full of promise. "Perfect."

A word about the author…

Debby Grahl lives on Hilton Head Island, South Carolina, with her husband, David. Besides writing, she enjoys biking, walking on the beach and a glass of wine at sunset. Her favorite places to visit are New Orleans, New York City, Captiva Island in Florida, the Cotswolds of England, and her home state of Michigan. She is a history buff who also enjoys reading murder mysteries, time travel, and, of course, romance. Visually impaired since childhood by Retinitis Pigmentosa (RP), she uses screen-reading software to research and write her books.

http://www.debbygrahl.com